河北省高等学校人文社会科学研究重点项目：
合作学习理论视域下的英语专业基础课教学模式探究
（SD201025）研究成果

Understanding English Poetry
理解英语诗歌

英语诗歌赏析入门

刘涵 著

中央民族大学出版社
China Minzu University Press

图书在版编目（CIP）数据

理解英语诗歌：英语诗歌赏析入门：汉、英/刘涵著.—北京：中央民族大学出版社，2024.1（2025.3重印）

ISBN 978-7-5660-2252-3

Ⅰ.①理… Ⅱ.①刘… Ⅲ.①英语诗歌—诗歌欣赏-汉、英 Ⅳ.①I106.2

中国国家版本馆CIP数据核字（2023）第213842号

理解英语诗歌：英语诗歌赏析入门

著 者	刘 涵
策划编辑	由伟峰
责任编辑	杨爱新
封面设计	舒刚卫
出版发行	中央民族大学出版社
	北京市海淀区中关村南大街27号　　邮编：100081
	电话：（010）68472815（发行部）　　传真：（010）68933757（发行部）
	（010）68932218（总编室）　　　　　（010）68932447（办公室）
经 销 者	全国各地新华书店
印 刷 厂	北京鑫宇图源印刷科技有限公司
开 本	787×1092　1/16　印张：15.5
字 数	210千字
版 次	2024年1月第1版　2025年3月第2次印刷
书 号	ISBN 978-7-5660-2252-3
定 价	76.00元

版权所有　翻印必究

目 录

第一章　引言 ·· 1
  1.1　什么是诗歌 ··· 1
  1.2　诗歌的内容和形式 ··· 3
  1.3　诗歌的功能和作用 ··· 4

第二章　英诗的韵律 ··· 11
  2.1　引言 ·· 11
  2.2　英诗的节奏 ··· 12
    2.2.1　节奏与格律 ·· 13
    2.2.2　节奏的类型 ·· 22
    2.2.3　节奏的作用 ·· 28
  2.3　英诗的押韵和音效 ··· 35
    2.3.1　押韵的种类 ·· 36
    2.3.2　单词的音效 ·· 42
    2.3.3　素体诗 ··· 50

第三章　英诗的语言 ··· 56
  3.1　引言 ·· 56
  3.2　隐含义与字面义 ·· 57
  3.3　象征与典故 ··· 65
  3.4　意象 ·· 75
  3.5　重复与平行结构 ·· 83
  3.6　比喻 ·· 93

    3.6.1 明喻和暗喻 ·· 94
    3.6.2 拟人、呼语和夸张 ································· 100

第四章　英诗的体裁 ·· 116
  4.1 引言 ·· 116
  4.2 叙事诗 ··· 117
    4.2.1 民谣 ··· 118
    4.2.2 史诗 ··· 125
    4.2.3 戏剧独白 ·· 129
  4.3 抒情诗 ··· 136
    4.3.1 十四行诗 ·· 137
    4.3.2 颂歌 ··· 143
    4.3.3 挽歌 ··· 152
  4.4 说教诗 ··· 158
  4.5 传统诗歌和自由体诗歌 ····························· 163
    4.5.1 传统诗歌 ·· 164
    4.5.2 自由体诗歌 ······································· 171

第五章　英诗的题材 ·· 178
  5.1 引言 ·· 178
  5.2 有关自然主题的诗歌 ································ 179
  5.3 有关爱情主题的诗歌 ································ 187
  5.4 有关死亡主题的诗歌 ································ 192
  5.5 有关哲思主题的诗歌 ································ 199

第六章　经典英语诗歌选注 ································ 206

参考文献 ·· 230
后　　记 ·· 239

第一章　引言

作为本书的第一章，笔者在此重点探讨了什么是诗歌，诗歌具有哪些文体特点以及诗歌作为一种文学体裁具有哪些功能和作用等三个问题。

1.1 什么是诗歌

诗歌是一种重要的文学体裁。

文学理论界对于文学体裁（literary genres）的划分历来没有统一的标准。"genre"一词来源于法语，是"种类、性别"的意思，可以用来指文学、艺术、电影、音乐等等的体裁或是类型。文学体裁就是指某一文学作品的类型，它可以由该文学作品所应用的文学技巧、语气、内容甚至长度（例如小说）来决定。我们通常可以先将文学作品归入更为抽象和更具包容性的大类，然后再根据其具体特征进一步细分为某种特定的体裁。然而需要注意的是，不同文学体裁之间的关系并非非此即彼、严格区分的，而文学体裁划分的标准也是灵活多变的（Pavel, 2003）。

通常来讲，文学文体可以划分为四种最基本的类型：诗歌、小说、戏剧和散文。其中，作为文学文体的诗歌历史最为悠久、影响最为深远、形式最为优美，当然也最为广大文学爱好者所喜闻乐见。

有关诗歌的定义可以说是多种多样。不列颠百科全书中是这样定义诗歌的：诗歌是这样一种文学体裁——诗人通过选择合适的语言并且依其意义、声音和节奏对其进行组合安排，从而激发出读者对于某种集中且富于想象力的体验的认知，抑或是某种特殊的情感反应（Nemerov，2021）。这一定义读起来有些拗口，不过我们还可以把它概括一下，或许更为清楚明白——诗歌就是运用某种特殊的语言形式唤起读者某种集中的审美和情感体验的一种文学艺术形式。

我国古代文论认为诗歌是一种抒情言志的文学体裁。《尚书·尧典》中记载："诗言志，歌永言，声依永，律和声。"《毛诗序》中有言："诗者，志之所之也。在心为志，发言为诗，情动于中而形于言。言之不足，故嗟叹之；嗟叹之不足，故咏歌之；咏歌之不足，不知手之舞之足之蹈之也。"所谓"诗言志"，其核心就是通过诗歌表达诗人的思想；所谓"歌永言"是指诗歌是唱出来的语言。除了表达思想以外，诗歌还是诗人情感的集中抒发，正所谓"情动于中而形于言"。由此可见，诗歌是一种表达思想、抒发情感的文学样式。古今中外，莫不如此。

对于什么是诗歌，英国文学史上的著名诗人华兹华斯（William Wordsworth，1770-1850）曾给出了自己的解释，他的解释也历来为广大文学爱好者特别是英国文学爱好者们所推崇。我们在此不妨引述如下，供大家仔细品味：诗歌是对强烈情感的充满想象力的表达，是诗人在恬静安宁当中所蓄积的强烈情感的自然流露（Poetry is the spontaneous overflow of powerful feelings: it takes its origin from emotion recollected in tranquility.）（Wordsworth, 1802）。由此可见，除了表达思想的功能以外，诗歌还是一种特殊的、充满想象力的、高度情绪化的艺术表达方式。

1.2 诗歌的内容和形式

　　第一节中所介绍的内容，笔者以为在某种程度上可以代表我们大多数文学爱好者对于诗歌这种文学体裁的认知。此外，为了加深各位读者对于诗歌作为一种文学体裁的理解，笔者还将从诗歌与散文的区别的角度来讨论一下诗歌的内容和形式。

　　先看内容。与散文相较而言，诗歌的内容更强调情感的抒发。诗歌的内容通常包括以下几个方面。首先，诗歌是情感的表达。诗人的创作活动基本上都是对某个场景、思想或是经历有所触动才开始的。诗人表达情感的语言富于想象力，他们通过运用那些生动的、形象的、具有画面感的词汇来帮助读者体会与自己类似的情感。其次，诗人之所以创作诗歌，是因为他们相信自己在诗歌当中所描摹的经历是重要的和有意义的，是能够帮助读者透视宇宙人生的真谛的。此外，诗人还会凭借其对于美的敏锐感知，而对于美的各种形式加以描摹。因此，诗歌的内容可以总结为诗人运用富于想象力的语言表达的情感；而诗歌的语言则是对于重要的和美的信息的传递。诗歌的具体内容则表现为其题材的多样性：爱情、友谊、死亡、哲思、心理的探究、宗教的虔诚、四季的轮替以及道德的说教，等等，都可以包括其中。

　　其次是诗歌的形式。诗歌的外在形式与散文是不同的。尽管诗歌中的诗节（stanzas）可以对应散文中的段落（paragraphs），而诗章（cantos）则相当于散文中的章节（chapters），然而诗歌的基本形式却是单独分隔的诗行（lines），而非段落和章节。更为重要的是，诗歌的节奏要远比散文的节奏更为规整；而节奏的妙趣则在于它与诗歌内容的相关性以及其自身的一致性和多样性。诗歌形式的第二个特点体现在其词语的顺序上。传统诗歌当中的词语安排通常要满足诗歌格律的要求；而在自由体诗歌当中，诗人则常常会为了表意的需要而安排词语的顺序。此外，诗歌的语言通常简洁而凝练，能将思想和语言的表达高度融合。换句话说，诗歌当中的每一个单词和短语都意涵丰富，微言大义。最后，诗歌以其独特的语言形式诉诸读者的感官，创造出各种意象。借此，诗歌的语言会使得抽象的思想和情感变得触手可及、形象立体。因此，在诗歌创作中，诗人会更倾向于选择那些隐含意义丰富的词汇以及那些能够充分调动读者听觉、视觉、嗅觉、触觉以及味觉等感官的词语。

综上所述，诗歌的内容和形式是非常大的两个范畴。诗歌的内容实际上是在讨论诗歌的题材；诗歌的形式实际上是在讨论诗歌的音韵、语言和体裁。因此，我们会在本书接下来的各个章节当中对诗歌的内容和形式进行更为深入和细致的讨论。

1.3 诗歌的功能和作用

诗歌的功能是指它要达到的表达效果。诗歌本身的题材、体裁、格调多种多样；同时，诗人也可以凭借创作技巧和方法从多个方面影响读者。诗歌可以用来描摹美丽的大自然，阐明宇宙人生的真谛，升华读者的思想，对读者进行说教，开拓读者认识自我和世界的视野，等等。然而，诗歌创作的终极目的不外乎是给读者留下新鲜、独特、深刻而富有教益的审美体验。与散文相较而言，这种审美体验来得更集中，更具想象力，更能让读者身临其境，更能让读者心潮澎湃。法国诗人保尔·瓦雷里（Paul Valéry, 1871—1945）曾经说过，诗歌之于散文就如同舞蹈之于行走——这一比喻很好地说明了诗歌与散文在表达效果方面的不同（Valéry, 1954）。

下面笔者就举一些具体的例子来说明诗歌的各种主要功能。

首先，诗歌可以描摹美丽的大自然。请看下面这段摘自华兹华斯的

《我独自行走如孤云》中的第一个诗节：

> I wandered lonely as a cloud
> That floats on high o'er vales and hills,
> When all at once I saw a crowd,
> A host, of golden daffodils;
> Beside the lake, beneath the trees,
> Fluttering and dancing in the breeze.
> —— *I Wandered Lonely as a Cloud* by William Wordsworth

诗歌还可以阐明宇宙人生的真谛。请看下面这两句选自济慈的《希腊古瓮颂》中的诗句：

> "Beauty is truth, truth beauty" — that is all
> Ye know on earth, and all ye need to know.
> —— *Ode on a Grecian Urn* by John Keats

诗歌还可以升华读者的思想。请看下面节选自弗罗斯特的《未择之路》中的诗句：

> I shall be telling this with a sigh
> somewhere ages and ages hence:
> Two roads diverged in a wood, and I —
> I took the one less traveled by,
> And that has made all the difference.
> —— *The Road Not Taken* by Robert Frost

诗歌还可以对读者进行说教。请看下面节选自爱默生的《国家的力量》中的最后两个诗节：

Not gold but only men can make

A people great and strong;

Men who for truth and honor's sake

Stand fast and suffer long.

Brave men who work while others sleep,

Who dare while others fly —

They build a nation's pillars deep

And lift them to the sky.

—— *A Nation's Strength* by William Ralph Emerson

诗歌还可以开拓读者认识自我和世界的视野。请看下面节选自莎士比亚《威尼斯商人》中的诗句：

Tell me, where is fancy bred,

Or in the heart, or in the head?

How begot, how nourished?

　　Reply, reply.

It is engendered in the eyes,

With gazing fed; and fancy dies

In the cradle where it lies.

　　Let us all ring fancy's knell:

I'll begin it — Ding, dong, bell.

Ding, dong, bell.

—— *The Merchant of Venice* by William Shakespeare

最后，也是最重要的，诗歌可以为读者带来集中而且富于想象力的审美体验。下面请读这首华兹华斯的《怦然心动》(My Heart Leaps Up)，并且体会这首诗的意象以及意境之美。

威廉·华兹华斯（William Wordsworth，1770—1850）是英国文学史上最伟大的诗人之一，是19世纪上半叶英国浪漫主义文学的奠基人，是"湖畔派诗人"（Lake Poets）当中成就最高者。他与柯勒律治（Samuel Taylor Coleridge，1772—1834）于1789年合作发表的《抒情歌谣集》(Lyrical Ballads)被认为是英国浪漫主义诗歌运动的宣言书。华兹华斯于1843年成为英格兰桂冠诗人并至死保有这一头衔。

下面这首《怦然心动》是华兹华斯见到雨后彩虹后有感而发创作而成。这首诗既抒发了华兹华斯对于自然的挚爱，又表达了他对于宇宙人生的思考。特别是那句"The Child is father of the Man"成了华兹华斯的名言——它告诉世人，一颗未泯的童心是成年人美好生活的源泉。同时，华兹华斯的诗歌总能将虔诚的宗教情感与纯粹的自然美景结合在一起；有评论家认为，在这首诗里，华兹华斯见到彩虹便肃然起敬、心潮澎湃，是因为他联想到了上帝将彩虹作为与诺亚（Noah）以及他的子孙后代订立契约的象征的典故（Twitchell，2004）。

请读下面这首诗歌并且回答问题：

My Heart Leaps Up

William Wordsworth

My heart leaps up when I behold
A rainbow in the sky:
So was it when my life began;
So is it now I am a man;
So be it when I shall grow old,

Or let me die!
The Child is father of the Man;
And I could wish my days to be
Bound each to each by natural piety.

思考题：

1. 诗人是如何展现自己与自然间的关系的？
2. 诗人试图在读者的心中激发出怎样的情感？
3. 你是如何理解"The Child is father of the Man"这句诗的？

译文鉴赏：

怦然心动

威廉·华兹华斯

每当看到彩虹
我便怦然心动：
有这种感觉，当我出生；
有这种感觉，当我长成；
希望心潮依旧汹涌，   5
直到我垂垂老矣，
哪怕是生命告终！
成人的父亲是那孩童；
唯愿活着的每一天
都对美景怦然心动。   10

下面我们再看一首法吉恩的《诗歌》(*Poetry*)。这首诗以"诗歌"为题，现身说法，很好地诠释了什么是诗歌。

第一章　引言

　　埃莉诺·法吉恩（Eleanor Farjeon, 1881–1965）是英国著名儿童文学作家。她出生于伦敦，家庭中的文学氛围非常浓厚：她的两个弟弟都是作家，长兄是一位作曲家。法吉恩自小视力很差且体弱多病，于是便整日待在家中的阁楼上面与书籍为伴。从五岁开始，法吉恩的父亲便鼓励她开始写作；而她的创作灵感很多都来自儿童时期与弟弟们的游戏和家庭的节日活动。成人后，法吉恩积极从事文学创作，并且广泛结交当时的著名作家，例如劳伦斯（D. H. Lawrence, 1885 — 1930）、弗罗斯特等人（Robert Frost, 1874 — 1963）（Bell & Millar, 2011）。法吉恩逝世后，由各出版商发起成立的"儿童图书协会（The Children's Book Circle）"开始每年向个人或组织颁发埃莉诺·法吉恩奖（Eleanor Farjeon Award），以表彰他们对儿童图书出版发行所做出的杰出贡献。

　　请读下面这首诗歌并且回答问题：

Poetry

Eleanor Farjeon

What is Poetry? Who knows?

Not a rose, but the scent of the rose;

Not the sky, but the light in the sky;

Not the fly, but the gleam of the fly;

Not the sea, but the sound of the sea;　　　　5

Not myself, but what makes me

See, hear, and feel something that prose

Cannot: and what it is, who knows?

思考题：

1. 这首诗歌中应用了哪些修辞手法？这些修辞手法达到了怎样的效果？
2. 这首诗歌是否读来朗朗上口？为什么？
3. 读过法吉恩的这首诗，你知道什么是诗歌了吗？请论述。

译文鉴赏：

诗歌
埃莉诺·法吉恩

有谁知道，什么叫作诗歌？
没有玫瑰，却让你闻到玫瑰的花香；
没有天空，却让你看到天空的光芒；
没有飞蝇，却让你触到飞蝇的颤抖；
没有海洋，却让你听到海洋的歌唱； 5
也没有我自己，却让我看到、听到、感觉到了
散文所言之不及：
什么叫作诗歌，有谁知道？

　　我们在引言的部分先后介绍了什么是诗歌以及诗歌的内容、形式和功能、作用。诗歌能够给我们带来独特的审美体验，能够让我们增长见识、开阔视野、提升品位、洞悉宇宙人生的真谛。所以，我们每个人都应当去阅读诗歌、欣赏诗歌，享受它所带给我们的乐趣。需要指出的是，对于英语诗歌相关知识的了解，对于英语诗歌赏析相关要素和角度的分析，将可以帮助广大英语文学爱好者更好地欣赏、品鉴英语诗歌，提升阅读英语诗歌的乐趣。这也是我们在下面几个章节中要做的事情。

第二章 英诗的韵律

2.1 引言

在详细探讨英语诗歌的韵律（rhythm and rhyme）之前，我们先简单介绍一下有关英诗形式的一些基本常识。

英诗是由"诗句"和"诗节"组成的。英诗当中的诗句（sentences）与散文当中的句子就其功能而言其实是一样的。通常来讲，一个句子就是对于某个事情的陈述。英诗当中的诗节（stanzas）就类似于散文当中的段落；有所不同的是，散文当中的段落通常会包含若干完整的句子，而诗节可以由一个或是多个句子组成，有时甚至可以是半句话。

我们在读一首英语诗歌的时候，特别是第一次读，请注意诗句当中的标点符号以及诗句的类型，弄清楚诗句是陈述句、疑问句、感叹句还是祈使句。此外，还要留意诗人是如何根据所要表达思想的不同而将整首诗歌分为几个诗节、几个部分的。

除了诗句和诗节的组织形式以外，节奏和押韵也是英语诗歌重要的组织形式。我们可以这样理解"诗句和诗节"同"节奏和押韵"之间的关系，即如果说诗句和诗节是整首诗歌的组织形式，那么节奏和押韵则是在词语、诗行或是几组诗行层面上运作的英诗的组织形式。

此外，在详细探讨英语诗歌的节奏以前，我们还有必要首先对英汉两种语言的节奏模式加以概述和比较；这是因为，汉语和英语的节奏模式并不相同，而由于受到母语的影响，中国学生在学习、朗读、分析、鉴赏其他英语文学作品和英语诗歌的时候往往会面临诸多的困扰。

汉语是音节节拍语言（syllable-timed language）；而英语是重音节拍语言（stress-timed language）。所谓音节节拍语言是指汉语基本上每一个字就是一个音节，而在语流当中每个汉字读音的音长基本相等，因此汉语的节奏是以音节为最小单位的，所以也被称为音节节拍语言。可以划归音节节拍语言的语言还有法语、意大利语、朝鲜语，等等。而所谓重音节拍语言是指，在英语语流当中存在明显的轻重读音节，而每两个重读音节间所间隔的时间大体相当（无论中间有多少轻读音节）——这被称作音步等时性（isochrony），所以英语的节奏是以重读音节为最小单位划分的，也被称作重音节拍语言。可以划归重音节拍语言的语言还有德语、俄语、波斯语，等等（Nespor, 2011）。

由于英汉两种语言节奏模式不同，就经常会造成对中国学生学习英语的负迁移作用，即汉语自身的语言习惯干扰和阻碍了英语的学习——使得他们在使用英语进行朗读、口语交流的时候，特别是在朗读英语诗歌的时候，会一个单词一个单词地念出英文，把每个单词作为一个重读单位，出现难以把握节奏的情形，从而造成了英语学习特别是英语诗歌赏析方面的困难。

我们可以将诗歌的语言比喻为歌词，而将节奏和押韵比喻为诗歌的律动和曲调。除此以外，诗歌所包含的节奏、押韵和声音本身也具有意义——它会为诗歌当中的词语增添新的意涵。本章当中，我们就会集中讨论节奏、押韵和单词的声音效果在英语诗歌当中的重要作用。

2.2 英诗的节奏

本节当中我们将要探讨如下三个主题：英诗的节奏与格律、英诗节奏的类型和英诗节奏的作用。在第一部分中，我们将首先厘清节奏、格律的概念以及二者间的关系；接下来，我们会对节奏的类型与作用加以详细的讨论。

2.2.1 节奏与格律

广义而言，节奏（rhythm）是指所有受控的或是有规则的律动。它既可以诉诸我们的听觉也可诉诸我们的视觉。例如，我们会说"这首歌的节奏比较慢"，我们也会说"这张画的节奏很好"，等等。节奏通常是由某种媒介当中的相对立的构成要素有序交替出现而产生的（Crossley-Holland, Nov. 12, 2020）。节奏是所有艺术形式的基本特征之一，特别是在音乐、舞蹈和诗歌等方面表现得尤为突出。即便是在自然现象当中，我们也可以感受到节奏的存在，例如一波一波的海浪、起伏的山峦、大都市高层建筑所勾勒出的天际线，等等。

当然，我们更多的时候会将节奏与音乐和诗歌联系起来；然而事实上，我们每天的日常语言当中也存在节奏。这一点对于英语语言来说尤为重要。例如，如果你大声地朗读一句英文，那么你就会注意到这个句子当中的某些词语或是某些词语的某些部分需要得到强调，需要重读；而在一组词语与另外一组词语之间则需要有不同时间长短的停顿。在连续的英语口语表达当中，我们会意识到节奏的存在。也就是说，在语流当中，我们会识别出以重读音节及其组合变化为表征的所谓节奏（参见本章第一节当中所述，英语为重音节拍语言）。由此，我们引导出以下这个重要的概念：格律（meter, also metre）。

英语诗歌的格律，就是指在单个诗行或是整首诗歌当中，由于轻重读音节的有规律的交替出现而产生的最基本的节奏类型。因此，所谓"格律"其实就是对英语诗歌节奏类型的技术性描述。英诗的格律依据诗行当中的重读音节的数量来划分，而对中间的轻读音节的数量则没有严格的规定。也就是说，由轻重读音节构成的每一个不断重复的节奏单位（即音步——foot，我们会在下一个小节详细讨论）不见得完全一致，只要求大致相同即可。许多传统的英语诗歌形式会要求某一个或某一组特定的格律以特定的顺序交替出现，而最常见的英诗格律（节奏类型）则是抑扬格五音步（iambic pentameter）：一句诗行当中共包含十个音节，组成五个抑扬格的音步，每个音步由一个轻读音节加上一个重读音节组成（Britannica, April 25, 2018）。

英语当中的节奏非常重要。例如，在日常英语口语的表达当中，人们经常通过改变句子的重读和停顿，也就是通过改变句子节奏的方式改变句子所表达的含义。同样，诗人在诗歌创作当中也会应用这种节奏上的变化，来充分表达出自己的情感和态度。

此外，节奏还有其他的用途。例如，根据经验，人们认为如果傍晚天空呈现出微红的颜色，那么第二天的天气一定会很好。相反，如果早晨天空呈现出微红的颜色，那么这一天的天气就会变坏。大多数的人很难记得清楚，什么时候什么颜色会预示怎样的天气变化。然而，如果我们将这种规律用有特定节奏的诗歌语言表达出来，人们记忆起来就会简单得多。请看下面这句谚语：

> Red sky at night sailor's delight;
> Red sky at morning sailor take warning.（T. Watson, 2009）

再如，在西方，人们刻在墓碑上的铭文经常会采用具有鲜明节奏的押韵的语言：

> Beneath this stone, this lump of clay,
> Lies Uncle Peter Daniels,
> Who too early in the month of May

第二章　英诗的韵律

Took off his winter flannels.（Kelly，1996）

在墓志铭中使用韵文，除了幽默的效果以外，节奏和韵律还能够使得这些话语变得更有文采，易读易记，从而长远地流传。就如同莎士比亚曾经说过的那样：

Not marble, nor the gilded monuments
Of princes, shall outlive this pow'rful rhyme.（Shakespeare，1609）

因此，在叙述重要的事件和表达重要的思想的时候，人们通常会使用具有鲜明节奏的押韵的语言，即所谓"诗语"（poetic diction）。最早见于文献的，有关"诗语"的评论来自亚里士多德的《诗学》。他认为，所谓"诗语"就是清晰而不落俗套的语言（Britannica，Nov. 1，2007a）。此评论言简意赅，直中要害。在这里，笔者认为有必要对其内涵加以进一步的阐发。

笔者以为，所谓"诗语"是更适宜诗歌内容的语言；是比普通语言更为高级的语言；是具有整齐、有规律和精心设计的韵律的语言。同时，我们还应当注意到，很多现代诗歌并不押韵，同时节奏也略显杂乱无章。出现这种现象的主要原因在于，现代诗人经常会尝试新的表达方式，其目的是赋予他们的诗歌作品以更多的新鲜感和冲击力。

我们在朗读一首诗歌的时候要充分注意到节奏的重要性，因为诗歌的节奏通常会帮助我们理解诗歌所传达的意义、情感、态度以及诗人的创作意图。反过来说，诗人在安排诗歌当中的词语的时候，其目的就是让读者在朗读的时候能够自然而然地找到它们的节奏。所以，在我们朗读诗歌的时候，一定要让词语"达意"，即让词语表达出诗人的真实意涵。这就要求我们既不能过度地强调节奏，又不能无视它的存在——我们要充分理解节奏和韵律的设计初衷，充分地相信诗人，以一种自然的态度进行朗读，以期表现出诗歌的意涵和意境。

下面我们以两首诗为例，帮助大家理解英语诗歌当中节奏的重要性。

第一首是洛威尔写的《男人和妻子》(Man and Wife)。

罗伯特·洛威尔（Robert Lowell, 1917—1977）生于美国马萨诸塞州波士顿市，卒于纽约，以复杂艰涩的、自传式的诗歌而闻名。他于1947年和1974年先后两次分别凭借诗歌集《威利爵爷的城堡》(Lord Weary's Castle)和《海豚》(The Dolphin)荣获普利策诗歌奖。

下面这首《男人和妻子》(Man and Wife)选自洛威尔的诗歌集《生活研究》(Life Studies, 1959)，诗中的主人公为洛威尔本人和他的第二任妻子伊丽莎白·哈德威克（Elizabeth Hardwick）。这首诗理解起来有些难度，希望读者可以借助工具书、参考译文以及相关文学评论来加深理解。

请读下面这首诗歌并且回答问题：

Man and Wife
Robert Lowell

Tamed by Miltown, we lie on Mother's bed;
the rising sun in war paint dyes us red;
in broad daylight her gilded bed-posts shine,
abandoned, almost Dionysian.
At last the trees are green on Marlborough Street,   5
blossoms on our magnolia ignite
the morning with their murderous five days' white.
All night I've held your hand,
as if you had
a fourth time faced the kingdom of the mad —   10
its hackneyed speech, its homicidal eye —

and dragged me home alive ⋯ Oh my petite,

clearest of all God's creatures, still all air and nerve:

you were in our twenties, and I,

once hand on glass   15

and heart in mouth,

outdrank the Rahvs in the heat

of Greenwich Village, fainting at your feet —

too boiled and shy

and poker-faced to make a pass,   20

while the shrill verve

of your invective scorched the traditional South.

Now twelve years later, you turn your back.

Sleepless, you hold

your pillow to your hollows like a child;   25

your old-fashioned tirade —

loving, rapid, merciless —

breaks like the Atlantic Ocean on my head.

思考题：

1. 为什么诗人说他妻子的"old-fashioned tirade"是"loving"而且"merciless"？
2. 请说一说节奏对这首诗的幽默表达起到了怎样的作用？
3. 请大声朗读这首诗并且注意诗歌是如何通过节奏组织、安排词语的。

译文鉴赏：

男人和妻子

罗伯特·洛威尔

被眠尔通驯服的我们，躺在妈妈的床上；
战争油画上升起的太阳将我们染得血红；
白日里她镀金的床柱如酒神的权杖，
挥舞，几近疯狂。
最后马尔伯勒街上的树变成绿色，　　　　　　5
木兰花用它横扫一切的白色
连续五天，将清晨点燃。
我整晚握住你的手，
似乎
你在第四次陷入疯狂——　　　　　　　　　　10
陈腐的言辞，夺人的眼光——
将我拖回家中……啊，我的宝贝儿，
上帝的宠儿：
那时我们二十出头儿，
我手端酒杯　　　　　　　　　　　　　　　　15
心头惴惴，
在格林尼治村的盛夏里喝得大醉，
热血沸腾又羞涩难当，
强作镇静却晕厥在你的身旁。
而此时，　　　　　　　　　　　　　　　　　20
你粗鲁澎湃的神韵
烧毁了一本正经的南方。

十二年后，回眸凝望，

无眠而又消瘦的你

怀抱枕头，孩子一样

老一套的激烈言辞——

像大西洋

爱抚，迅速而又无情地

砸在我的头上。

下面再读一首丁尼生的《碎了，碎了，碎了》(*Break, Break, Break*)。

阿尔弗雷德·丁尼生（Alfred Tennyson，1809—1892）是英国维多利亚时代最具代表性的诗人之一。他于1827年考入剑桥大学三一学院；然而由于父亲病亡，家道中落，不得不于1831年辍学谋生，并未获得学位。在大学期间，丁尼生结识了同为诗人的亚瑟·哈勒姆（Arthur Hallam），并且从此成为终生挚友；而后者又向丁尼生的妹妹求婚，并且于1833年得到其家人的应允。然而，天妒英才，哈勒姆却在同年突然亡故（一说是死于中风）。痛失挚友使得丁尼生伤心欲绝。下面这首《碎了，碎了，碎了》就是诗人悼念亡友之作。丁尼生这样描述创作这首诗时的情形：作于林肯郡的一条小路上，那时是凌晨5点，路两旁的树篱上鲜花开放。(Made in a Lincolnshire lane at five o'clock in the morning, between blossoming hedges.)（Barry，2013）。

请读下面这首诗歌并且回答问题：

Break, Break, Break

Alfred Tennyson

Break, break, break,

On the cold gray stones, O Sea!

And I would that my tongue could utter

   The thoughts that arise in me.

O, well for the fisherman's boy,   5

   That he shouts with his sister at play!

O, well for the sailor lad,

   That he sings in his boat on the bay!

And the stately ships go on

   To their haven under the hill;   10

But O for the touch of a vanished hand,

   And the sound of a voice that is still!

Break, break, break,

   At the foot of thy crags, O Sea!

But the tender grace of a day that is dead   15

   Will never come back to me.

思考题：

1. 请大声朗读诗歌的第一行。在诗歌的开始部分，第一行诗句发挥了怎样的作用？
2. 这首诗当中各个诗行的轻重读音节有规律吗？如果有，请描述一下。
3. 这首诗中有多种修辞手法的运用。请简要分析。

译文鉴赏：

碎了，碎了，碎了

阿尔弗雷德·丁尼生

碎了，碎了，碎了
那拍打在冰冷礁石上的海水
我的心中纵有思绪万千
而此时却有口难言

渔家的男孩是多么快乐　　　　　　　　　　　　　5
同自己的姐妹追逐打闹
年轻的水手是多么快乐
哼唱着歌子在湾畔停靠

雄壮的船队驶回了
山下停泊的港湾　　　　　　　　　　　　　　　10
而我再也听不到你的声音
触不到你的笑脸

碎了，碎了，碎了
那拍打在峭壁岩石上的海水
曾与你共度的美好时光　　　　　　　　　　　　15
再难回到我的身旁

2.2.2 节奏的类型

英诗中对于诗行节奏类型的分析叫作格律分析，也称韵节分析（scansion）。在做格律分析的时候我们要清点并确认每个诗行当中的轻重读音节及其数量，并且要将它们划分成若干音步（feet）（Greene & Cushman, 2016）。格律分析的主要作用就在于，它从"机械技巧"的视角解释了诗歌的节奏是如何为诗歌的内容、意义以及审美效果服务的。通过格律分析，通过对诗人创作技巧的研究，读者就可以弄明白诗人所要达到的表达效果，从而进一步加深对于诗歌的理解。换个角度看，格律分析的知识也可以为我们将来可能的诗歌创作提供方法上的指导。

进行格律分析首先要弄清楚什么是音步（feet）。音步就是诗行当中的一个单独的节奏单位，或是叫作一个单独的格律（meter）构成单位。通常来讲，每一个音步至少要包含一个重读音节以及一个或是多个轻读音节。在对这一节奏单位进行描述时，我们用"扬"指称其重读音节，用"抑"指称其轻读音节。

为了增加对于音步的感性认识，我们不妨先看一下下面这个诗节。该诗节选自克里斯托弗·马洛的《激情的牧人致心爱的姑娘》：

> Come **live** with **me**, and **be** my **love**,
> And **we** will **all** the **plea**sures **prove**,
> That **Va**lleys, **groves**, **hills**, and **fields**,
> **Woods**, or **stee**py **moun**tain **yields**.
> —— *The Passionate Shepherd to His Love* by Christopher Marlowe

这个诗节当中下划线并且加粗的部分就是应当重读的音节。这样看来，此诗节的四行诗都是由四组"轻读音节+重读音节"，共计八个音节构成的诗行；也就是说，这四行诗句分别都是由四个音步组成，每个音步都是由一个轻读加一个重读音节组成。

下面我们开始对英诗节奏类型进行具体的、专业性的描述。

英诗中有五种常见的音步。其中有两种是基于两个音节的音步。它们分别是抑扬格（iambic）和扬抑格（trochaic），例如单词děstróy就是抑扬格，而单词wánděr则是扬抑格。其中抑扬格是英诗当中最为常见的音步类型。此外，还有两种基于三个音节的音步。它们分别是抑抑扬格（anapestic）和扬抑抑格（dactylic），例如单词iňtěrvéne就是抑抑扬格，而单词mérrĭlў则是扬抑抑格。第五种常见的音步叫作扬扬格（spondaic），例如单词foótbáll——它同时包含两个重读音节。

同时请注意，在英诗当中存在很多上述音步类型的变体，这就使得我们的格律分析变得很棘手。不过，需要提醒大家的是，不同的人对同一首诗歌的格律分析不见得完全相同。事实上，大多数的诗歌都会有一种最主要的节奏类型，例如"抑扬格"；而同一首诗歌当中偶尔出现其他的节奏类型也是再正常不过的事情。大家试想一下，如果一首诗歌当中的节奏始终如一，那么读起来就会变得非常枯燥乏味。所以，当你读一首英语诗歌的时候，既要留意某种主要节奏类型所产生的效果，又要明晰诗歌在节奏类型上的变化。有时候你会发现某些诗行当中非重读音节的数量与主要的节奏类型要求出入较大，那么这些音节就叫作松散音节（slack syllables）。之所以会出现这种情况，多半是因为诗人想要通过节奏的变化来强调某些重要的词语，从而突出某些特殊的思想。

除了对诗行当中主要音步类型进行描述，当我们对整首诗歌进行格律分析（scan the poem）的时候，还需要说明每一句诗行当中的音步的数量。对于音步数量的描述需要使用下面这些来自拉丁语的词汇：

mono — one	di — two
tri — three	tetra — four
penta — five	hexa — six
hepta — seven	octa — eight

如果我们将这些数字前缀与格律（meter）相结合，就会生成如下这些用以描述音步数量的术语（Cummings, 2006）：

monometer — one feet	dimeter — two feet
trimeter — three feet	tetrameter — four feet
pentameter — five feet	hexameter — six feet
heptameter — seven feet	octameter — eight feet

明白了上述知识以后，我们就已经准备好描述英语诗歌的节奏类型（格律）了。还以上文所举的克里斯托弗·马洛的诗节为例，其节奏类型就是抑扬格四音步，用英文表述就是"iambic tetrameter"。

下面我们以两首诗为例，帮助大家加深对于英诗节奏的认识。第一首是朗斯顿·休斯的《梦想》（*Dreams*）。

朗斯顿·休斯（Langston Hughes, 1901—1967）是美国著名黑人小说家、剧作家、诗人兼社会活动家。他是所谓"爵士诗歌"（jazz poetry——一种展现出爵士乐节奏或是即兴创作感觉的诗歌艺术形式）（Wallenstein, 1993）艺术流派的创始人之一，同时还是"哈莱姆文艺复兴"（Harlem Renaissance——一场以美国纽约曼哈顿哈莱姆区为中心的，时间跨越20世纪二三十年代的，以美国黑人在文学、音乐、戏剧和视觉艺术等方面取得非凡成就为特征的非洲裔美国人文化复兴运动）（Hutchinson, Sep. 14, 2021）的重要领袖之一。

《梦想》最初发表于1923年5月出版的《明天的世界》（*The World Tomorrow*）杂志上，同期出版的还包括杜波伊斯（W. E. B. Du Bois, 1868—1963）、莫顿（Robert R. Moton, 1867—1940）等著名黑人作家的文章。这首诗歌所探讨的主题思想贯穿了整首作品：面对现实困难时保持梦想的重要性，以及放弃梦想后所要面临的严峻问题。

请读下面这首诗歌并且回答问题：

Dreams

Langston Hughes

Hold fast to dreams

For if dreams die

Life is a broken-winged bird

That cannot fly.

Hold fast to dreams   5

For when dreams go

Life is a barren field

Frozen with snow.

思考题：

1. 请对这首诗进行格律分析。
2. 从哪些意义上来说梦想是可以死亡或是消失的呢？
3. 这首诗当中有哪些暗喻是贯穿始终的呢？
4. 找到这首诗中的意象，并且分析这些意象所达到的效果。

译文鉴赏：

梦想

朗斯顿·休斯

抓紧梦想

如果梦想死去

生活就如折翼的鸟儿。

不能飞翔。

> 抓紧梦想 5
> 如果梦想远离
> 生活便如贫瘠的土地
> 覆盖冰霜。

下面我们再看一首叶芝的《当你老了》(*When You are Old*)。

爱尔兰诗人威廉·巴特勒·叶芝（William Butler Yeats, 1865—1939）是20世纪最伟大的英语诗人之一。除了创作诗歌，他还是一位剧作家和散文家，并于1923年荣获诺贝尔文学奖。叶芝的诗歌创作受到了诸如浪漫主义、神秘主义、唯美主义、现实主义等诸多文艺思潮的影响，最终形成了自己独特的艺术风格。

我们这里所选的《当你老了》是叶芝写给初恋女友茅德·冈（Maud Gonne, 1866—1953）小姐的一首情诗。后者是一位爱尔兰民族主义者，终其一生投身于爱尔兰独立运动。有趣的是，叶芝曾先后四次向茅德·冈小姐求婚，都惨遭拒绝。自1889年在伦敦与茅德·冈小姐相识后，叶芝便开始了对她长达三十年的不懈追求——直到1916年，茅德·冈小姐的丈夫由于参与"复活节起义"（Easter Rising, 1916）而被处决后，叶芝最后一次向她求婚，却仍被拒绝。

叶芝曾经告诉茅德·冈，没有她自己就不会高兴。而茅德·冈的回答则颇为有趣："不，你是高兴的，因为正是你所谓的'不高兴'才让你写出了美丽的诗歌，而你因为写诗而高兴。婚姻是一桩枯燥无聊的事情。诗人不应当结婚。这世界应当因为我拒绝和你结婚而对我说声谢谢。"（Oh yes, you are, because you make beautiful poetry out of what you call your unhappiness and are happy in that. Marriage would be such a dull affair. Poets should never marry. The world should thank me for not marring you.）（McNally, Dec. 5, 2014）诚如斯言，叶芝应当感谢茅德·冈小姐的不嫁之恩；而文学爱好者们也欠茅德·冈小姐一声"谢谢"！

请读下面这首诗歌并且回答问题:

When You are Old
William Butler Yeats

When you are old and grey and full of sleep,
And nodding by the fire, take down this book,
And slowly read, and dream of the soft look
Your eyes had once, and of their shadows deep;

How many loved your moments of glad grace, 5
And loved your beauty with love false or true,
But one man loved the pilgrim soul in you,
And loved the sorrows of your changing face;

And bending down beside the glowing bars,
Murmur, a little sadly, how Love fled 10
And paced upon the mountains overhead
And hid his face amid a crowd of stars.

思考题:

1. 请对这首诗的格律加以分析。
2. 第八诗行中使用了"pilgrim soul",请解释其含义。
3. 第三诗节运用了怎样的修辞手法?请说明。
4. 最后一行诗中运用了怎样的意象?有何象征意义?

译文鉴赏：

当你老了

叶芝

当你老了，鬓发如霜，
睡意昏沉，独坐炉旁，
手把诗篇，缓缓吟唱，
想起，曾有的深深眼影，
和温柔目光；　　　　　　　　　　　　　　　　　　　　5

多少人为了你片刻的娇颜
痴迷轻狂，
只有一人爱着你朝圣的灵魂
和脸上掠过的
点点忧伤；　　　　　　　　　　　　　　　　　　　　10

当你老了，蜷缩炉旁，
喃喃低语，暗自神伤，
任时光飞逝，爱成过往，
叹息，她已如夜空中的星斗，
嵌入永恒的苍茫。　　　　　　　　　　　　　　　　　15

2.2.3 节奏的作用

英诗当中的节奏具有非常重要的作用。不同的节奏类型会创造出一种所谓的"文学音乐"（literary music）以抚慰、取悦读者。这些节奏类型会吸引读者的注意力，让他们不知不觉地沉浸其中，从而鼓励他们继续阅读。重读和非重读的音节则会让诗人们根据表意的需要而特别强调某些词语，从而得到更强大的语义表达效果。此外，不同的节奏类型还会帮助读者记忆，甚至背诵诗歌。当然，诗人们也会应用特定的节奏类型来突出诗歌的主题思想或意义（Attridge，1982）。

下面我们就根据具体的节奏类型分析一下它们在英诗当中的作用。

大家知道，抑扬格是英诗当中最为常见的节奏类型。这可能是出于以下两点原因。第一，英文当中的多音节单词大部分的重读会落在第二个音节上面，这样就会很自然地在语流当中形成很多"轻读音节+重读音节"的组合。第二，在英语语流当中，大多数的虚词只有一个音节，而紧随其后的实词则大多需要重读。例如下面这句英文：the dog has run to school——很自然地形成了抑扬格三音步（iambic trimeter）的节奏。因此，英语当中抑扬格的节奏听起来最自然、最接近人们的日常口语表达。

与抑扬格相反，扬抑格的节奏类型则是把自然的语流表达颠倒过来了，所以听起来会有些吃力，语流涩滞。抑抑扬格由两个轻读音节加上一个重读音节构成，听起来会有一种跳跃、轻快的感觉，所以经常会在表达幽默或是描写快速运动状况的诗句当中出现。扬抑抑格起首是一个重读音节，所以听起来会带有一种向前冲刺的感觉。而扬扬格则因为同时包含两个重读音节，所以听起来掷地有声，严肃而庄重（Fussell，1979）。

除了声音效果以外，诗人有时还会通过使用更多的重读单音节单词来达到改变诗歌行进节奏的目的。一般来说，使用更多的非重读音节会加快诗歌的节奏；相反，使用更多的重读音节则会减缓诗歌行进的节奏。

下面我们看一些例证以加深对于英诗节奏及其作用的理解。请注意在下面即将讨论的诗歌当中，诗人都使用了怎样的节奏类型以及这些节奏类型的实际应用效果如何。同时，还请留意，在诗歌的哪些地方诗人对主要的节奏类型作出了改变以及这样做达到了怎样的效果。

先看拜伦的诗歌《夜美人》（*She Walks in Beauty*）。

乔治·戈登·拜伦（George Gordon, Lord Byron, 1788—1824）是为中国广大外国文学爱好者所熟知的一位重要作家。作为19世纪初英国伟大的浪漫主义诗人，他的代表作长篇叙事诗《恰尔德·哈洛尔德游记》（*Childe Harold's Pilgrimage*）和《唐璜》（*Don Juan*）在我国流传甚广，深受好评。

拜伦以其诗笔塑造了无数"拜伦式的英雄"——他们叛逆、抗争、热爱自由，同时又忧郁、徘徊和苦闷。我们此处所选的是拜伦的一首抒情短诗。这首诗里面的"她"是拜伦的表兄威尔莫特（Sir Robert Wilmot）的妻子安妮（Mrs. Anne Beatrix Wilmot）。1814年6月，拜伦在伦敦的一次聚会当中见到了身着点缀着闪闪发光的金属亮片黑色长裙的安妮。他被眼前的美人深深打动，于是诗兴大发，第二天便创作出了这首脍炙人口的绝妙短诗（Cummings, 2008）。

请读下面这首诗歌并且回答问题：

She Walks in Beauty

George Gordon, Lord Byron

1

She walks in beauty, like the night
　Of cloudless climes and starry skies;
And all that's best of dark and bright
　Meet in her aspect and her eyes:
Thus mellowed to that tender light　　　　　　　　5
　Which heaven to gaudy day denies.

2

One shade the more, one ray the less,
　Had half impair'd the nameless grace

第二章　英诗的韵律　　　　　　　　　　　　　　　　　　　　　　31

  Which waves in every raven tress,
   Or softly lightens o'er her face,   10
  Where thoughts serenely sweet express
   How pure, how dear their dwelling-place.

3

  And on that cheek, and over that brow,
   So soft, so calm, yet eloquent,
  The smiles that win, the tints that glow,   15
   But tell of days in goodness spent,
  A mind at peace with all below,
   A heart whose love is innocent!

思考题：

1. 请说出这首诗歌所运用的最主要的节奏类型。
2. 这种节奏类型在整首诗当中的哪些地方发生了哪些变化？这些变化的作用是什么？
3. 这首诗的节奏是怎样服务于诗歌的意义、情感、态度以及诗歌创作意图的？

译文鉴赏：

夜美人
拜伦

她
行走在

透明的星空下
黑暗与光线
汇聚   5
在她的身上和心间
释放出
柔和而醇香的光环
令灼眼的白天
艳羡   10

夜
再暗上一点
或是再亮上一丝
都会
减损她的万种风情   15
思绪
纯净而柔美地
将她的面庞照亮
在她乌黑的发丝上面
荡漾   20

她
一颦一笑
所有的
温柔、安静和善良
都藏在了眉头   25
写在了脸上
一个安宁的灵魂

高高在上

一颗纯净的心灵

为爱发光　　　　　　　　　　　　　　　　30

下面我们再以柯勒律治的诗作《韵步》(Metrical Feet)为例，帮助大家加深对英诗节奏的理解。

塞缪尔·泰勒·柯勒律治（Samuel Taylor Coleridge, 1772—1834）是英国19世纪初浪漫主义诗歌运动的奠基人之一，同时他还是著名的思想家和文学理论家。他与华兹华斯合作出版的《抒情歌谣集》(Lyrical Ballads)是英国浪漫主义文学的开山之作。柯勒律治一生作品不多，却影响巨大。其代表诗作有大家耳熟能详的《古舟子咏》(The Rime of The Ancient Mariner)和《忽必烈汗》(Kubla Khan)。此外，他于1817年出版的《文学传记》(Biographia Literaria)则对现代文学理论的发生、发展产生了深远的影响。

下面这首《韵步》创作于1807年，那时柯勒律治年仅七岁的三儿子德文特（Derwent Coleridge）刚刚开始学习希腊语。柯勒律治写这首诗的初衷是为了帮助儿子学习诗歌的格律，不曾想这首诗却广为传颂，成为他的代表作之一（Hainton, 1996）。这首《韵步》以诗歌的形式具体而生动地介绍了英语诗歌的格律，可谓是现身说法，诗中谈诗。由于本首诗歌的内容和形式所限，笔者将不再提供参考译文，而是对内容中的一些重点、难点做了注解，希望能够帮助到各位读者。

Metrical Feet

— A Lesson for a Boy

Samuel Taylor Coleridge

Tróchĕe[1] trĭps frŏm lóng tŏ shórt;

From long to long in solemn sort

Slów Spóndeé[2] stálks; stróng foót! yet ill able

E'vĕr tŏ cóme ŭp wĭth Dáctўl's[3] trĭsýllăblĕ.

Ĭ́ ámbĭcs[4] márch frŏm shórt tŏ lóng—   5

Wĭth ă leáp ănd ă boúnd thĕ swĭft A'năpĕsts[5] thróng;

One syllable long, with one short at each side,

A˘ mphíbrăchўs[6] hástes wĭth ă státelў stríde—

Fiŕst ańd lást béiňg lońg, míddlĕ shórt, A˘ mphímăcĕr[7, 8]

Stríkes hĭs thúndérińg hoófs líke ă próud hígh-brĕd Rácer.   10

If Derwent[9] be innocent, steady, and wise,

And delight in the things of earth, water, and skies;

Tender warmth at his heart, with these meters to show it,

With sound sense in his brains, may make Derwent a poet—

May crown him with fame, and must win him the love   15

Of his father on earth and his Father above.

My dear, dear child!

Could you stand upon Skiddaw[10], you would not from its whole ridge

See a man who so loves you as your fond S. T. COLERIDGE.

Notes:

1. 扬抑格
2. 扬扬格
3. 扬抑抑格
4. 抑扬格
5. 抑抑扬格
6. 抑扬抑格

7. 扬抑扬格
8. 最后两种格律类型（amphibrach和amphimacer）划分的依据是音节的长短而非音节的轻重。此两种格律主要出现在希腊和拉丁语诗歌当中。
9. 德文特（Derwent）是柯勒律治的小儿子。这首诗本来是写给他的长子哈特利（Hartley）的，可是后来柯勒律治对此进行了修改。诗歌当中的轻重读符号是诗人自己加到相关音节上面的。
10. 斯基多山（Skiddaw）是英格兰西北部的一座山峰，位于柯勒律治早年曾经生活过的城镇附近。

2.3 英诗的押韵和音效

一提到诗歌的韵律，我们就会自然而然地想到押韵（rhyme）。所谓押韵是指相互关联的两个或是两个以上的单词的最后一个音节发音近似，从而使得这些单词产生相互呼应的效果（Britannica, Feb. 4, 2020）。然而，诗歌的韵律不仅仅涉及押韵和我们上个小节讨论过的节奏，还会涉及其他的方面，例如单词的声音效果。所以，本节当中我们会首先讨论英诗的押韵，然后再讨论诗人是如何运用英语词汇的声音来传情达意的，即所谓"单词的音效"。

押韵在英诗当中的作用类似于节奏。它会将诗歌的语言提升到高于我们日常用语的水平；并且，押韵还会使得诗歌的思想内容听起来更为强烈、优美，使得诗歌更易传唱。此外，押韵还是将一首诗歌组织成一个整体的重要方式。例如，如果诗歌中的各个诗行都押尾韵的话，那么这种押韵的方式就会将所有诗行联系起来，同时各个诗行的意义也就不再彼此孤立了。同时，押韵还是一种诗人表达强调的方法，因为彼此押韵的单词会显得更为突出；而且，当押韵出现在诗歌当中更为重要的位置的时候，就会给相关词语带来额外的强调效果。

下面我们就分三个小节——押韵的种类、单词的音效和素体诗（这是一种不押韵但是有节奏的诗歌形式。由于其特征与韵律紧密相关，所以我们就将其放在本章当中加以讨论），对英诗的韵律加以探讨。

2.3.1 押韵的种类

在探讨英诗押韵的种类之前，需要首先说明的一点是，我们不能依据英语单词的拼写来对其是否押韵作出判断，因为我们判断英语单词是否押韵的依据是它们的发音而非拼写。

英诗当中押韵的种类很多。

我们首先看"正韵"和"斜韵"（exact and slant rhyme）。当押韵单词当中的重读的元音及紧随其后的辅音完全相同时，我们称之为"正韵"（exact/perfect rhyme）。例如 fight — delight; powers — flowers。反之，当押韵单词当中的重读元音或是紧随其后的辅音不完全相同时，我们称之为"斜韵"（slant/half rhyme）。斜韵还可以细分为三种：谐辅韵（consonance）——元音不同而辅音相同押韵，例如 black, block; creak, croak; 谐元韵（assonance）——元音相同而辅音不同，例如，lake, fate; time, mind; 头韵法（alliteration）——诗行当中相邻单词以同样的辅音开头的押韵方法，例如 wild woolly, threatening throngs。

其次，押韵的音节可以是一个音节，也可以是多个音节。我们据此将押韵划分为"阳韵"和"阴韵"（masculine and feminine rhyme）。由一个音节且押韵的单词或是重读音节为最后一个音节且押韵的单词构成的押韵方式叫作"阳韵"（masculine rhyme）。例如，pail — rail; divorce — remorse。与之对应，当押韵单词当中的重读音节以及紧随其后的一个、两个或是多个非重读音节押韵的时候，我们称之为"阴韵"（feminine rhyme）。例如，bitten — written; gladness — madness; merrily — verily。

此外，我们还可以根据押韵单词在诗行当中位置的不同将其划分为押尾韵和中间韵（end and internal rhyme）。我们将诗歌当中位于不同诗行末尾的一个或是多个音节押韵的形式称为押尾韵（end rhyme）；而在同一诗行之内出现押韵的情况则叫作押中间韵（internal rhyme），例如Just because of applause I have to pause。

需要补充的一点是，英诗当中还经常会出现所谓"假押韵"情况——即所谓押韵的单词的拼写非常类似，而发音实则不同。尽管这种情况严格来讲算不上押韵，但我们还是给它取了个名字，叫作"眼韵"（eye rhyme）。例如，cough — bough; love — move。

除了了解上述押韵的种类，我们在读英诗的时候还需注意以下两点。第一，由于英文单词的发音会随时代的不同而发生变化，所以会出现有些单词过去曾经押韵，到了现代英语中却不押韵的情况。例如，"tea"曾经与"say"是押韵的；而"die"与"me"也曾经是押韵的。所以我们在读20世纪以前的英诗的时候就要留心可能的发音变化，因为有些单词看似不押韵，其实有可能在创作之初它们却是押韵的。第二，不要认为英诗当中押韵越是严格、整齐就一定越好。事实上，过于严整的押韵可能会使整首诗歌变得枯燥乏味或是分散读者对于诗歌所传递思想的注意力。所以，好的押韵形式一定是新鲜的和出人意料的；一定是服务于诗歌内容表达的和能起到组织诗歌内容之功效的。下面我们就通过一些具体的例子来分析鉴赏英诗的押韵。

先看一首布雷克的《伦敦》（*London*）。

威廉·布雷克（William Blake，1757—1827）是英国文学史上最伟大的诗人之一，是英国浪漫主义文学运动的先驱，是神秘慈悲的幻想家和版画艺术家。然而，在其生前和死后的很长一段时间内，布雷克的艺术成就并没有引起人们的注意和认可。帕尔格雷夫（Palgrave）所编辑出版的英诗选集《金库》（*The Golden Treasury*，1875）当中仅仅收录了布雷克的一首诗作，就是最好的证明。直到20世纪初，叶芝等人重新编辑出版了布雷克的诗集。自此，他作为诗人的声名日隆，并且逐渐确立了其伟大艺术家的历史地位。

布雷克的代表诗作为诗歌集《诗歌素描》(*Poetical Sketches*，1783)、《纯真之歌》(*Songs of Innocence*，1789)和《经验之歌》(*Songs of Experience*，1794)。布雷克出生在伦敦，并且一生中大部分的时间生活在这座城市。在伦敦的生活和工作经历，对其文学创作产生了深刻而全面的影响；而彼时的伦敦是一个正在经历巨大的社会和政治动荡的大都市。下面的这首《伦敦》选自《经验之歌》，体现了布雷克对当时英国的社会现实的深入思考和猛烈抨击。

请读下面这首诗歌并且回答问题：

London

William Blake

I wander thro' each charter'd street,
Near where the charter'd Thames does flow,
And mark in every face I meet
Marks of weakness, marks of woe.

In every cry of every Man,　　　　　　　　　　5
In every Infant's cry of fear,
In every voice, in every ban,
The mind-forg'd manacles I hear:

How the chimney-sweeper's cry
Every blackening Church appalls,　　　　　　　10
And the hapless soldier's sigh

Runs in blood down Palace walls.

But most, thro' midnight streets I hear
How the youthful Harlot's curse
Blasts the new-born infant's tear, 15
And blights with plagues the Marriage hearse.

思考题：

1. 请标记这首诗歌的押韵格式（rhyme scheme），并且熟记下面这些标记押韵格式的方法：
   （1）诗行末尾的第一个押韵的地方标记为a。
   （2）所有诗行末尾与a押韵的单词后面都标记为a。
   （3）诗行末尾出现的第二个押韵的地方标记为b；所有诗行末尾与b押韵的单词后面都标记为b；并且以此类推。
   （4）请注意，对于长诗，可以对每个诗节单独标记押韵格式，而对于短诗则无须如此。
2. 就这首诗而言，整齐的押韵格式对于诗歌意义的表达是起到了正面还是负面的作用？请说明你的理由。

译文鉴赏：

伦敦

威廉·布雷克

伦敦的街头铜臭洋溢，
泰晤士河水奔忙不息，
每个行人的每张脸庞
都露出虚弱悲苦的印记。

每人发出的每声哀号， 5
每个婴儿的每声哭泣，
每个声音和每组禁条，
宛如精神的枷锁和镣铐：

扫烟囱孩子发出惨叫
让那熏黑的教堂战栗， 10
牺牲士兵的声声叹息
鲜血般染红了宫廷的墙壁。

年轻妓女的高声诅咒
将那午夜的街道穿透
吹干了新生儿的泪滴， 15
让那新婚的灵车染上瘟疫。

我们再看一首叶芝的《沉默良久》(*After Long Silence*)。

这首《沉默良久》发表于1933年，彼时的叶芝已经是一位白发老者。这首诗是叶芝写给另一位曾经的恋人——奥莉薇娅·莎士比亚（英国小说家、剧作家：Olivia Shakespear, 1863 — 1938）的。二人曾在年轻时短暂相爱，然而由于种种原因，有情人终究未成眷属。1926年，叶芝曾经给奥莉薇娅写过一封信表达自己的悔意。他在信中说：每当我回首青春的时候，就像是一个渴得要死的疯子，想起了当年那杯还剩一半未尝滋味的酒水。不知道你是否也有同感。(One looks back to one's youth as to a cup that a mad man dying of thirst left half tasted. I wonder if you feel like that.)（Hassett, 2010）

请读下面这首诗歌并且回答问题：

After Long Silence

William Butler Yeats

Speech after long silence; it is right,
All other lovers being estranged or dead,
Unfriendly lamplight hid under its shade,
The curtains drawn upon unfriendly night,
That we descant and yet again descant   5
Upon the supreme theme of Art and Song:
Bodily decrepitude is wisdom; young
We loved each other and were ignorant.

思考题：

1. 请标记本首诗的押韵格式。
2. 请看第三行。为什么说lamplight是unfriendly？
3. 请看第六行。指出押中间韵的单词，并且分析这一押韵方式对于突出诗歌主题有何帮助。
4. 诗中的第七行说，与身体衰老相伴而生的是智慧的增长。你认为透过这首诗，叶芝是在歌颂老年的从容与智慧，还是少年的单纯与活力呢？

译文鉴赏：

沉默良久

叶芝

沉默良久后的交谈
甚欢

所有曾经的情侣都已死去，或

各奔东西

亮闪闪的灯光暗藏着敌意 5

窗帘将险恶的黑夜，隔离

我们开始高谈阔论

艺术和诗歌的

至高话题

伴随着智慧的增长 10

是我们衰老的身体

年轻时

我们彼此相爱

却绝口不提

2.3.2 单词的音效

英诗当中单词的声音甚至每个单独字母的声音都很重要。这是因为，英文单词的声音效果可以与某些特定的人类情感相联系；而诗人也经常会在诗歌当中运用单词的声音传情达意。

在语音学上，英语的发音可以分为元音和辅音。除了极少数的情况以外，例如单独由一个元音构成的单词"I""Oh"，等等，英语单词的发音绝大多是由元音和辅音组合而成的。在英诗当中，无论是辅音还是元音都可以表达一定的意涵。

下面是一些辅音通常所能传达的意义（Feng, 1995）：

1) /b, p/：可以暗示轻蔑、嘲笑或是动作的迅速

2) /k, g, st, ts, ch/：可以暗示粗糙、残忍、噪声或是矛盾冲突

3) /m, n, ng/：可以暗示嗡嗡的声响、歌唱或是音乐的声音

4) /l/：可以暗示平静、柔和的动作、溪水的流动或是休憩

第二章 英诗的韵律

我们以柯勒律治（T. S. Coleridge）写的《古舟子咏》（*The Rime of the Ancient Mariner*）中的一个诗节为例说明辅音的常见音效。请大家注意引文当中斜体并且加粗的英文字母。

> The *f*air *b*reeze *b*lew, the white *f*oam *f*lew,
> The *f*urrow *f*ollowed *f*ree;
> We were the fir*st* that ever bur*st*
> Into that *s*ilent *s*ea.

大家可以看到，在这个诗节当中，诗人运用了多种语音技巧来传情达意。例如，在第一、第二行当中，诗人运用了"头韵法"（alliteration）的语音技巧。通过重复地使用/f/和/b/两个辅音，使得这两句诗行的运行速度加快，从而给读者留下小船快速行驶的印象。再看第三行。诗人运用了"中间韵"（internal rhyme）的语音技巧，特别是通过在单词的末尾重复地使用辅音/st/从而表达出船只快速地冲入平静海域所带来的震撼效果。再看第四行。诗人仍然使用了"头韵法"（alliteration）的语音技巧，通过重复使用辅音/s/，并且让其分别与两个重读的长元音连用，从而达到强调大海的广阔和安宁的效果。

我们再看元音。通常来讲，长元音听起来更为平和、肃穆；而短元音则更多用来暗指迅速的动作或是激越的情绪（ibid.）。例如，短元音/i/，多数人认为会给人一种明快、跳跃和欢乐的感觉。例如，下面所选取的是托马斯·纳什（Thomas Nashe）所写的《春天》（*Spring*）当中的一个诗节。我们对其中发音为短元音/i/的字母进行了斜体和加粗的标注，请读者仔细体会。

> Spr*i*ng, the sweet Spr*i*ng, *i*s the year's pleasant k*i*ng;
> Then blooms each th*i*ng, then maids dance in a r*i*ng,

Cold doth not sting, the pretty birds do s*i*ng,
Cuckoo, jug-jug, pu-we, to-w*i*tta-woo!

我们再举一例说明英语当中元音可能的表达效果。在英语单词的读音当中，圆唇的、开口或是半开口的、长元音或是短元音，读起来通常带有一种庄严肃穆的感觉（ibid.）。请看下面托马斯·格雷（Thomas Gray）有名的《墓园挽歌》（*Elegy Written in a Country Churchyard*）中的片段，并请各位读者留意斜体并且加粗的字母在单词当中的发音，仔细体会其所传达的情绪或是意涵。

The c*ur*few t*o*lls the kn*e*ll of p*ar*ting d*ay*,
The l*o*wing h*er*d winds slowly *o*'er the l*ea*,
The pl*ou*ghman h*o*meward pl*o*ds his w*ea*ry w*ay*,
And l*ea*ves the w*or*ld to d*ar*kness and to m*e*.

综上所述，读者在朗读英语诗歌的时候，应当注意诗歌当中单词的声音效果，并且应当设法将声音与诗歌的意涵联系起来。不过，在这里也需要特别提醒各位读者：不要过度地夸大单词的声音效果，这是因为对于单词音效的过度解读可能会导致对于诗歌内容的片面理解，牵强附会，从而导致偏离诗歌所要传达的主旨。事实上，所谓"好听"的单词不见得"意思"就一定好。此外还需要注意，英诗当中单词的声音效果通常不会单独达成；它经常会与诗歌的节奏结合起来，通过增加或是减缓我们朗读诗歌时的语流的速度表达出诗人所预期的效果。

下面，我们就以完整的诗歌为例，说明单词的声音效果在英诗当中的重要作用。

我们先看一首狄兰的《不要温柔地同人生说再见》（*Do Not Go Gentle into That Good Night*）。

第二章　英诗的韵律

出生于威尔士的狄兰·托马斯（Dylan Thomas，1914 — 1953）是20世纪早期重要的英语诗人之一。他最重要的诗歌集是出版于1946年的《死亡与出场》(*Deaths and Entrances*)。狄兰·托马斯的诗歌具有强烈的浪漫主义色彩，并且以其充沛的情感、生动的意象和富于想象力的语言而闻名。然而不幸的是，由于受困于经济的窘迫和大量饮酒，诗人在39岁的年纪便英年早逝了。

下面所选的这首《不要温柔地同人生说再见》创作于1947年，收录并发表于1952年的诗集 *In Country Sleep, And Other Poems*，是诗人最为人所熟知和喜爱的一首诗歌。据信，这是狄兰写给他垂死的父亲的一首诗，尽管他的父亲直到1952年的圣诞节前才去世（Thomas，2008）。原诗没有标题，所以这里就以诗歌的第一句为题；而这一句连同第一个诗节的最后一行是作为"叠句"（refrain：音乐作品当中称为"副歌"，诗歌作品当中叫作"叠句"，是作品当中反复重复的部分）贯穿于整首诗歌当中的。

请读下面这首诗歌并且回答问题：

Do Not Go Gentle into That Good Night
Dylan Thomas

Do not go gentle into that good night,
Old age should burn and rave at close of day;
Rage, rage against the dying of the light.

Though wise men at their end know dark is right,
Because their words had forked no lightning they   5
Do not go gentle into that good night.

Good men, the last wave by, crying how bright

Their frail deeds might have danced in a green bay,
Rage, rage against the dying of the light.

Wild men who caught and sang the sun in flight,   10
And learn, too late, they grieved it on its way,
Do not go gentle into that good night.

Grave men, near death, who see with blinding sight
Blind eyes could blaze like meteors and be gay,
Rage, rage against the dying of the light.   15

And you, my father, there on the sad height,
Curse, bless me now with your fierce tears, I pray.
Do not go gentle into that good night.
Rage, rage against the dying of the light.

思考题：

1. 请注意诗歌当中的第一个诗节中的第一行和最后一行。这两行诗在整首诗歌当中曾多次重复。请深入分析这两行诗的意义。
2. 最后一个诗节当中的"curse"和"bless"是什么意思？为什么要这样说？
3. 在这首诗歌当中，诗人是如何通过意象、节奏和单词的音效传达出诗歌主旨的？

译文鉴赏：

不要温柔地同人生说再见

狄兰·托马斯

不要温柔地同人生说再见
老年人应当在日暮时分，狂欢
怒斥那将要来临的黑暗

聪明的人知道黑夜在所难免
即便是长夜漫漫也要发出雷鸣电闪　　　　　　　5
他们不会温柔地同人生说再见

善良的人对着最后一波浪涛哭喊
即便是惋惜再也不能搅动绿色的港湾
他们怒斥将要来临的黑暗

狂放的人一路追逐着、歌颂着太阳的光线　　　　10
即便有时驻足叹息，为时已晚
他们不会温柔地同人生说再见

快要离去的人会变得沉默寡言
然而浑浊的眼中有时也会流星闪现
他们怒斥将要来临的黑暗　　　　　　　　　　　15

你啊，我亲爱的爸爸，此时悲伤难掩
诅咒并且祝福我吧，即使泪流满面

请不要温柔地同人生说再见

对着那将要来临的黑暗，呼喊

我们再读一首斯宾塞的十四行诗。

埃德蒙·斯宾塞（Edmund Spenser，1552—1599）是英国文学史上最具影响力的诗人之一。他出身于伦敦当地一个普通的布商家庭；然而由于1566年的伦敦大火烧毁了所有有关斯宾塞所在教区的出生记录，所以有关他的出生年代不过是后人的推断。斯宾塞的第一部重要诗作《牧羊人日记》(*The Shepheardes Calendar*)出版于1579年，是对维吉尔的古典牧歌集（Virgil's *Eclogues*）的模仿之作；而其代表作史诗《仙后》(*The Faerie Queene*，1590）则是对都铎王朝和女王伊丽莎白一世的歌功颂德之作。除此之外，他还是斯宾塞诗节和斯宾塞体十四行诗（Spenserian stanza and the Spenserian sonnet）的开创者。所有这些都是斯宾塞对推动英国文学的发展和繁荣所做出的重要贡献。

斯宾塞死后葬入西敏寺的诗人角（Poets' Corner of Westminster Abbey），成了自"英国诗歌之父"乔叟（Geoffrey Chaucer，1340s-1400）之后的第二位在此长眠的诗人（Poetry-Foundation，2021c）。

下面的这首"Sonnet 75"选自斯宾塞的系列十四行诗集《爱情小唱》(*Amoretti*，1595），是斯宾塞体十四行诗的代表作，是传诵至今的爱情诗歌经典。

请读下面这首诗歌并且回答问题：

Sonnet 75
Edmund Spenser

One day I wrote her name upon the strand,

But came the waves and washed it away:

第二章　英诗的韵律　　　　　　　　　　　　　　　　　　　　　　　　49

Agayne I wrote it with a second hand,

But came the tyde, and made my paynes his pray.

"Vayne man," sayd she, "that doest in vaine assay　　　　　5

A mortall thing so to immortalize,

For I my selve shall lyke to this decay,

And eek my name bee wyp'ed out lykewise."

"Not so," quod I, "let baser things devize,

To dy in dust, but you shall live by fame:　　　　　　　　10

My verse your vertues rare shall eternize,

And in the hevens wryte your glorious name.

Where whenas death shall all the world subdew,

Out love shall live, and later life renew."

思考题：

1. 请分析这首诗歌的韵律（rhythm and rhyme）。
2. 诗中使用了大量的古英语的拼写。请转换成现代英语的拼写并且查看拼写的变化对诗歌的节奏和韵律是否有影响。
3. 诗歌当中运用了大量的意象。请分析"tyde"这一意象的象征意义。
4. 这首诗歌的主旨是什么？请分析。

译文鉴赏：

《爱情小唱》第75首
斯宾塞

一天，我将她的名字写在沙滩上，

潮水袭来，名字便踪影难觅：

我又一次写下了她的名字，

潮水再次将它残忍地抹去。
痴心的人啊，她说，不要再枉费心机，　　　　　　　　5
凡夫俗子难免一死，
终有一天我也会老去，不再有人记起。
不，不，那是鄙俗的人们在玩弄机巧，
他们终会消灭于尘土，而你，
我的爱人，将会声名永续：　　　　　　　　　　　　10
我的诗歌和你的美德将会一同不朽，
你闪光的名字会被镌刻在天堂里。
死神会征服世间的一切，而我们的爱
将会永世长存，往生更替。

2.3.3 素体诗

素体诗（blank verse），也称作无韵体诗歌，是由不押韵的诗行组成的。不押韵并非意味着没有节奏；相反，素体诗大多采用了较为规整的抑扬格五音步（iambic pentameter）的节奏类型（Shaw, 2007）。

素体诗起源于意大利。由于它与古典的、不押韵的诗歌相类似，所以在文艺复兴时期成为诗人们广泛使用的诗体。英国文艺复兴时期诗歌的重要奠基人萨里伯爵，亨利·霍华德（Henry Howard, Earl of Surrey）是第一位将古罗马史诗《埃涅伊德》（*Aeneid*, 1540）以素体诗的形式翻译成英文的诗人（ibid.）。就英诗而言，素体诗由于使用抑扬格五音步的格律形式，与英语日常语言的节奏最为接近，所以成了诗人和剧作家们在诗歌和戏剧创作当中乐于采用的形式。著名的美国文化和文学史学家保罗·福塞尔（Paul Fussell）认为，"大约四分之三的英语诗歌是由素体的形式写成的"（Fussell, 1979）。

下面我们就举莎士比亚戏剧《哈姆雷特》（*Hamlet*）当中有名的戏剧

独白片段为例，说明素体诗的魅力所在。

威廉·莎士比亚（William Shakespeare，1564—1616）是英国文学史上最伟大的剧作家和最伟大的诗人之一，是在世界范围内享有崇高声誉的文学家。他于1564年出生于埃文河畔的斯特拉特福镇（Stratford-upon-Avon）。莎士比亚童年时生活优渥，七岁时进入当地的文法学校——King's New School读书，十八岁时便与长自己八岁的安妮·海瑟薇（Anne Hathaway）结婚，婚后育有三个子女。1587年莎士比亚只身来到伦敦，直到1592年英国枢密院下令关闭伦敦剧院之前的这几年当中一直从事戏剧演员的工作并开始尝试戏剧创作。1594年伦敦剧院再次开放后，莎士比亚便加入了一个叫"宫内大臣剧团"（Lord Chamberlain's Men）的剧团（后改名为"国王剧团"），并且迎来了戏剧创作的高峰时期。1613年前后，49岁的莎士比亚离开伦敦返回故乡，并于三年后故去（Schoenbaum，1991）。

莎士比亚一生共创作了37部戏剧，其中最为著名的作品大多集中在1589—1613年期间。按照创作时期划分的话，他的戏剧创作可以分为三个主要的时期：早期以喜剧和历史剧为主（histories and comedies）；中期，直到1608年为止，以悲剧（tragedies）为主；晚期以悲喜剧（tragicomedies，也称作romances）为主（Bevington，2002）。这些作品中就包括最为我国广大读者所熟知的四大悲剧：《哈姆雷特》《奥赛罗》《李尔王》和《麦克白》（*Hamlet*，*Othello*，*King Lear*，*Macbeth*），以及四大喜剧《仲夏夜之梦》《威尼斯商人》《皆大欢喜》和《第十二夜》（*A Midsummer Night's Dream*，*The Merchant of Venice*，*As You Like It*，*Twelfth Night*），等等。当然还有其他作品，诸如凄美绝伦的爱情悲剧《罗密欧与朱丽叶》（*Romeo and Juliet*）等，更是为无数的少男少女们所痴迷。然而，莎士比亚有生之年并未结集出版自己的作品；1623年出版的《第一对开本》（*The First Folio*，全称是 *Mr. William Shakespeare's Comedies*，*Histories & Tragedies*，现代学者们通常简称其为《第一对开本》）是其最早的戏剧作品集，其中包括了他的36部戏剧作品（没有收录 *Pericles and The Two Noble Kinsmen*），是研究莎剧最重要的版本。

有关莎士比亚的诗歌，特别是他的十四行诗，我们会在"英诗的体裁"一章中有较为详尽的介绍，这里就不再赘述了。

下面的素体诗节选自莎士比亚的著名悲剧《哈姆雷特》第三幕第一场。该段独白记述了哈姆雷特从鬼魂那里得知其叔父杀己父、娶己母，并且篡夺王权的罪行后内心的悲愤、痛苦以及疑虑重重、犹豫不决的心境。由于该段独白篇幅较长，内容较难理解，所以笔者对其做了较为详尽的注释。另外，还请各位读者在朗读这段诗歌的时候仔细体会其中英语语言的节奏，并且分析素体诗是如何在不押韵的情形下传情达意的。对于之后的译文鉴赏，也请读者带着节奏和感情大声朗读；因为唯其如此才能理解诗歌的含义，体味英语语言之美。

请读下面这首诗并且参阅注释加深理解：

Hamlet（III. i. 56-88）

Hamlet: To be[1], or not to be, that is the question:
Whether 'tis nobler in the mind to suffer
The slings[2] and arrows of outrageous fortune
Or to take arms against a sea of troubles[3],
And by opposing end them. To die— to sleep—　　　　5
No more; and by a sleep to say we end
The heartache, and the thousand natural shocks
That flesh is heir to[4]. 'Tis a consummation
Devoutly to be wish'd. To die— to sleep.
To sleep— perchance[5] to dream: ay[6], there's the rub!　　　10
For in that sleep of death what dreams may come

When we have shuffled off[7] this mortal coil[8],

Must give us pause. There's the respect

That makes calamity of so long life.

For who would bear the whips and scorns of time,   15

Th' oppressor's wrong[9], the proud man's contumely,

The pangs of despis'd love[10], the law's delay,

The insolence of office[11] and the spurns

That patient merit of th' unworthy takes[12],

When he himself might his quietus[13] make   20

With a bare bodkin[14]? Who would these fardels bear,

To grunt[15] and sweat under a weary life,

But that the dread of something after death—

The undiscover'd country[16], from whose bourn

No traveller returns— puzzles the will,   25

And makes us rather bear those ills we have

Than fly to others[17] that we know not of?

Thus conscience does make cowards of us all,

And thus the native hue of resolution[18]

Is sicklied o'er with[19] the pale cast of thought[20],   30

And enterprises of great pith and moment[21]

With this regard their currents turn awry[22]

And lose the name of action.

Notes:

1. To be, or not to be: 活着（to be是存在的意思）或者死去。
2. slings: 投石器。
3. a sea of troubles: 苦难的海洋（暗喻）。

4. 这句诗的正常语序是：and（it is）to say（that）by a sleep we end the heartache and the thousand natural shocks to which the human body is an heir.

5. perchance：perhaps.

6. ay /eɪ/：yes.

7. shuffled off：去除掉。

8. this mortal coil：尘世的牵挂。

9. wrong：不公正。

10. despi'd love = despised love：受到轻视的爱情。

11. office：官员们。

12. That patient merit of th' unworthy takes：（the kicks）that a person of merit patiently receives from the unworthy.

13. quietus：死亡（委婉语）。

14. a bare bodkin：匕首。

15. grunt：groan.

16. The undiscover'd country：无知的境地——阴曹地府。

17. fly to others：go to others（other ills of evils）.

18. the native hue of resolution："决断"的本来面色（拟人："决断"的脸色是红色的）。

19. Is sicklied o'er with：is covered with a sickly color（覆盖上了病容）。

20. the pale cast of thought：思想的面色是灰色的（拟人）。

21. of great pith and moment：伟大的，重要的。

22. their currents turn awry：turn awry their currents（改变了行动的轨迹）。

译文鉴赏：

哈姆雷特：活着，还是死去，这是个问题：
在心中默然承受着多舛命运的枪弹
还是拿起武器对抗着无边的苦海，将其终结

怎样做才更高贵呢？死去，睡去
一切都结束了；睡去，我们的心　　　　　　　　　　　　　　5
就不再痛，肉体就不会再承受千万次的摧残。
这似乎是我们求之不得的结局。死去，睡去。
然而，睡去难免就会做梦：没错，这就是问题的症结所在！
因为当我们摆脱了这尘世的纷扰
在死亡的沉睡中或许还会有梦境　　　　　　　　　　　　　10
这使得我们犹豫不决，只得在煎熬中了却残生。
如果仅仅一把小小的匕首就能让我们自我了断
那么谁还会忍受人世的嘲讽和鞭挞，
压迫者的不公，傲慢者的凌辱，
备受冷落的爱情的痛楚，法律的迁延，　　　　　　　　　　15
官员的怠慢，以及卑劣小人对心地良善者的唾弃呢？
那么谁还会忍辱负重
在困顿的生活中痛苦地呻吟，挥汗如雨呢？
这一切无非是出于对于身后事的恐惧——
那个未知的世界，没有哪个人曾经去而复返——　　　　　　20
于是这动摇了我们的意志，
使得我们宁愿忍受尘世的痛楚，而不愿投身那未知的阴曹地府。
所以，正是思考让我们变成了懦夫，
而决断的红颜则遮盖上了纠结的灰色的病容，
于是乎，伟大的事业偏离了原本的航线　　　　　　　　　　25
失去了行动的力量。

第三章 英诗的语言

3.1 引言

英语诗歌的语言在本质上与人们在日常生活中所使用的语言是相同的。我们日常运用词汇的时候经常会赋予某些词汇与其字面意义不同的含义，而诗歌当中的语言也是如此。例如，我们可能会说："太阳从云层中跳了出来（The sun leaps out of the clouds.）。"很明显，这里我们是将"太阳"拟人化了——他像一个可爱的顽童一样从云层的遮蔽中露出真身。再比如，我们还经常说"这是一片富饶的农田（This is a rich farmland.）"，或是"我的心在滴血（My heart is bleeding.）"，等等。在这些句子当中，我们都赋予了某些词汇以新的意义（如rich和bleeding），从而使得语义的表达更为生动，更加具有感染力。

此外，无论是在日常表达还是诗歌创作当中，我们都经常会想要抒发、表达自己的强烈情感。例如，当一群小孩子让我们感到不胜其烦的时候，我们可能会说，"这些孩子简直让我快疯掉了！（These kids are driving me up the wall! 或是These kids are driving me crazy!）"，等等。这些话听起来就比"这些孩子调皮捣蛋（The children are misbehaving.）"所表达出的语气强烈得多。因此，相同或是类似的词语，依据不同的使用语境往往会表达出比其字面意义更为丰富的意涵。与人们日常说话或是其他文学文体，特别是非文学类的文体中词语的运用不同的是，诗人会在诗歌当中经常地、大量地、创造性地使用词语，从而使得诗歌的语言听起来更为清新、更为生动、更加震撼人心。

因此，在英语诗歌当中，即便最为普通的词汇，经过诗人的创造性运用也可以显得熠熠生辉。本章当中我们将会讨论如下有关英语诗歌语言的内容：隐含义与字面义（Connotation and Denotation）、象征与典故（Symbol and Allusion）、意象（Imagery）、重复与平行结构（Repetition and Parallel Structure）和比喻（Figurative Language）。这些方面并不能体现出英语诗歌语言的全部特点；然而毫无疑问的是，这些方面都是对英语诗歌从语言层面进行分析和鉴赏的重要视角。

3.2 隐含义与字面义

所谓"隐含义（connotation）"是指某个单词或短语所承载的文化或情感联系，是"暗示"给读者的意义；与之对应的就是"字面义（denotation）"，是指单词或短语的原始或词典义，是"明示"给读者的意义。例如，"一枝红红的玫瑰"：其字面义就是"一枝绿叶衬托下的红颜色玫瑰花"；而其隐含义则很有可能是"充满了激情的爱恋"。

此外，由于隐含义是与特定的情感相联系的，而人类的情感则大体上可以区分为愉快的、不愉快的或是不带感情色彩的情感；所以，某个词语的隐含义就通常可以描述为正面的（positive）、负面的（negative）或是中性的（neutral）（White，1993）。下面我们就以两组词语为例，请各位读者仔细区分它们在字面义基本相同的情况下所包含的隐含义（感情色彩）的不同：

1	thin, bony, slim, anorexic, slender
2	guerilla, freedom fighter, mercenary, soldier, terrorist

在英语诗歌当中，诗人当然会使用日常语言。然而由于诗歌的篇幅有限，所以诗人会仔细挑选每一个词语以传达特定的情感、强调特殊的观点以及定义精准的意涵。因此，英诗当中的词语往往具有多重含义——不仅仅有直白的字面义，还经常会有带着强烈感情色彩的隐含义。

很多词语的字面意义是多重的。因此，词典会同时给出某个词语几个、十几个、甚至几十个字面意义。例如，《牛津现代高级英语学习词典》中就给单词"run"列举出了26个动词义项以及15个名词义项。读者如果要在某首特定诗歌当中确定"run"的含义，他就必须在它的上下文当中对其加以考察。例如，如果"run"的上下文当中出现了诸如"candidate""election""office"或是"vote"，等等词汇，那么它可能就是"参加""管理"等的意思；而如果"run"的上下文当中出现了诸如"color""sweater"或是"wash"等的词汇，那么它就很有可能是"使…褪色"的意思。所以，读者在阅读英语诗歌的时候要结合诗歌的上下文，仔细揣摩某个特定词语的意义。

与字面义相比较，词语的隐含义则要更多，更复杂。这是因为读者在阅读英语诗歌的时候，会不自觉地将自己所有的个人经历与其联系起来进行理解，从而赋予了诗歌本身更多的意涵。对于不同的读者来说，诗歌当中的词语经常带有不同感情色彩，甚至这些感情色彩可以是截然相反的。例如，"红旗（red flag）"，对于我国读者来说，这一词汇基本上是正面的、积极的色彩——它象征了革命、进步和一往无前；然而在一些西方读者心目中，"红旗（red flag）"的隐含意义则更多表现为中性的甚至是消极的色彩。所以，要正确理解诗歌当中词语的隐含意义，读者就必须联系起诸如字面意义、情感态度以及历史文化背景等，诸多要素进行全面而深刻的剖析。

下面就请各位读者通过几个具体的例子体会一下诗人是如何在诗歌当中运用词语的隐含意义的。请大家特别注意这些例句当中斜体并且加粗的词语。

1. 民谣《帕特里克·斯彭斯爵士》(*Sir Patrick Spens*) 当中是这样描绘一位国王的：

> The King sits in Dunfermline town,
> Drinking the **blood-red** wine;
> "O where shall I get a skeely skipper
> To sail this ship or mine?"

2. 勃朗宁（Robert Browning）在诗歌《期待》(*Prospice*) 中说他不惧怕死亡而是期待死亡的到来，因为他在死亡中可以获得爱和安宁：

> O thou soul of my soul! I shall clasp thee again,
> And with God be the **rest**!

3. 史蒂文森（Robert Louis Stevenson）将下面的诗句镌刻在自己的墓碑上：

> Home is the **sailor**, home from the **sea**,
> And the **hunter** home from the **hill**.

下面我们通过朗费罗的诗《箭与歌》(*The Arrow and the Song*) 进一步说明英语诗歌语言当中的隐含义和字面义。

亨利·沃兹沃思·朗费罗（Henry Wadsworth Longfellow, 1807 —

1882）是19世纪美国文学史上的一位重要作家；他在美国国内和欧洲都获得了极高的声誉，事实上他是第一位半身雕像被安放在西敏寺诗人角的美国作家。

朗费罗的代表作包括他的第一部诗集《夜吟》(Voices of the Night)、长篇叙事诗《伊凡吉林》(Evangeline)和《海华沙之歌》(The Song of Hiawatha)，等等。除了诗人头衔以外，朗费罗还是一位翻译家和学者。他曾三次远赴欧洲游学，精通欧洲几国语言，并在哈佛大学现代语言系（Modern Languages Department of Harvard University）任教长达十八年之久。然而，朗费罗的个人生活却颇为不幸。1835年他的第一任夫人玛丽（Mary Storer Potter）在随他游学欧洲期间死于小产；痛苦不堪、孑然一身的诗人于是便埋头钻研德国文学。1861年的一场火灾又使得他的第二任妻子范妮（Fanny Appleton）命丧黄泉，而诗人也被大火烧伤。由于面部烧伤导致剃须不方便，朗费罗自此便蓄起了胡须，而这也成了他的一个标签。之后，为了摆脱丧妻之痛，朗费罗便开始埋头翻译但丁用意大利语写成的《神曲》(Divine Comedy)（Calhoun, 2004）。该书的英文译作于1867年出版，使得诗人成了第一个翻译《神曲》的美国人。

朗费罗的诗歌韵律轻快自然，读来朗朗上口；他的诗歌主题简单易懂，充满积极乐观的人生态度。下面我们就选这首《箭与歌》与大家共同品鉴。

请读下面这首诗歌并且回答问题：

The Arrow and the Song
Henry Wadsworth Longfellow

I shot an arrow into the air,
It fell to earth, I knew not where;
For, so swiftly it flew, the sight

Could not follow it in its flight.

I breathed a song into the air, 5
It fell to earth, I knew not where;
For who has sight so keen and strong,
That it can follow the flight of song?

Long, long afterwards, in an oak
I found the arrow, still unbroke; 10
And the song, from beginning to end,
I found again in the heart of a friend.

思考题：

1. 这首诗歌的主旨很大程度上体现在其题目当中。请分析诗歌题目当中的两个名词具有怎样的隐含意义？
2. 诗歌当中与"arrow"相关联的词语有哪些？与"song"相关联的又有哪些呢？请分析这些词语是如何与它们相关联的呢？

译文鉴赏：

箭与歌
亨利·沃兹沃斯·朗费罗

我的箭射向天空，
掉落，不知所踪；
它飞行迅疾，
逃脱了视线的掌控。

我的歌唱响天空, 5
飘散, 不知所踪;
谁的眼睛如此敏锐,
能捕捉到飞翔的歌声?

许久许久以后,
一棵橡树上 10
找见了我未折的箭羽;
而我的歌,
一直回荡在
朋友的心中。

我们下面再看一首克劳德·麦凯的《白宫》(The White House),以加深对于诗歌语言当中的隐含义与字面义的理解。

克劳德·麦凯(Claude Mckay, 1889—1948)是牙买加裔美国人(Jamaican-American),是哈莱姆文艺复兴(Harlem Renaissance)运动当中的重要诗人和小说家。

麦凯是一位出生于牙买加的黑人诗人。他的第一部重要作品是于1912年出版的名为《牙买加之歌》(Songs of Jamaica)的诗集。在诗集当中,他用牙买加方言记录了当地黑人的生活图景。同年,他用出版诗集赚到的钱离开了牙买加,开始了在美国的学习、生活。初到美国,他便读到了杜波伊斯的《黑人的灵魂》(The Souls of Black Folk),该部作品对麦凯以后的文学创作和政治倾向起到了至关重要的作用。1914年麦凯前往纽约,并在哈莱姆住了下来。他的代表诗作《如果我们必须死》(If We Must Die, 1919)就是这一时期的作品。1922年,麦凯的诗集《哈莱姆的阴影》(Harlem Shadows)出版,奠定了他在哈莱姆文艺复兴运动当中的历史地位。20世纪二三十年代时,麦凯曾长期旅居欧洲和北非并创作了很多文

第三章　英诗的语言

学作品，其中，《回到家乡哈莱姆》（*Home to Harlem*，1928）是一部广受好评的小说。

《白宫》这首诗发表于1922年，是与其他三首麦凯的诗歌一同发表于一本叫作《解放者》（*The Liberator*）的杂志上的。麦凯后来称这首诗"表达了我自己的痛苦、仇恨和热爱（expressing my bitterness, hate and love）"，是其系列十四行诗当中的一首（Sigler, Feb. 16, 2017）。

请读下面这首诗歌并且回答问题：

The White House
Claude Mckay

Your door is shut against my tightened face,
And I am sharp as steel with discontent;
But I possess the courage and the grace
To bear my anger proudly and unbent.
The pavement slabs burn loose beneath my feet,　　　5
A chafing savage, down the decent street,
And passion rends my vitals as I pass,
Where boldly shines your shuttered doors of glass.
Oh, I must search for wisdom every hour,
Deep in my wrathful bosom sore and raw,　　　10
And find in it the superhuman power
To hold me to the letter of your law!
Oh, I must keep my heart inviolate
Against the poison of your deadly hate.

思考题：

1. 诗歌标题对于身为黑人的诗人来说具有什么隐含意义吗？
2. 这首诗歌的读者是谁？可能的阅读情境是怎样的？
3. 诗人使用了非常有力的词语表达他的愤怒。请找出这些词语。
4. 你认为这首诗歌的主题是什么？诗人创作这首诗歌的目的又是什么？

译文鉴赏：

白宫

克劳德·麦凯

怒气冲冲的我被你拒之门外，
屈辱如钢刀般锋利；
然而，带着勇气和风度
我骄傲不屈，压抑着所有的愤怒。
脚下的便道砖似乎要被踩碎，　　　　　　　　　　5
我如疯狂的野兽般走过这繁华的都会。
当路过你耀眼而紧闭的玻璃大门时，
我怒火中烧，五脏俱焚。
哦，在苦楚而灼伤的内心深处，
我时刻都在搜寻着圣人的教导，　　　　　　　　10
只为了能说服自己相信你的法条！
哦，我只有保持心灵的圣洁
才能化解你仇恨的毒药。

3.3 象征与典故

我们先看什么是象征。

为了论述的准确，我们有必要首先区分什么是象征手法（symbolism），什么又是象征（symbol）。

狭义来讲，"symbolism"可以翻译为"象征手法"——是指一种在文学创作当中，通过使用象征或是符号来代表某些思想和品质，从而赋予这些象征或是符号以不同于它们字面意义的象征意义的文学创作手法。广义来讲，"Symbolism"还可以翻译为"象征主义"，是指19世纪晚期起源于法国的一场文艺运动，是对先前"自然主义（Naturalism）"和"现实主义（Realism）"文艺运动的一次反动（Britannica, May 22, 2013）。

而象征（symbol）则是指任何用于替代或是代表其他事物（通常是与某种具体事物相联系的抽象的思想或是情感）的事物（通常为具体的事物，例如某件物品、某个人、动物，等等）。例如，红玫瑰是忠贞爱情的象征，鸽子是和平的象征，而黑色在西方文化当中则经常用来代表邪恶和死亡，等等。由于象征具有丰富的隐含意义，所以诗人常常会在诗歌当中大量使用。

下面就来看两首充分运用象征手法的英语诗歌。

第一首是威廉·布雷克的《病玫瑰》（*The Sick Rose*）。

这首《病玫瑰》选自1794年发表的布雷克的诗集《经验之歌》（*Songs of Experience*）。诗人以"玫瑰"和"蠕虫"作为象征符号讲述了一个"纯真无邪"被"丰富的经验"所吞噬的故事（Riffaterre, 1973）。诗中最主要的意象就是"玫瑰"；然而，与传统意义上象征爱情的玫瑰不同的是，这却是一支"生病的"玫瑰。作为一名多才多艺的艺术家，布雷克不仅创作了诗歌本身，而且还亲手包办了诗歌的插图和雕版；而印刷和上色的工作则是在其妻子凯瑟琳（Catherine Blake, 1762—1831）的帮助下完成的。

请读下面这首诗歌并且回答问题：

The Sick Rose
William Blake

O Rose, thou art sick.
The invisible worm,
That flies in the night
In the howling storm:

Has found out thy bed   5
Of crimson joy:
And his dark secret love
Does thy life destroy.

思考题：

1. 除了象征以外，这首诗当中还应用了哪些修辞手法呢？
2. 诗歌当中的"the invisible worm"有何象征意义？
3. 诗歌当中的"the night"和"the howling storm"具有象征意义吗？如果有，它们象征的是什么？
4. 请从象征的角度对这首诗歌的主旨进行阐释。

译文鉴赏：

病玫瑰
威廉·布雷克

啊，玫瑰，你病了

第三章　英诗的语言

>   那隐匿的蠕虫
>   趁着夜色
>   在暴风雨中
>   飞行   5
>
>   它找见了你
>   欢愉的温床
>   种下暗色的密爱
>   使你的生命
>   凋零   10

下面我们再看一首弗罗斯特的《雪夜林边停》(*Stopping by Woods on a Snowy Evening*)。

罗伯特·弗罗斯特（Robert Frost, 1874 — 1963）是20世纪美国最著名的诗人之一。他曾先后四次荣获普利策诗歌奖（Pulitzer Prizes for Poetry），并享有"美国非官方的桂冠诗人（the unofficial poet laureate of the United States）"的美誉。弗罗斯特的诗作内容常常与美国新英格兰（New England）的乡村生活密切相关。他经常在诗歌中以新英格兰的风物为背景，以口语化的美国英语为表现形式，探索复杂的哲学和社会主题。既不同于惠特曼（Walt Whitman, 1819 — 1892）的自由奔放，也不同于狄金森（Emily Dickinson, 1830 — 1886）的实验创新，弗罗斯特的诗歌风格更多地表现为清新自然、朴实无华，而同时又遵循传统、寓意深刻（Stine, Broderick, & Marowski, 1983）。1961年1月，弗罗斯特于87岁高龄受邀参加约翰·肯尼迪（John F. Kennedy）的总统就职典礼，并且现场朗诵了自己的诗歌《彻底奉献》(*The Gift Outright*)。1963年1月29日弗罗斯特逝世。

弗罗斯特一生总共出版10余部诗集，影响较大的有《波士顿以北》

（*North of Boston*，1914）、《山间》（*Mountain Interval*，1916）、《新罕布什尔》（*New Hampshire*，1923）、《西流的小溪》（*West-Running Brook*，1928）、《见证树》（*A Witness Tree*，1942），等等。他最受广大读者欢迎的短诗有《修墙》（*Mending Wall*）、《桦树》（*Birches*）、《未择之路》（*The Road Not Taken*）、《雪夜林边停》（*Stopping by Woods on a Snowy Evening*）、《冰与火》（*Fire and Ice*）、《美景易逝》（*Nothing Gold Can Stay*）、《摘苹果后》（*After Apple Picking*），等等。我们这里所选的就是他的代表诗作之一——《雪夜林边停》。

《雪夜林边停》（*Stopping by Woods on a Snowy Evening*）选自弗罗斯特的诗集《新罕布什尔》（*New Hampshire*，1923）。这首诗描绘了诗人在白雪覆盖的树林中停下马拉的雪橇，一番苦思冥想之后却被现实生活的责任从诱人的黑暗中唤醒的故事。在写给友人路易斯·昂特迈耶（Louis Untermeyer，美国著名诗人、编辑和评论家，1885—1977）的一封信中，弗罗斯特曾经说过，这是"我最值得纪念的一首诗歌"（my best bid for remembrance）（Romano，2014）。

请读下面这首诗歌并且回答问题：

Stopping by Woods on a Snowy Evening
Robert Frost

Whose woods these are I think I know.
His house is in the village though;
He will not see me stopping here
To watch his woods fill up with snow.

My little horse must think it queer 5
To stop without a farmhouse near

Between the woods and the frozen lake
The darkest evening of the year.

He gives his harness bells a shake
To ask if there is some mistake.   10
The only other sound's the sweep
Of easy wind and downy flake.

The woods are lovely, dark and deep,
But I have promises to keep,
And miles to go before I sleep,   15
And miles to go before I sleep.

思考题：

1. 诗中的"woods"和"village"分别代表了什么？有什么象征意义吗？
2. 诗中的"sleep"具有怎样的意涵？
3. 本首诗歌的主旨是什么？请具体说明。
4. 诗人在这首诗歌当中使用了重复的手法，请分析其修辞效果。

译文鉴赏：

雪夜林边停

罗伯特·弗罗斯特

我认得这片森林的主人
他的家就在附近的农村
他不会看到我在此停留
欣赏这大雪覆盖的丛林

我的小马驹一定不明白　　　　　　　　　　5
为什么要远离人家徘徊
停在树林和结冰的湖间
在一年中最黑暗的夜晚

他摇了摇马具上的铃铛
似乎在询问自己的主人　　　　　　　　　10
此外再听不到其他声响
除了雪片在随微风飘荡

这森林可爱黑暗而幽深
而我却难逃世间的责任
要在睡去之前打起精神　　　　　　　　　15
要在睡去之前打起精神

  我们再看典故（allusion）。
  典故同样也是英语诗歌当中最为常见的修辞方式之一。典故通常是指文学作品当中的一个用以指示历史或是文学方面的某人或是某事的单词或是短语。通过使用典故，诗人可以将与某著名人物或事件相关的故事融入当前的诗歌当中，从而增进、加深读者对于诗歌所要表达含义的理解。当然，典故的使用也有一个前提，那就是作者要确信自己与读者享有共同的历史、文化和文学传统。唯其如此，典故的使用才会在读者中引起共鸣，否则就会因为晦涩难懂而变成对牛弹琴（Britannica, Jan. 15, 2020）。
  如上所述，典故的应用和理解需要作者和读者之间更多的理解和默契。例如，西方文学当中说某个人年纪大、受尽折磨、成就也颇高时，经常会说他就如同尤利西斯（Ulysses）一样。对于谙熟古希腊英雄尤利西

第三章　英诗的语言

斯漂泊历险故事的读者来说这很容易理解，此典故的应用就能够传达更为丰富而生动的信息。然而对于中国读者而言，特别是对那些对西方文学、历史以及文化传统知之甚少的读者来说，这种典故可能就很难理解，使读者一头雾水。相反，如果我们在中国文学作品中看到"廉颇老矣"或是"老骥伏枥"等等的句子，恐怕大多数的中国读者会心领神会，因为此处所用的典故（"廉颇老矣，尚能饭否"出自南宋词人辛弃疾的《永遇乐·京口北固亭怀古》；"老骥伏枥，志在千里；烈士暮年，壮心不已"出自东汉曹操的《龟虽寿》）是我们再熟悉不过的了。

再说回英语典故。如果追根溯源的话，英语典故大多数来自两个部分。一个是普罗大众所熟悉的文学形式：儿歌或童谣、童话故事、历史传说、希腊神话和圣经故事，等等（nursery thymes, fairy tales, legends, Greek mythology and Bible stories）；另一个则是受过良好教育的人们所熟知的重要作家的重要文学作品，比如莎士比亚、狄更斯、福克纳、菲茨杰拉德，等等的重要文学作品（Feng, 1995）。

下面我们看几个诗歌当中应用典故的例子。如果你对这些典故不熟悉，请使用词典或其他工具书找出这些典故的出处，并且思考这些典故为原诗增添了怎样的意涵。

(1) Sophocles long ago
　　Heard it on the Aegean, and it brought
　　Into his mind the turbid ebb and flow
　　Of human misery
　　(*Dover Beach* by Matthew Arnold)

(2) So, till the judgement that yourself arise,
　　You live in this, and dwell in lover's eyes.
　　(*Sonnet 55* by William Shakespeare)

(3) Teach me to hear Mermaids singing,
　　Or to keep off envy's stinging,

And find

　　What wind

Serves to advance an honest mind.

（*Song* by John Donne）

（4）That I might once more reach that plain,

　　Where first I left my glorious train;

　　From whence th'enlighten'ed spirit sees

　　That shady City of Palm trees!

（*The Retreat* by Henry Vaughan）

下面我们以爱伦·坡的诗歌《致海伦》(*To Hellen*)为例，说明典故在诗歌当中的重要作用。

埃德加·爱伦·坡（Edgar Allan Poe, 1809—1849）是19世纪美国著名的短篇小说家、诗人和文学评论家。他在短篇小说方面的贡献主要体现在促进了推理和恐怖小说的发展。他的《莫格街谋杀案》(*The Murders in the Rue Morgue*, 1841)被认为是最早的侦探小说（detective fiction）之一，开创了现代侦探小说的先河；而他在小说当中对于恐怖氛围的营造也是无与伦比的，例如他的《厄舍府的倒塌》(*The Fall of the House of Usher*, 1839)就是此类小说的典范。在诗歌方面，他的代表作《乌鸦》(*The Raven*, 1845)是美国文学史上最著名的诗作之一。在文学理论方面，坡是19世纪欧洲文学中为艺术而艺术运动（Art for Art's Sake）的主要先驱。他的文学创作理论集中体现在以下两点：第一，成功的作品必须对读者产生统一的影响（a unity of effect on the reader）；第二，这种单一效果的产生并非来自意外或是灵感，而应当是在作者理性的思考之下，通过作品的最细微之处体现出来的（the result of rational deliberation on the part of the author）(Poetry-Foundation, 2021b)。

然而不幸的是，坡在四十岁的年纪便英年早逝了。有关他的死因至今仍是未解之谜——可能的原因包括疾病、酗酒、药物滥用甚至是自杀

（Meyers，1992）。

《致海伦》的创作灵感来自一位坡童年时期朋友的母亲，叫作简·斯坦纳德（Jane Stanard）。坡幼年丧母，简美丽贤惠并且支持坡进行诗歌创作；所以坡对她非常迷恋，将她当作是心目中的母亲。然而不幸的是，简在坡十五岁的时候便去世了。几年以后，坡写了这首诗，对她进行讴歌（Burns，2002）。《致海伦》最初发表于1831年的诗集《爱伦·坡的诗歌》（*Poems of Edgar A. Poe*）当中；1836年，该诗通过杂志《南方文学通讯》（*Southern Literary Messenger*）再版发行；1945年，坡对该诗进行了修改，最终收入诗集《乌鸦和其他诗歌》（*The Raven and Other Poems*）中。

请读下面这首诗歌并且回答问题：

To Helen
Edgar Allan Poe

Helen, thy beauty is to me
Like those Nicéan barks of yore,
That gently, o'er a perfumed sea,
The weary, way-worn wanderer bore
To his own native shore.　　　　　　　　　　5

On desperate seas long wont to roam,
Thy hyacinth hair, thy classic face,
Thy Naiad airs have brought me home
To the glory that was Greece,
And the grandeur that was Rome.　　　　　10

Lo! in yon brilliant window-niche

How statue-like I see thee stand,

The agate lamp within thy hand!

Ah, Psyche, from the regions which

Are Holy Land! 15

思考题：

1. 这首诗歌中使用了哪些典故？请分析。
2. 请分析这首诗歌当中的象征手法。
3. 谁是"The weary, way-worn wanderer"，哪里又是"his own native shore"呢？为什么这样说？
4. 有评论称这首诗歌颂了"nurturing power of woman"（Kennedy, 1993）。谈谈你对此的看法。

译文鉴赏：

致海伦

埃德加·爱伦·坡

海伦，你的美丽

宛如西尼亚的古船，

载着我，

一个疲倦而迷途的行者，

轻柔地驶过香馨的海面， 5

回到了

故国的港湾。

我已在绝望的大海中漂泊许久，

是你风信子般的头发，古典的面庞

和水中仙子的气质， 10

将我带回了久别的家园——
在那里有光荣的希腊
在那里有伟大的罗马！
看，在那光辉闪耀的神龛里，
你如雕塑一般站立，　　　　　　　　　　　　　　　　15
手中还擎着玛瑙的灯盏。
啊！人类的精灵，
你来自那片神圣的土地！

3.4 意象

  如果说诗歌语言是血肉之躯，那么意象（imagery）就是诗歌语言跳动的灵魂。

  所谓意象，也叫作"形象的描述"，是指在文学文本当中能够在读者头脑中创造出画面的、生动形象的描述性语言。它诉诸读者的各个感官，帮助读者清晰地想象作品中的人物和场景，从而加深读者对于文学作品的理解。意象的形式可以涉及所有的人类感官，而具体意象（images）的创造则大多是通过比喻语言（figurative language）达成的，例如明喻、暗喻、拟人、拟声，等等。

  除了广大读者所熟知的视觉、听觉、嗅觉、味觉和触觉意象（visual, auditory, olfactory, gustatory and tactile imagery），英诗当中还能够看到其他两种意象：动觉和主观意象（kinesthetic and subjective/ organic imagery）。这里需要解释一下的是，所谓的动觉意象是指与运动或是肢体动作相关联的意象；所谓的主观意象是指与个人体验（比如悲伤、饥饿、疲劳、疼痛，等等）相关联的意象（Team, 2021）。

对于诗歌当中意象的理解极为重要，因为从某种意义上来说，读者对于诗歌的阐释就是建立在对于诗歌当中意象的理解和分析的基础之上的。有些诗歌会为读者呈现出一系列相关联的意象（例如流水、云雀、海洋，等等）；而另外一些诗歌则会呈现出一系列对此鲜明的意象（例如光明和黑暗、沼泽和荒漠、出生和死亡，等等）。而诗人所要传递的情感、态度和主旨则会通过诗歌当中的这些意象自然而然地展现出来。

因此，当我们要对意象进行解读、阐释的时候，最好是将诗歌视为一个整体——将其中的所有意象作为一个整体进行考量；并且将诗歌当中的意象与诗歌的主旨联系起来。唯其如此，我们才有可能对诗歌的意涵进行更深层次的挖掘。

我们先看几个有关意象的例子。

请各位读者从下面诗句当中找出诗人所创造的意象，并且分析这些意象与我们的哪些感官经验相联系，在诗句当中起到了怎样的作用。

（1）Life's but a walking shadow, a poor player

That struts and frets his hour upon the stage,

And then is heard no more: it is tale

Told by an idiot, full of sound and fury,

Signifying nothing.

(*Macbeth* by William Shakespeare)

（2）Or sinking as the light wind lives or dies;

And full-grown lambs loud bleat from hilly bourn;

Hedge-crickets sing; and now with treble soft

The redbreast whistles from a garden-croft,

And gathering swallows twitter in the skies.

(*To Autumn* By John Keats)

（3）Beside the ungathered rice he lay,

His sickle in his hand;

> His breast was bare, his matted hair
>
> Was buried in the sand.
>
> Again, in the mist and shadow of sleep,
>
> He saw his Native Land.
>
> (*The Slave's Dream* by H. W. Longfellow)

下面我们就以整首英语诗歌为例，说明意象的重要作用。

我们先看一首狄金森的《头脑大过天空》(*The Brain—is wider than the sky*)。

艾米莉·狄金森（Emily Dickinson, 1830 — 1886）是美国文学史上最伟大也是最具独创性的诗人之一。狄金森于1830年出生于美国马萨诸塞州阿默斯特市（Amherst, Massachusetts）的一个律师家庭。她在阿默斯特学院（Amherst Academy）上了7年学，之后又在曼荷莲女子神学院（Mount Holyoke Female Seminary）学习了不到一年，之后便辍学回家了。没有确凿的证据可以证明她回家的真实原因——有人认为是由于健康问题，有人认为是她与学校的福音派（evangelical）宗教氛围格格不入，也有人认为她辍学仅仅是因为太想家了（Sewall, 1974）。尽管狄金森没有正式皈依任何宗教，然而毫无疑问的是，她家乡小镇浓重的清教氛围对其宗教观念产生了重要影响。

狄金森的诗歌深受17世纪英国玄学派诗人的影响，因此她的诗歌中常常会出现新奇的比喻、抓人眼球的意象和独创的诗歌形式。以诗歌形式为例，我们在狄金森的诗歌手稿（manuscript versions）中可以看到大量的破折号和非常规使用的大写字母，再加上独特的词汇和意象，所有这一切都使得她的作品呈现出远超人们想象的多样化的风格和形式（Hecht, 1996）。在诗歌韵律方面，狄金森放弃了诗人们最常使用的五音步诗行（pentameter），而是更多地使用三音步（trimeter）或是四音步（tetrameter）诗行，个别时候也会使用双音步（dimeter）诗行。在诗节方面，她经常使用的是民谣体诗节（ballad stanza）——四行一个诗节（quatrains），每个诗节的押韵格式为 a b c b（Ford, 1966）。

　　狄金森的个人生活充满了矛盾和传奇的色彩——作为一位隐居诗人（a reclusive poet），她一生未婚，甚至没有真正地谈过恋爱，然而她的诗歌当中却充满了对于爱情的讴歌；她二十五岁之后便居家生活，不与外界接触，然而她却终生与很多文学界名人保持定期的书信往来；她从学校毕业后便只穿白色的长裙，显得不食人间烟火，然而她却擅长园艺和烹饪，成为家中技艺高超的园丁和大厨。

　　狄金森是一位非常多产的诗人，她经常在给朋友的信中附上诗歌，所以她究竟写了多少首诗歌至今也没有明确的统计。然而，由于她生前只发表了7首诗歌，所以她的诗才在其有生之年并未得到公众的认可。在她死后，狄金森的家人发现了她的40本手工装订的诗集，总计将近1800首诗歌，于是她的第一部诗集在她去世四年后得以出版；自此，狄金森的诗名得以确立。然而，此后出版的狄金森的诗集都进行了大量的编辑甚至篡改；直到1955年托马斯·约翰逊（Thomas H. Johnson）出版《狄金森诗歌全集》（*The Complete Poems of Emily Dickinson*），这一局面才得以改观（Ford, 1966）。

　　请读下面这首诗歌并且回答问题：

The Brain—is wider than the sky

Emily Dickinson

The Brain — is wider than the sky —
For — put them side by side —
The one the other will contain
With ease — and You — beside —

The Brain is deeper than the sea —　　　　　5

第三章 英诗的语言

> For — hold them — Blue to Blue —
> The one the other will absorb —
> As Sponges — Buckets — do —
>
> The Brain is just the weight of God —
> For — Heft them — Pound for Pound —
> And they will differ — if they do —
> As Syllable from Sound —

10

思考题:

1. 请分析这首诗歌当中的意象,并且回答,诗中有哪些形成鲜明对照的意象?
2. 请分析这首诗歌当中所运用的修辞手法。
3. 请分析诗人是如何运用标点符号和大写字母表达思想的?

译文鉴赏:

头脑大过天空
艾米莉·狄金森

> 头脑大过天空
> 不信比比就行
> 一个能将另一个装下
> 连你一起轻轻松松
>
> 头脑深过海洋
> 不信量量就行
> 一个能将另一个吸收

5

恰如海绵和木桶

头脑和上帝一样沉重
不信称称就行　　　　　　　　　　　　　　　　10
若非要分出个彼此
就如曲调和歌声

下面我们再看一首坎皮恩的《她的脸上有座花园》（*There Is a Garden in Her Face*）。

托马斯·坎皮恩（Thomas Campion，1567—1620）是著名作曲家、诗人和医生。他在诗歌艺术方面的成就主要体现在他将诗歌和音乐有机地结合起来，写出了具有持久文学价值的与音乐相融合的抒情诗。

珀西瓦尔·维维安（Percival Vivian，1880—1958）在其编辑出版的《坎皮恩作品集》（*Campion's Works*）序言当中这样评价他：坎皮恩早年挥霍无度；晚年的他是一位和蔼的绅士，充满成熟的经验和判断，珍视旧爱、友谊和青春不羁的幻想；他一生致力于诗歌、音乐和医学的研究，是阿波罗的真正儿子；他同时还兼具一名好医生应有的机智和同情心（Vivian，1909）。

下面这首《她的脸上有座花园》又名《樱桃熟了》（*Cherry-Ripe*）发表于1617年，收录在坎皮恩的代表性诗集《第三及第四部艾尔丝之书》（*The Third and Fourth Booke of Ayres*）当中——这是一部可以在鲁特琴（lute——一种古老的、外形类似吉他的拨弦乐器，也叫作"诗琴"）的伴奏下演唱的歌曲集，为该系列歌书的第三、第四部。这首《她的脸上有座花园》充分展现了诗人掌控节奏和旋律的能力，将音乐同诗歌有机地结合起来。在诗集开始的部分，坎皮恩曾提醒读者注意：在阅读他的诗歌的时候，心中一定要伴有音乐的旋律（Hart，1976）。

请读下面这首诗歌并且回答问题：

There Is a Garden in Her Face

Thomas Campion

There is a garden in her face,
Where roses and white lilies grow,
A heavenly paradise is that place,
Wherein all pleasant fruits do flow.
There cherries grow, which none may buy   5
Till "Cherry ripe!" themselves do cry.

Those cherries fairly do enclose
Of orient pearl a double row;
Which when her lovely laughter shows,
They look like rosebuds filled with snow.   10
Yet them nor peer nor prince can buy,
Till "Cherry ripe!" themselves do cry.

Her eyes like angels watch them still;
Her brows like bended bows do stand,
Threatening with piercing frowns to kill   15
All that attempt with eye or hand
Those sacred cherries to come nigh,
— Till "Cherry ripe!" themselves do cry.

思考题：

1. 请分析这首诗歌的节奏和韵律。
2. 请分析这首诗歌当中的意象，其中哪个意象最为重要？为什么？

3. 请注意每个诗节的最后一行，并且分析诗歌的整体感是如何营造的？诗歌的主题是怎样突出的？

译文鉴赏：

她的脸上有座花园
托马斯·坎皮恩

她的脸上有座花园，
玫瑰百合竞相开放，
那美景如乐园天边，
各色鲜果枝头摇荡。
樱桃虽美不能买，   5
除非你听到"樱桃熟了！"
——是她自己高声叫卖。

娇艳的樱桃笑红脸，
璀璨的珍珠排成行，
可爱的笑声刚听见，   10
含苞的玫瑰冰雪藏。
公子王孙不能买，
除非你听到"樱桃熟了！"
——是她自己高声叫卖。

天使的明眸看花园，   15
弯弓的眉毛果实守，
紧蹙的眉头如利剑，
神圣的樱桃可保留。

轻狂之徒莫要来，
除非你听到"樱桃熟了！"　　　　　　　　　　　　　　20
——是她自己高声叫卖。

3.5 重复与平行结构

"重复"（repetition）的文学手法古已有之，特别是在古希腊、古罗马时期尤为突出。这一方面是由于在文学作品中需要突出、强调某些内容；另一方面还是由于古时候的文学作品大都以口头方式传播，而"重复"则可以帮助讲故事的人或是诗歌的背诵者更为容易地记忆、背诵相关的内容。

那么什么是"重复"呢？作为一种文学手法，重复是指在文学作品当中，为了达到清晰地表达、强调、突出某些深层次含义的目的，作者有意地、多次地、在相临近的上下文当中重复地使用一个单词、短语或是句子的做法（Glatch, Sep. 21, 2021）。重复同样是诗歌语言的一大特色。

作为一种文学修辞手法，重复的细分种类多达十几种。这里，为了简明、扼要，我们就将诗歌当中的重复分为两大类：递增重复/叠加体（incremental repetition/adding style）以及句子部分的重复（repetition of sentences in part）。所谓递增重复/叠加体是指每个诗节当中对于之前诗节当中部分句子的重复（措辞不见得完全一致）。这种重复的方法多见于口头传统的诗歌形式，特别是多出现在英格兰、苏格兰的民谣当中（Britannica, Aug. 4, 2017）。第二种句子部分的重复则是指诗歌当中某些句子成分和/或句子结构的重复，它又可以细分为联珠法、首语重复法、尾语重复法和首尾语重复法（anadiplosis, anaphora, epiphora/epistrophe and epidiplosis）。所谓联珠法是指后句的句首单词与前句句尾单词重复；

所谓首语重复法是指几个连续的句子的起首部分的单词重复；所谓尾语重复法是指几个连续的句子的结尾部分单词重复；所谓首尾语重复法是指一个句子或是诗节的开头和结尾重复同一个或是几个单词（Glatch, Sep. 21, 2021）。

下面我们看几个有关重复的例子，请各位读者思考其中运用了怎样的重复手法。

(1) Cold in the earth — and the deep snow piled above thee,

　　Far, far removed, cold in the dreary grave!

　　Have I forgot, my only Love, to love thee,

　　Severed at last by Time's all-severing wave?

　　……

　　Cold in the earth, and fifteen wild Decembers

　　From those brown hills have melted into spring：

　　Faithful indeed is the spirit that remembers

　　After such years of change and suffering!

　　……

　　No later light has lightened up my heaven；

　　No second morn has ever shone for me：

　　All my life's bliss from thy dear life was given,

　　All my life's bliss is in the grave with thee.

　　　　　　　　　　（*Remembranc*e by Emily Brontë）

(2) Tell zeal it wants devotion；

　　Tell love it is but lust；

　　Tell time it is but motion；

　　Tell flesh it is but dust.

　　　　　　　　　　（*The Lie* by Sir Walter Ralegh）

(3) Do not weep, maiden, for war is kind,

> Because your lover threw wild hands toward the sky
>
> And the affrighted steed ran on alone,
>
> Do not weep.
>
> War is kind.
>
> (*War Is Kind* by Stephen Crane)

我们再看平行结构（parallelism）。

可能有人会说"parallelism"就相当于中文修辞里面的"排比"；然而事实上，英文中的"parallelism"与中文中的"排比"的含义并非完全相同。这是因为英文中的"parallelism"既可以包含中文中的"排比"，也可以部分地包含中文修辞中的"对偶"；换言之，中文中的"排比"只是英文中的"parallelism"的一部分，而英文中的"antithesis（平行对照）"则相当于中文中的"对偶"的一部分——前者是指结构平行而意思相反的句子，而后者则是指结构平行而意思相近或相反。当然，如果从广义的视角来看，英文中的"parallelism"可以包括"antithesis"，而中文中的"对偶"也可以算作是"排比"的一种特殊类型。所以，为了不与中文相关修辞概念混淆，笔者这里就使用"平行结构"来指代"parallelism"。

所谓"平行结构"是指，为了达到某些特定的修辞目的，例如强调，而在句子当中重复地使用相近似的单词、短语、从句、句子结构、时态、语态等语法要素的修辞手法。具体来说，在平行结构当中我们会发现，相互协调一致的思想会以单词对单词、短语对短语、从句对从句、句子对句子的平衡的形式（balanced form）在文本中呈现出来。例如，下面这句培根在《论学习》（Francis Bacon, *Of Studies*）当中的话："Reading maketh a full man, conference a ready man, and writing an exact man."再如，下面这句林肯在《葛底斯堡演说》（Abraham Lincoln, *Gettysburg Address*）中的名言："… and that government of the people, by the people, for the people shall not perish from the earth."

下面我们再看几个英语诗歌当中应用平行结构的例子。请各位读者思考一下平行结构在这些诗歌当中营造了怎样的修辞效果。

（1）The warm sun is falling, the bleak wind is wailing,

　　 The bare boughs are sighing, the pale flowers are dying.

　　（*Autumn: A Dirge* by Percy Bysshe Shelley）

（2）Ant. I pray you, think you question with the Jew:

　　 You may as well go stand upon the beach,

　　 And bid the main flood bate his usual height;

　　 You may as well use question with the wolf,

　　 Why he hath made the ewe bleat for the lamb;

　　 You may as well forbid the mountain pines

　　 To wag their high tops and to make no noise

　　 When they are fretten with the gusts of heaven;

　　 You may as well do anything most hard,

　　 As seek to soften that — than which what's harder?--

　　 His Jewish heart: therefore, I do beseech you,

　　 Make no more offers, use no farther means;

　　 But with all brief and plain conveniency,

　　 Let me have judgment and the Jew his will.

　　（*The Merchant of Venice*, Act IV, Scene I by William Shakespeare）

英语诗歌当中的重复和平行结构有着大致相同的修辞效果：加重语气，突出主旨；渲染气氛，抒发情感；前后呼应，融为一体——使得读者在诵读诗歌的时候朗朗上口，在理解诗歌的时候清晰明澈，而在诵读之后则难以忘怀。

此外，在实际的文学文本当中，重复的手法经常会与平行结构合并使用，所以有些学者干脆称这种情况为平行重复（parallel repetition），或是就简称为重复。这里我们需要明确的一点是，尽管二者都运用了"重复"的手法，然而平行结构和重复还是各有侧重的：平行结构强调的是句子与句子之间在相似的语法要素和/或结构上的重复；而重复的重点则是在于相同单词、短语甚至句子的反复吟唱。例如，下面这句肯尼迪在《总统就职演说》（John F. Kennedy, *Presidential Inaugural Address*）当中的话："Let every nation know, whether it wishes us well or ill, that we shall **pay any price**, **bear any burden**, **meet any hardship**, **support any friend**, **oppose any foe** to assure the survival and the success of liberty."请读者注意体会句子当中的加粗的"平行结构"和"重复"的部分。

下面我们就以两首诗歌为例具体说明重复和平行结构在英诗当中的重要作用。

《兰德尔勋爵》（*Lord Randal*）是一首盎格鲁—苏格兰边境民谣（Anglo-Scottish border ballad），这是一首由对话组成的传统民谣。尽管此首民谣有不同的语言版本，然而大都遵循相同的故事主线：歌谣中的主要角色（此处是兰德尔勋爵，故事可以发生在不同的地点）中了毒，而下毒的人就是他的爱人；歌谣借由对话方式，通过主人公的叙述来揭秘事件的经过和可能的投毒者（Child, 1965）。

这首民谣一共有九个诗节。在每一个诗节中，兰德尔勋爵的母亲都要求他讲述更多的故事，而他也都做了相应的回答。此外，在每个诗节的副歌部分（refrain——歌词中反复出现的部分，也叫叠句），兰德尔勋爵都表示他感觉不舒服，需要躺下休息。歌谣的前五个诗节当中，母亲询问了整个事件的详细经过；接下来的三个诗节当中，母亲询问兰德尔勋爵，如果他死了，会给家人留下什么；而在歌谣的最后一个诗节当中，勋爵的母亲问他将会给自己的爱人留下什么，他的回答是"地狱与火"（hell and fire）。

请读下面这首诗歌并且回答问题：

Lord Randal

I

"O where hae ye been, Lord Randal, my son?
O where hae ye been, my handsome young man?" —
"I hae been to the wild wood; mother, make my bed soon,
For I'm weary wi' hunting, and fain wald lie down."

II

"Where gat ye your dinner, Lord Randal, my son?　　　　5
Where gat ye your dinner, my handsome young man?" —
"I dined wi' my true-love; mother, make my bed soon,
For I'm weary wi' hunting, and fain wald lie down."

III

"What gat ye to your dinner, Lord Randal, my son?
What gat ye your dinner, my handsome young man?" —　　10
"I gat eels boil'd in broo'; mother, make my bed soon,
For I'm weary wi'hunting, and fain wald lie down."

IV

"What became of your bloodhounds, Lord Randal, my son?
What became of your bloodhounds, my handsome young man?" —
"O they swell'd and they died; mother, make my bed soon,　　15
For I'm weary wi'hunting, and fain wald lie down."

V

"O I fear ye are poison'd, Lord Randal, my son!
O I fear ye are poison'd, my handsome young man!" —
"O yes! I am poison'd; mother, make my bed soon,
For I'm sick at the heart, and I fain wald lie down."　　20

VI

"What d'ye leave to your mother, Lord Randal, my son?
What d'ye leave to your mother, my handsome young man?"
"Four and twenty milk kye; mother, mak my bed soon,
For I'm sick at the heart, and I fain wad lie down."

VII

"What d'ye leave to your sister, Lord Randal, my son? 25
What d'ye leave to your sister, my handsome young man?"
"My gold and my silver; mother, mak my bed soon,
For I'm sick at the heart, an I fain wad lie down."

VIII

"What d'ye leave to your brother, Lord Randal, my son?
What d'ye leave to your brother, my handsome young man?" 30
"My house and my lands; mother, mak my bed soon,
For I'm sick at the heart, and I fain wad lie down."

IX

"What d'ye leave to your true-love, Lord Randal, my son?
What d'ye leave to your true-love, my handsome young man?"
"I leave her hell and fire; mother, mak my bed soon, 35
For I'm sick at the heart, and I fain wad lie down."

思考题：

1. 重复的手法在本首歌谣当中得到了充分的体现，取得了很好的修辞效果。请结合诗歌具体分析。
2. 在诗歌的第五诗节当中，我们看到兰德尔勋爵的母亲不再提问，而是对儿子的遭遇做出推断；而副歌的部分也由"For I'm weary wi' hunting"变成了"For I'm sick at the heart"。请分析这个诗节在整个歌谣当中的作用以及"For I'm sick at the heart"的含义。

3. 在歌谣的每个诗节的第三行当中，兰德尔勋爵都说让他母亲给他铺床（mak my bed soon），这里有什么特殊含义吗？

4. 请分析为什么兰德尔勋爵的故事虽然发生在遥远的古代，却仍然能在现代读者当中产生共鸣？

　　考虑到本首诗歌篇幅较长，语言和内容却简单易懂，所以笔者这里不再提供参考译文。读者朋友们可以结合上文的题解和思考题对其进行深入的理解。

　　我们再看一首赫伯特的《美德》（*Virtue*）。

　　乔治·赫伯特（George Herbert, 1593 — 1633）是著名的英国宗教诗人（devotional poet），17世纪玄学派诗人（metaphysical poets）的重要代表人物之一，其诗歌以选词精妙、技巧圆熟、韵律自然、意象新奇而著称。

　　赫伯特出生在贵族家庭，先后于威斯敏斯特学校和剑桥大学三一学院接受教育。他于1625年受戒成为执事（deacon），1630年成为英国国教牧师（priest of the Church of England）并进而获得布雷默顿教区牧师（rector of Bemerton）的职位。作牧师期间，他善待会众，口碑甚好（Vaughan, 1652）。不幸的是，赫伯特身体状况欠佳，不到四十岁便死于肺结核了。

　　赫伯特的诗歌与音乐联系紧密。据与其同时代的约翰·奥布里（英国博物学家兼作家：John Aubrey, 1626 — 1697）说，赫伯特的鲁特琴（也称诗琴）弹得很好，还曾为他自己创作的抒情诗和圣诗（lyrical and sacred poems）谱曲（Aubrey, 1898）。赫伯特在世时并没有发表自己的诗作，只是在临终前把诗作的手稿交给了友人费拉尔（Nicholas Ferrar, 1592 — 1637），请他决定是出版还是销毁——"如果这些诗作能够给沮丧而可怜的灵魂带来些许好处的话就将其出版；否则就将其烧掉，因为我和我的诗歌与上帝的仁慈相较而言不值一提。（If he can think it may turn to the advantage of any dejected poor soul, let it be made public; if not let him burn

it; for I and it are less than the least of God's mercies.）（Maycock, 1938）"
在他死后，费拉尔以《神庙》（*The Temple*, 1633）为题结集出版了这些诗歌，而下面这首《美德》正是其中的一首。

请读下面这首诗歌并且回答问题：

Virtue

George Herbert

Sweet day, so cool, so calm, so bright,
The bridal of the earth and sky:
The dew shall weep thy fall tonight,
    For thou must die.

Sweet rose, whose hue, angry and brave,   5
Bids the rash gazer wipe his eye:
Thy root is ever in its grave,
    And thou must die.

Sweet spring, full of sweet days and roses,
A box where sweets compacted lie;   10
My music shows ye have your closes,
    And all must die.

Only a sweet and virtuous soul,
Like seasoned timber, never gives;
But though the whole world turn to coal,   15
    Then chiefly lives.

思考题：

1. 请分析这首诗歌当中重复及平行结构手法的运用。除了重复和平行结构，这首诗歌还应用了哪些修辞手法呢？
2. 请解释诗歌的第一节第三行（The dew shall weep thy fall tonight）的含义。其中的"fall"有什么特指吗？
3. 这首诗歌当中有很多新奇的意象。请找出它们并加以分析。
4. 这首诗歌的主题思想是什么？这一主题思想得到充分的表达了吗？请论证你的观点。

译文鉴赏：

美德

乔治·赫伯特

甜美的日子，多么清新、平静而明媚，
你是天空和大地的婚礼：
露水是因你落幕而垂下的泪滴，
　　因为你定会死去。

甜美的玫瑰，多么热情、奔放而刚毅，　　　　　　　　　　5
让轻率的看客也目不能移：
然而你就扎根在自己的坟茔，
　　因为你终会凋零。

甜美的春天，每天都开满了玫瑰花朵，
就像一只盒子塞满了糖果；　　　　　　　　　　　　　　10
你也终将逝去恰如我的诗歌，

因为一切都会衰落。

只有那甜美而高尚的灵魂
才会如风干的木材，不屈不折；
即便世界毁灭，分崩离析，　　　　　　　　　　　　　　15
　　你也会昂首挺立。

3.6 比喻

与我们的日常语言相比较，诗歌当中的"比喻（figurative language）"应用得更多一些。广义的"比喻"是指在语言运用当中，对任何正常的词序、词义和造词法进行改变后所使用的语言（中文经常翻译成形象语言、比喻语言或是修辞语言）。狭义的"比喻"通常涉及两个事物间的比较，发现这二者的相似性。我们中文当中所说的"比喻"一般是指"打比方""譬喻"，是一种常见的修辞手法，更接近于狭义的"比喻"。

关于此两种"比喻"，文学理论大家艾布拉姆斯（Meyer Howard Abrams，1912—2015）和乔纳森·卡勒（Jonathan Culler，1944—）分别给出了自己理解。艾布拉姆斯认为，比喻语言为了表达某种特殊的意义或取得特殊效果而明显地背离了语言使用者所理解的词语的常规意义或常规顺序。人们有时认为比喻主要应用于诗歌当中，而事实上比喻是所有语言的组成部分，是所有话语模式当中不可或缺的部分（Abrams，1999）。卡勒认为，比喻是认知的一种基本方式——通过把一种事物看成另一种事物而认识了它。也就是说找到甲事物和乙事物的共同点，发现甲事物暗含在乙事物身上不为人所熟知的特征，而对甲事物有一个不同于往常的重新的认识（Culler，1996）。

比喻的修辞效果往往取决于其准确与新鲜的程度。例如，吉姆和比利长得就像双胞胎一样（Jim and Billy look like twins）——这样的比喻虽然准确却毫无新意；如果我们换一种说法：吉姆和比利就像是一个模子里刻出来的（Jim and Billy are as like as two peas），效果就会好得多了。再举一个例子。我们在形容美女的时候说，她像花儿一样美丽（She is as beautiful as a flower）——平淡无奇，索然寡味；再看看雪莱是怎么形容美女的：

For she was beautiful — her beauty made

The bright world dim, and everything beside

Seemed like the fleeting image of a shade.

(*The Witch of Atlas* by P. B. Shelley)

由此可见，准确且新鲜的比喻能够使得原本平淡无奇的表达变得生动有趣，给人们留下深刻的印象。

基于对于狭义的"比喻"概念的理解，除了我们司空见惯的明喻、暗喻以外，比喻还可以包括其他多种修辞手法（figures of speech）——例如转喻（metonymy——以一事物名称代替与之有密切关系的另一事物）和提喻（synecdoche——以某一事物的部分代替其整体或是以其整体代替其部分），等等。然而由于篇幅所限，我们在这里仅仅讨论在英诗当中最为常见的五种比喻手法：明喻、暗喻、拟人、呼语和夸张。

3.6.1 明喻和暗喻

明喻和暗喻（simile and metaphor）是最为常见的比喻形式。这是将两种本质上不同的事物进行比较的修辞手法。不同之处在于，在明喻中，两个事物的比较关系是通过连词，诸如like, as, than；或是通过动词，诸如seem, resemble等等体现出来的；而在暗喻（也称作"隐喻"）当中，上述这些连词都省略掉了，诗人会直接说某事物是另一事物；或者是使用

第三章 英诗的语言

"be"动词（am, is, are）的某种形式对两者进行连接。在潜喻（implied metaphor——比较的双方有一方未被提及的暗喻）当中，连词或是"be"动词均不出现，所以就要求读者对词语的语义具有相当的敏感性才会发现其中的奥妙。

下面我们首先举一些有关明喻的例子，并请大家在下列运用明喻的句子当中找到比较的双方，并且试着考虑这些明喻给相关词语增加了哪些额外的意涵。

（1）Records fell like ripe apples on a windy day.

　　（E. B. White）

（2）Keep love in your heart. A life without it is like a sunless garden when the flowers are dead.

　　（Oscar Wilde）

（3）Her hair, like golden threads, play'd with her breath.

　　（William Shakespeare）

（4）Day after day, day after day,

　　　We stuck, nor breath nor motion;

　　　As idle as a painted ship

　　　Upon a painted ocean.

　　（S. T. Coleridge）

下面我们以罗塞蒂的《生日》（*A Birthday*）为例说明明喻在英诗当中的运用。

克里斯蒂娜·乔治娜·罗塞蒂（Christina Georgina Rossetti, 1830—1894）是英国维多利亚时代最著名的女诗人之一。罗塞蒂于1830年出生于伦敦的一个意大利移民家庭，父亲是一名研究但丁的学者和意大利语教授。在母亲的督促和教导下，她兄弟姐妹四人都受到了良好的家庭教育，并且都在各自的领域取得了相当的成就。例如，她的大哥但丁·加布里尔·罗塞蒂（Dante Gabriel Rossetti, 1828—1882）也是著名的诗人，同时还是知名的画家。

  罗塞蒂的诗歌艺术从未从人们的视野当中消失过。她在世的时候，普通读者和评论家们更多的是关注她和另一位同时代的女诗人伊丽莎白·芭蕾特·勃朗宁（Elizabeth Barrett Browning, 1806—1861）谁的成就更高。普遍的观点认为，二者都是维多利亚时代最伟大的女诗人，而二人的艺术又各有特色：勃朗宁夫人的诗歌更显理性、政治性和多样性；而罗塞蒂的诗歌则更长于抒情性和绝美的措辞、韵律和诗歌形式。罗塞蒂的大哥但丁·罗塞蒂曾经这样评价妹妹的艺术成就：毫无疑问，她是继勃朗宁夫人之后最优秀的女性诗人。而就艺术的质朴和自然而言，她则比勃朗宁夫人还要高明得多（Sharp, 1895）。在20世纪的最后几十年当中，借助女性主义批评（feminist criticism）的兴起，罗塞蒂的诗歌再次引起文学批评家们的强烈兴趣，而这些评论则大多集中在罗塞蒂诗歌当中的性别议题（gender issues）和她作为女性诗人的独特身份。

  罗塞蒂是一位多产的诗人，一生诗作甚丰。她的代表诗集有《妖魔集市》（*Goblin Market and other Poems*, 1862）、《王子的历程》（*The Prince's Progress and Other Poems*, 1866）、《赛会》（*A Pageant and other Poems*, 1881）、《大海的面孔》（*The Face of the Deep: A Devotional Commentary on the Apocalypse*, 1892），等等。

  下面的这首《生日》是罗塞蒂的代表诗作之一。这首诗传达出一种纯粹的、快乐的情绪。自第一次出版以来，它优美的旋律就令评论家们和广大读者欣喜不已。时至今日，在英美国家人民的贺卡或是婚礼请柬上还经常能看到这首诗中的文字。然而，如果我们不仅仅停留在对于这首诗歌的表层意涵的理解上面，而是深入挖掘其中的精神内涵，那么我们就会获得对该诗全新的解读方式（Kumar, March 11, 2017）。

  请读下面这首诗歌并且回答问题：

A Birthday

Christina Georgina Rossetti

My heart is like a singing bird

Whose nest is in a watered shoot;

My heart is like an apple tree

Whose boughs are bent with thickset fruit;

My heart is like a rainbow shell   5

That paddles in a halcyon sea;

My heart is gladder than all these

Because my love is come to me.

Raise me a dais of silk and down;

Hang it with vair and purple dyes;   10

Carve it in doves, and pomegranates,

And peacocks with a hundred eyes;

Work it in gold and silver grapes,

In leaves and silver fleurs-de-lys;

Because the birthday of my life   15

Is come, my love is come to me.

思考题：

1. 请在这首诗歌当中找到诗人所运用的明喻，并且解释它们的含义。
2. 人的心灵与诗中的"a singing bird, an apple tree, a rainbow shell"有哪些相似之处呢？
3. 这首诗歌当中的明喻运用得当吗？请阐明你的观点。

译文鉴赏：

生日

克里斯蒂娜·罗塞蒂

我的心如同一只歌唱的鸟儿，
在鲜嫩的枝丫间筑巢；
我的心如同一棵丰收苹果树，
累累果实压弯了腰；
我的心如同那七彩的贝壳儿，　　　　　　　　　5
在静谧的大海中飘摇；
我的心比这些都要快乐，
因为我的爱人就要来到。

请搭起丝绸铺就的高台，
再挂上紫色的松鼠皮毛；　　　　　　　　　　10
台座要刻上鸽子和石榴，
还有开屏的孔雀在鸣叫；
再装点上银色的百合花朵，
和绿叶掩映下晶莹的葡萄；
因为我的新生即将开始，　　　　　　　　　　15
因为我爱的人就要来到。

　　下面我们再举一些有关暗喻的例子，并请大家试着回答如下问题：这些暗喻当中的本体和喻体分别是什么？这些例子当中的暗喻是否加强了语义的表达？为什么？

　　（1）The world is a stage, and we are all players.

第三章　英诗的语言

(2) Tom is a fox.

(3) There is a garden in her face.

(4) She was strangled in the net of gossip.

(5) He is the black sheep in his family.

接下来我们看一首罗伯特·弗罗斯特（Robert Frost, 1874—1963）的《冰与火》(Fire and Ice)。

这首《冰与火》最初发表于1920年出版的《新罕布什尔》(New Hampshire)，是弗罗斯特的代表诗作之一。这首诗歌探讨的主题是世界末日（the Apocalypse: the end of the world as described in the last book of the New Testament of the Bible）。作家杰弗里·迈尔斯（Jeffrey Myers, 1939— ）在《弗罗斯特传》(Robert Frost: A Biography)当中这样介绍《冰与火》的创作灵感：它的创作灵感来自但丁的《地狱》篇中的第三十二章（Canto 32 of Dante's Inferno in Divine Comedy）中的一段——在烈焰燃烧的地狱中，最恶劣的灵魂都淹没在冰湖里，只露出因羞耻而发红的脸颊（Myers, 1996）。

请读下面这首诗歌并且回答问题：

Fire and Ice

Robert Frost

Some say the world will end in fire,
Some say in ice.
From what I've tasted of desire
I hold with those who favor fire.
But if it had to perish twice,   5
I think I know enough of hate
To say that for destruction ice

Is also great

And would suffice.

思考题：

1. 诗中的"fire"和"ice"分别具有什么象征意义？
2. 请找出并分析这首诗歌当中所运用的各种修辞手法。
3. 请分析这首诗歌的主题思想。

译文鉴赏：

冰与火

罗伯特·弗罗斯特

有人说世界将在烈焰中毁灭，
有人说它会在冰冻中完结。
以我对于欲望的了解
火焰的说法更加准确。
然而，如果世界要毁灭两次的话，　　　　　5
以我对于仇恨的了解
冰冻的说法同样正确
结局
同样惨烈。

3.6.2 拟人、呼语和夸张

我们先看拟人（personification）。

作为一种修辞方式，拟人事实上是暗喻的一种类型。所谓拟人，就是给动物、无生命的物体、思想或是抽象概念，等等赋予了人类的外形、情感或是个性特征的修辞手法。简言之，就是将"非人"比喻成了"人"。通过拟人的手法，抽象的品质或是思想可以变得更具体；无生命的物体或是事物可以变得活灵活现；动物们也可以像我们一样开口讲话。因此，拟人手法的运用会使得文学作品表达的意义更生动形象，更加具有感染力。

我们看一下有关拟人的例子，并请回答：下面句子中的本体和喻体分别是什么？诗人将物体或是品质拟人化后产生了怎样的效果？

（1）My heart danced when he came to me.

（2）The geographic core, in Twain's early years, was the great valley of the Mississippi River, main artery of transportation in the young nation's heart.

（*Mark Twain—Mirror of America* by Noel Grove）

（3）Because I could not stop for Death,

　　He kindly stopped for me;

　　The carriage held but just ourselves

　　And Immortality.

（*Because I could not stop for Death* by Emily Dickinson）

需要注意的是，与拟人相反，还有一种修辞叫作"拟物（zoosemy）"，也叫作"动物隐喻（animal metaphor）"。所谓拟物，就是一种用动物的名字或形象来比喻人类的品质和特征的修辞手法。请大家看下面这些例句并且找出其中应用拟物的地方：

（1）He is a wolf in sheep's clothes.

（2）She is shedding crocodile tears.

（3）"A lucky dog you are!" exclaimed Jim.

（4）The boy's full-fledged now, and he will fly far and wide.

（5）Terribly hungry, the man wolfed down all the cakes.

下面我们看一首德·拉·梅尔的诗歌《银色》（*Silver*），并且分析其中拟人手法的运用。

沃尔特·德·拉·梅尔（Walter de la Mare, 1873 — 1956）是英国

著名小说家和诗人。他生于伦敦,曾在圣保罗大教堂唱诗班学校（St. Paul's Cathedral Choir School）读书。他十六岁便离开学校开始工作,并且从1890—1908年的18年间,在英美石油公司（Anglo-American Oil Company）的伦敦办事处工作。

德·拉·梅尔的诗歌继承发展了18世纪英国诗歌的浪漫主义传统。他的第一部重要作品是诗集《童年之歌》(*Songs of Childhood*, 1902)。这部诗集以其创造性的意象和多变的韵律而著称,是德·拉·梅尔儿童文学的代表作。他在1908年成功出版了第二部诗集《诗歌》(*Poems*, 1908),并且因此获得了皇室专用年金（Civil List pension）,从而得以辞去石油公司的工作,专门从事写作。他的代表作还包括诗歌《聆听者》(*The Listeners*)、短篇小说集《谜语》(*The Riddle*, 1923)等。

下面这首《银色》描述了在黑暗的夜晚,银色的月光照耀在各种物体和动物身上所造成的视觉冲击。这首诗采用克莱尔十四行诗（Clare Sonnet）的形式——一种对句押韵的十四行诗模式,韵脚安排为a a b b c c d d e e f f g g（Baldwin, April 3, 2019）。这首诗韵律优美、节奏轻快、意象生动,请各位读者仔细体会。

请读下面这首诗歌并且回答问题：

Silver

Walter de la Mare

Slowly, silently, now the moon
Walks the night in her silver shoon;
This way, and that, she peers, and sees
Silver fruit upon silver trees;
One by one the casements catch
Her beams beneath the silvery thatch;
Couched in his kennel, like a log,

5

With paws of silver sleeps the dog;

From their shadowy cote the white breasts peep

Of doves in a silver-feathered sleep; 10

A harvest mouse goes scampering by,

With silver claws and a silver eye;

And moveless fish in the water gleam,

By silver reeds in a silver stream.

思考题：

1. 请分析这首诗歌的节奏和韵律。
2. 这首诗中的月亮是如何被拟人化的？除了拟人，这首诗歌当中还运用了哪些修辞手法呢？请分析。
3. 这首诗歌当中有哪些意象？这些意象与我们的哪些感官相联系？

译文鉴赏：

银色

沃尔特·德·拉·梅尔

一弯明月亮，银鞋穿脚上；

左走右看看，银果枝头荡；

窗户亮闪闪，茅屋泛银光；

髭须闪闪亮，狗儿入梦乡；

银鸽挺起胸，梦里在低唱； 5

老鼠街中过，小眼透贼光；

鱼儿水中游，银色满池塘。

我们再看呼语（apostrophe）。

所谓呼语是指诗歌当中对于一个不在场的人或是死人，或是无生命的物体或是拟人化的事物的呼唤语。呼语经常被用来引导读者注意到所呼唤的对象，表明其重要性或意义。此外，诗人们还会使用呼语作为一种诗歌中角色向无法回应的人或物表达内心想法和感受的方式（Tsykynovska, May 5, 2017）。呼语是一种诗歌当中常见而在其他文学体裁当中不常见的修辞格。

下面是有关呼语的例子，请分析呼语在各个诗句当中的作用。

（1）O wild West Wind, thou breath of Autumn's being,

　　Thou, from whose unseen presence the leaves dead

　　Are driven, like ghosts from an enchanter fleeing.

　　(*Ode to the West Wind* by Percy Bysshe Shelley)

（2）Milton! thou shouldst be living at this hour：

　　England hath need of thee; she is a fen

　　Of stagnant waters.

　　(*Sonnet: London, 1802* by William Wordsworth)

（3）Little Lamb, who made thee?

　　Dost thou know who made thee?

　　Gave thee life, and bid thee feed,

　　By the stream and o'er the mead.

　　(*The Lamb* by William Blake)

我们下面以一首史蒂文森的《风》（*The Wind*）为例说明呼语在英语诗歌当中的作用。

罗伯特·路易斯·史蒂文森（Robert Louis Stevenson, 1850—1894）是著名苏格兰小说家、诗人、旅行作家。他的经典小说作品包括《金银岛》（*Treasure Island*, 1882）、《化身博士奇案》（*The Strange Case of Dr. Jekyll and Mr. Hyde*, 1886）以及《绑架》（*Kidnapped*, 1886），等等。

史蒂文森出生于苏格兰的爱丁堡，是家中的独子。他从小体弱多病，需要有人照看。他在1885年出版的诗歌集《儿童诗园》(*A Child's Garden of Verses*, 1885) 就是史蒂文森在法国南部的耶尔（Hyeres）养病期间创作并且献给幼年时曾经照看过自己的护士艾莉森·坎宁安（Alison Cunningham）的一部作品。1890年，史蒂文森偕同妻儿移居南太平洋岛国萨摩亚，并且在乌波卢岛的韦亚山（Mount Vaea on the island of Upolu in Samoa）下安顿下来，结庐而居。不幸的是，作家于1894年，年仅44岁的时候便死于脑出血，留下了未完成的小说《赫米斯顿的韦尔》(*Weir of Hermiston*, 1896)。在他死后，近60名萨摩亚人开辟了一条通往韦亚山顶的道路，将史蒂文森葬在了那里（Balfour, 1906）。

史蒂文森的诗歌语言生动、韵律优美而严谨并且充满了想象力。下面这首《风》很好地突出了这些特点。

请读下面这首诗歌并且回答问题：

The Wind
Robert Louis Stevenson

I saw you toss the kites high
And blow the birds about the sky;
And all around I heard you pass,
Like ladies' skirts across the grass —
　O wind, a-blowing all day long,　　　　　　　　5
　O wind, that sings so loud a song!

I saw the different things you did,
But always you yourself you did.
I felt you push, I heard you call,
I could not see yourself at all —　　　　　　　　　10

O wind, a-blowing all day long,
O wind, that sings so loud a song!

O you that are so strong and cold,
O blower, are you young or old?
Are you a beast of field and tree,　　　　　　　　　　15
Or just a stronger child than me?
O wind, a-blowing all day long,
O wind, that sings so loud a song!

思考题：

1. 这首诗的整体风格是轻松的还是严肃的？请论证你的观点。
2. 诗歌当中哪些有关风的问题诗人并未作出回答？
3. 诗人是怎样在这首诗当中将风拟人化的？
4. 这首诗当中的说话人是一个孩子吗？你是如何判断的？

译文鉴赏：

风

罗伯特·路易斯·史蒂文森

你将风筝高高抛起，
又将鸟儿吹向天空；
你在我身边匆匆走过，
如女士的裙摆掠过草丛——
啊风，你没日没夜地吹动，　　　　　　　　　　5
啊风，你时刻都在尽情歌颂！

你做过各种事情，
而且要事必亲躬。
我感到你的推搡，我听到你的呼声，
然而却见不到你的行踪——   10
　　啊风，你没日没夜地吹动，
　　啊风，你时刻都在尽情歌颂！

啊，你是如此强劲凛冽，
啊，你是年老还是年轻？
你是田野和丛林中的野兽，   15
抑或是比我更有力的孩童？
　　啊风，你没日没夜地吹动，
　　啊风，你时刻都在尽情歌颂！

最后是夸张（hyperbole）。

夸张是一种通过刻意地夸大其词（exaggeration）来达到更加突出的表达效果的修辞手法，其实质就是夸大的比喻。作为一种修辞手法，夸张经常应用于各类文体，特别是在诗歌当中应用得就更为广泛；同时，夸张也经常会出现在人们的日常讲话当中。夸张可以用来唤起人们的强烈的情感共鸣或留给人们深刻的印象；但需要注意的是，夸张的目的是强调，是为了增强表达效果，而并非是要求读者从字面意思对其加以理解。

理解夸张非常重要，因为它可以传递出强烈的情绪——依据说话者使用它的语境的不同，夸张可以表达出忧郁、兴奋、悲伤、喜悦、愤怒，等等多种复杂的情感。所以，很好地理解夸张将有助于我们准确、深刻地理解文学作品所传达的信息。

我们先看一下有关夸张的几个例子。请各位读者找出其中应用夸张的部分，并且思考夸张手法的运用收到了怎样的修辞效果。

（1）My car is a million years old.

（2）My aunt is so fat that when she walks by the TV, I miss three shows.

（3）Was this the face that launched a thousand ships,

　　And burnt that topless towers of Ilium?

　　Sweet Helen, make me immortal with a kiss!...

　　Oh, thou art fairer than the evening star,

　　Clad in the beauty of a thousand stars …

　　（*Doctor Faustus* by Christopher Marlowe）

（4）Macbeth:

　　Whence is that knocking? —

　　How is't with me, when every noise appals me?

　　What hands are here? Ha! They pluck out mine eyes.

　　Will all great Neptune's ocean wash this blood

　　Clean from my hand? No, this my hand will rather

　　The multitudinous seas incarnadine,

　　Making the green one red.

　　（*Macbeth* by Shakespeare）

我们再看一首奥登的《那夜我独自漫步》（*As I walked out one evening*）来继续体会夸张手法在英诗当中的应用。

威斯坦·休·奥登（Wystan Hugh Auden, 1907—1973）出生于英国，毕业于牛津大学，后移居纽约并加入美国籍。他是20世纪最有影响力的英语诗人之一，同时还是一位剧作家和批评家。

奥登的第一部重要诗集《诗歌》（*Poems*）是在艾略特（T. S. Eliot: 1888—1965）的帮助下于1930年结集出版的，自此他作为年轻一代诗人的杰出代表登上了文坛。在第二次世界大战爆发之前，奥登移民到了美国。在那里他遇到了同样是诗人的切斯特·卡尔曼（Chester Kallman,

1921 — 1975），并成为他一生的爱人。值得一提的是，奥登曾于1938年偕同友人兼作家克里斯托弗·伊舍伍德（Christopher Isherwood，1904 — 1986）访问中国，并且依据这段经历，同伊舍伍德共同创作了以十四行诗为主兼有散文和照片的著作《战地行纪》(*Journey to a War*, 1939）。1948年，他凭借《焦虑时代》(*The Age of Anxiety*: *A Baroque Eclogue*, 1947）获得普利策诗歌奖。

奥登知识广博，涉猎广泛，他往往能够从各种各样的文学、艺术形式以及社会政治理论和科学技术知识当中汲取营养，并且在自己的诗歌当中加以体现。此外，他还谙熟各种诗歌形式和诗歌创作技法，常常能够模拟其他诗人的写作风格进行创作。

下面的这首奥登的《那夜我独自漫步》选自兰登书屋（Random House）1940年为他出版的诗集 *Another Time*。

请读下面这首诗歌并且回答问题：

As I walked out one evening

W. H. Auden

As I walked out one evening,
Walking down Bristol Street,
The crowds upon the pavement
Were fields of harvest wheat.

And down by the brimming river   5
I heard a lover sing
Under an arch of the railway:
'Love has no ending.

'I'll love you, dear, I'll love you
Till China and Africa meet,   10

And the river jumps over the mountain
And the salmon sing in the street,

'I'll love you till the ocean
Is folded and hung up to dry
And the seven stars go squawking   15
Like geese about the sky.

'The years shall run like rabbits,
For in my arms I hold
The Flower of the Ages,
And the first love of the world.   20

But all the clocks in the city
Began to whirr and chime:
'O let not Time deceive you,
You cannot conquer Time.

'In the burrows of the Nightmare   25
Where Justice naked is,
Time watches from the shadow
And coughs when you would kiss.

'In headaches and in worry
Vaguely life leaks away,   30
And Time will have his fancy
To-morrow or to-day.

'Into many a green valley

Drifts the appalling snow;

Time breaks the threaded dances   35

And the diver's brilliant bow.

'O plunge your hands in water,

Plunge them in up to the wrist;

Stare, stare in the basin

And wonder what you've missed.   40

'The glacier knocks in the cupboard,

The desert sighs in the bed,

And the crack in the tea-cup opens

A lane to the land of the dead.

'Where the beggars raffle the banknotes   45

And the Giant is enchanting to Jack,

And the Lily-white Boy is a Roarer,

And Jill goes down on her back.

'O look, look in the mirror,

O look in your distress: 50

Life remains a blessing

Although you cannot bless.

'O stand, stand at the window

As the tears scald and start;

You shall love your crooked neighbour 55
With your crooked heart.

'It was late, late in the evening,
The lovers they were gone;
The clocks had ceased their chiming,
And the deep river ran on. 60

思考题：

1. 这首诗歌当中运用了大量的修辞手法，特别是拟人和夸张。请分析这两种修辞手法在诗中的作用。
2. 这首诗歌的前五个诗节与后十个诗节所描写的内容截然不同。请分析前后两个部分的中心思想分别是什么？
3. 这首诗歌当中运用了很多新奇的意象。请找出这些意象并且分析它们在诗中的意涵。

译文鉴赏：

那夜我独自漫步

W. H. 奥登

那夜我独自漫步，
走在布里斯托尔街上，
人行道就像丰收的麦田
熙熙攘攘。

在那奔流不息的河边， 5
铁路的桥拱下面

一个恋人在歌唱:
"爱的河水永远流淌。

"我会爱你,亲爱的,
直到中国和非洲相撞,   10
直到河流越过那高山,
直到鲑鱼在街上歌唱。

我会爱你,直到大海
折叠起来,挂起晾干,
直到天上的北斗七星   15
像家鹅般嘎嘎叫喊。

岁月如兔子般飞奔,
而我的怀抱里面
拥着永不凋零的花朵,
还有对这世界最初的爱恋。   20

但此刻城市里所有的钟表
都开始了嗡嗡轰鸣:
"啊,你永远无法征服时间,
千万不要让它将你欺骗。

"在噩梦的洞穴中,   25
是赤裸裸的正义,
时间躲在阴影中窥伺,
时刻提醒你将梦想抛弃。

"在痛苦和忧虑中，
生命悄然消逝，　　　　　　　　　　　　　　　30
而时间的幻想却从未落空，
在明天或是今日。

可怕的积雪吹进了
绿色的山谷；
时间打断了缠绵的舞步　　　　　　　　　　　35
还有跳水者精彩的弧度。

"啊，把你的手伸进水里，
直到水漫过你的手腕；
盯着，紧盯着盆子看啊，
想一想错过了哪些精彩瞬间。　　　　　　　　40

冰川在碗柜中撞击，
荒漠躺在床上叹气，
一条裂缝在茶杯上打开，
如小路通向那阴曹府邸。

"在那儿乞丐们抽得了钞票，　　　　　　　　　45
杰克倾心于愚蠢和残暴，
纯洁的男孩大声吼叫，
吉尔则仰面躺倒。

"啊看，看一看镜子的里面，
看一看那张痛苦不堪的脸：　　　　　　　　　50

生活依旧是上帝的眷顾,
尽管你已无力祈福。

啊,站起来,站在窗前,
任泪水滚烫,夺出眼眶;
你只有用受伤的心灵 55
去爱同样受伤的宾朋。"

天色已晚,很晚了,
恋人们已经走散;
时钟停止了轰鸣,
河水在寂静中前行。 60

第四章 英诗的体裁

4.1 引言

为了帮助大家更好地理解英语诗歌的体裁（genres of English poetry），我们在这里先粗略地谈一谈汉语诗歌的体裁划分方法。

根据划分标准的不同，对于汉语诗歌体裁的划分可以有多种方法。例如，根据时代、语言和诗歌形式的不同，汉语诗歌可以划分为古代诗歌和新诗。其中新诗包括自由体诗歌、散文诗以及民歌。而按照韵律对诗歌进行划分的话，汉语诗歌则可以分为古体诗、近体诗、词和曲。其中古体诗又包括了古诗、楚辞和乐府诗；而近体诗又可以划分为律诗和绝句。当然，我们也可以根据诗歌内容的不同将它们划分为抒情诗、叙事诗、悼亡诗、田园诗、边塞诗，等等很多种类型。这里需要注意的是，一首诗歌是可以同时划归为多种类型的。例如，《孔雀东南飞》既是汉乐府诗的巅峰之作，同时又是我国文学史上的第一部长篇叙事诗。当然你也可以说它是我国古代诗歌当中描写爱情悲剧的代表作之一。再如，苏轼的《水调歌头·明月几时有》既是一首宋词，又是一首抒情诗，同时还是我国古代诗歌当中抒发思念亲人的强烈情感的代表诗作之一。

下面我们再说英诗。

同汉语诗歌一样，根据诗歌的形式、韵律、内容，等等，英语诗歌的体裁也可以有多种不同的划分方法。然而，所有这些方法当中没有一种方法是完全令人满意的；这是因为我们划分诗歌体裁的方法通常有赖于自身看待诗歌的角度和对诗歌进行划分的目的。所以无论怎样对英诗的体裁进行划分，都难免有主观武断之嫌。事实上，如同汉语诗歌一样，依据分类标准的不同，我们也可以给同一首英语诗歌贴上多个标签；而与此同时，还会有一些诗歌是根本无法贴上任何标签的。尽管如此，为了便于学习、鉴赏英语诗歌，我们还是要对其体裁进行简要的划分。

对于英语诗歌，最古老和最广为人们所接受的划分方法是将其分为两大类：史诗（epic：围绕某个民族英雄而展开的长篇叙事诗）和抒情诗（lyric：抒发强烈感情的短诗）。这种划分方法尽管清楚明了，却有些过于笼统。所以在本章当中，我们就以诗人创作诗歌的目的为最主要的依据对英诗的体裁加以分类。据此，我们可以大体上将英语诗歌分为三类：叙事诗、抒情诗和说教诗（Narrative Poetry, Lyric Poetry and Didactic Poetry）。叙事诗要讲故事（to tell a story）；抒情诗要抒发情感或是表达浸透情感的思想（to express emotions）；说教诗要解释某些观点或是陈述诗人的思辨（to teach a lesson）。此外，为了弥补这样划分英诗所造成的缺失，我们还额外地，根据英诗的音韵将其划分为传统诗歌和自由体诗歌，并且在本章的最后一个小节对此加以讨论。

下面我们就从叙事诗开始。

4.2 叙事诗

叙事诗（narrative poetry）主要讲述发生在特定人物或人群身上的一系列重要事件。与其他的叙事类文学文体（例如短篇或是长篇小说，等等）相类似，叙事诗也同样包括诸如人物、背景、环境、情节、叙事角度等的要素；也同样以矛盾冲突为基础；诗歌当中的情节也同样会被逐渐推向高潮，等等。同时，叙事诗的篇幅可长可短；故事情节可以简单也可以复杂；诗行间通常要有节奏，却不见得非要押韵（Meyer，2015）。下面我们就具体看一看这三种形式的叙事诗：民谣、史诗和戏剧独白。

4.2.1 民谣

民谣（ballad）是最为广大读者所喜闻乐见的一种叙事诗形式。它是一种聚焦于故事当中最为戏剧化的部分的民间歌谣（folk song）。它经常会采取对话以及穿插一系列偶发事件的方式叙述整个故事。

英文中的"ballad"一词源自法语"ballade"，是古普罗旺斯语中的"ballada"；其词源还可以进一步追溯到后期拉丁语（Late Latin）中的"ballare"一词，意为"跳舞"——这主要是因为，中世纪的时候人们跳舞要以歌曲伴奏，而用于伴奏的舞曲大都是记述英雄故事的诗歌，也就是民谣（Collins English Dictionary，2021）。早期的英语民谣是作为乡村社会的一种口头传统（oral tradition），由吟游诗人（minstrels）进行演唱或背诵的。其内容通常是流传于当地的传说和故事，而作者是谁一般也无从知晓。这类民谣有时也被称为流行民谣（popular ballads），以区别于后世诗人在模仿传统歌谣的形式和精神实质的基础上，进行刻意创作的所谓文学民谣（literary ballads）。

一般来说，民谣只讲述一个短小的故事，只关注于故事最具戏剧化的那一刻。这种叙事方式是作者通过蓄意的、朴素和突兀的表达，达到一种大胆、煽情和戏剧性的效果。然而，与这种惜字如金的叙事方式不同的是，民谣作者往往会通过大量地应用修辞手法来延长故事中的紧张时刻，从而营造出故事当中浓厚的情感氛围。在这些修辞方法当中，最为典型的当属递增重复，也叫作叠加体（incremental repetition/adding style）。在民谣中，我们经常会看到一个短语或一个诗节重复几次，只是在同一个关键点上进行轻微但重要的替换；而留给读者的悬念会随着每一次替换而累积；直到诗歌的最后，最终的启示性替换打破了这种模式，故事达到高潮，强烈的紧张感才瞬间得以释放（Friedman，Dec. 1, 2016）。

再说一下民谣的常见形式。一般来讲，民谣多由几个四行诗节（quatrains）组成；每个诗节的押韵形式多为 a b c b；每个诗节的第一行和第三行为抑扬格四音步（iambic tetrameter），而第二行和第四行则为抑扬格三音步（iambic trimeter）。这样的诗节也被称为"民谣诗节"（ballad stanza）。需要请各位读者注意的是，并不是所有的民谣的主要目的都是讲故事，而民谣的形式也不一定都严格地采取所谓的"民谣诗节"。

下面我们举两个实例帮助各位读者对民谣进行更深入的了解。

第一首是华兹华斯的《我曾远走他乡》（*I Travelled Among Unknown Men*）。

这首《我曾远走他乡》创作于1801年，最早收录于华兹华斯的《两卷本诗集》（*Poems, in Two Volumes*，1807），是华兹华斯《露西组诗》（*Lucy Poems*）当中的第三首。《露西组诗》一共有五首，其中的主人公都是露西，然而华兹华斯却从未指明露西的真实身份，这便引起了文学史学家们对于"谁是露西"的种种猜测（Abrams，2000）。

《我曾远走他乡》表达了诗人对祖国英格兰的热爱以及不再漂泊海外的决心。这首诗共由四个诗节组成，每个诗节的叙事口吻（tone）都有变化——从怀旧的到忧郁的，再到温馨的，最后是喜忧参半、充满哲思的口吻，希望大家可以仔细体味。

请读下面这首诗歌并且回答问题：

I Travelled Among Unknown Men

William Wordsworth

I traveled among unknown men,
  In lands beyond the sea;
Nor, England! did I know till then
  What love I bore to thee.

'Tis past, that melancholy dream!   5
  Nor will I quit thy shore
A second time; for still I seem
  To love thee more and more.

Among thy mountains did I feel
  The joy of my desire;   10
And she I cherished turned her wheel
  Beside an English fire.

Thy mornings showed, thy nights concealed,
  The bowers where Lucy played;
And thine too is the last green field   15
  That Lucy's eyes surveyed.

思考题：

1. 请分析这首诗歌的韵律。
2. 诗歌当中运用了哪些修辞手法？
3. 诗人对露西和家乡的爱是怎样紧密相连的？

4. 为什么诗人对英格兰的爱越来越深切呢?

译文鉴赏:

我曾经远走他乡
威廉·华兹华斯

我曾远走他乡
也曾海外流浪
然而却浑然不知
自己如此地深爱着英格兰
——我的故乡 5

忧郁的梦境已经散去
游子再不会扬帆起航
因为我仍旧爱着你
越发地热烈滚烫

在你的群山之中 10
我能感到生命的热望
在你炉火旁转动纺车的
有我心爱的姑娘

露西曾经玩耍过的草房
给你的晨光照亮 15
被你的夜色隐藏
露西留下的最后的凝望
是你绿色的田野

是我可爱的家乡

下面再看一首彭斯的《我的心呀在高原》(*My Heart's in the Highlands*)。

罗伯特·彭斯（Robert Burns，1759—1796）是著名的苏格兰民族诗人，广泛地受到世界各国人民的喜爱。他出生于一个佃农家庭，兄弟姐妹七人，他排行老大。彭斯家境窘迫，所以他并没有接受正规而完整的教育，只是在父亲的帮助下断续学习了文法和其他一些知识。

彭斯的诗歌自然、直接、真诚，情感充沛而且风趣幽默。彭斯是一位重要且复杂的文学家，这主要由以下三点决定：第一，他在苏格兰文学传统中的突出地位；第二，他作为早期浪漫主义诗人的开创性表现；第三，他所独有的农民出身并且代表广大苏格兰穷苦人民发声的特殊身份（Poetry-Foundation，2021d）。

彭斯第一部正式出版的诗集《主要以苏格兰方言写就的诗歌》(*Poems, Chiefly in the Scottish Dialect*)于1786年付梓。这部诗集当中收录了彭斯最优秀的诗歌作品。此外，彭斯曾广泛游历苏格兰各地，特别是高原地区，收集整理了大量的苏格兰民歌，使得很多濒于失传的古老民歌得以保存并且传承下来。这也是彭斯在苏格兰文学史上的一大贡献。

经过彭斯搜集、整理、改编过的苏格兰民歌很多都成了广为传诵的经典作品。例如，《友谊地久天长》(*Auld Lang Syne*)、《一枝红红的玫瑰》(*A Red, Red Rose*)、《苏格兰人》(*Scots Wha Hae*)，等等。下面这首《我的心呀在高原》就是彭斯的代表诗作之一。在诗中，彭斯充满激情地描摹了祖国的壮丽山河，充分表达了诗人对苏格兰故土的无限热爱。

请读下面这首诗歌并且回答问题：

My Heart's in the Highlands
Robert Burns

My heart's in the Highlands, my heart is not here,
My heart's in the Highlands, a-chasing the deer;
Chasing the wild deer, and following the roe,
My heart's in the Highlands wherever I go.

Farewell to the Highlands, farewell to the North,   5
The birth-place of Valor, the country of Worth;
Wherever I wander, wherever I rove,
The hills of the Highlands for ever I love.

Farewell to the mountains high-cover'd with snow,
Farewell to the straths and green valleys below;   10
Farewell to the forests and wild-hanging woods;
Farewell to the torrents and loud-pouring floods.

My heart's in the Highlands, my heart is not here;
My heart's in the Highlands, a-chasing the deer;
Chasing the wild deer, and following the roe,   15
My heart's in the Highlands, wherever I go.

思考题：

1. 请分析这首诗的节奏和韵律。
2. 这首诗歌的主题思想是什么？诗人通过怎样的方式进行表达？
3. 这首诗歌的语言有哪些特点？请结合具体词语和诗句加以说明。

译文鉴赏：

我的心呀在高原
罗伯特·彭斯

我的心呀在高原，不在这里
我的心呀在高原，追逐着群鹿
追逐着野鹿呀，跟随着雌鹿
我的心呀在高原，无论我在哪里

再见了高原，再见了北方   5
勇敢的源地，美德的故乡
无论我在哪里漂泊，无论我身在何方
我的最爱都是高原的山岗

再见了，白雪覆盖的山峰
再见了，绿色的山谷和坦阔的河床   10
再见了，郁郁葱葱的森林
再见了，奔腾的溪水和激流的鸣响

我的心呀在高原，不在这里
我的心呀在高原，追逐着群鹿
追逐着野鹿呀，跟随着雌鹿   15
我的心呀在高原，无论我在哪里

4.2.2 史诗

史诗（epic）是一种长篇的叙事诗。其最主要文体特点就是主题和风格的庄严与宏大。史诗所描述的内容通常为在某个国家、民族或是世界范围内具有重大影响的传说或是历史事件。大多数的史诗都以连续叙事的方式，复述某个个人或是某个群体的生活概貌和丰功伟绩；这个个人或是群体可以是现实中的人物也可以是神话传说中的虚构人物（Literary Devices, 2021）。

此外，史诗还具有以下几个典型特征：（1）通过引入某些超自然的力量推动故事情节的发展；（2）矛盾冲突的表现形式通常为战斗或是大规模的战争；（3）经常会出现下面这些文体特性：向缪斯（Muse —— 古希腊神话当中艺术和科学的守护神，引申为艺术家获得灵感的源泉）求助以获得灵感、在叙事当中正式提出故事主旨、列举大量的英雄人物、以华丽的辞藻发表长篇大论，等等（Harmon & Holman, 1999）。史诗当然也会记述日常的琐碎生活，然而这些记述都是为故事的展开提供背景铺陈的；同时，即便是对于日常琐碎的记述也会与史诗的其他部分保持同样的文体风格。

史诗一般分为两种类型：传统史诗和文学史诗。前者是以世代相传的歌谣为蓝本，经过后世的加工整理，以文字的形式记录下来的一种文学作品；后者是文学家或是诗人有意识地通过编写或是创作的方式而形成的文学作品。传统史诗的代表作有古巴比伦的《吉尔伽美什》（Babylonian epic of *Gilgamesh*）、古印度的《摩诃婆罗多》和《罗摩衍那》（classical Hindu epics of *Mahabharata and Ramayana*）、古希腊的《荷马史诗》——《伊里亚特》和《奥德赛》（Homer's *Iliad* and *Odyssey*）、英格兰的《贝奥武夫》（Old English epic of *Beowulf*），等等。而文学史诗的代表作则有维吉尔的《埃涅阿斯纪》（Virgil's *Aeneid*）、约翰·弥尔顿的《失乐园》（John Milton's *Paradise Lost*），等等。

我们下面就以弥尔顿的《失乐园》(*Paradise Lost*)当中的一个片段为例帮助大家理解、认识史诗的内容和形式。

约翰·弥尔顿(John Milton, 1608—1674)英国著名诗人和小册子作家(pamphleteer)。他在英国文学史上的地位被认为仅次于莎士比亚。

弥尔顿早在剑桥大学求学期间(1625—1932)便开始用拉丁文、意大利文和英文进行诗歌创作。之后的七年间，他曾游历欧洲，在意大利度过了最长的时间，并且先后创作了假面舞剧《科摩斯》(*Comus*, 1634)和挽歌《黎西达斯》(*Lycidas*, 1638)。之后弥尔顿返回了英国，在克伦威尔(Oliver Cromwell, 1599—1658)共和国政府内任职直到1660年。他在政府任职期间为宣扬公民和宗教信仰自由创作了大量的"小册子"(pamphlet)。其中最著名的当数他的《论出版自由》(*Areopagitica*, 1644)。1660年斯图亚特王朝复辟后(Stuart Restoration)，弥尔顿由于其政治立场而被捕入狱，但不久便被释放回家。

弥尔顿悲惨的个人境遇很好地诠释了"逆境出人才，烈火见真金"的道理。1651年弥尔顿双目失明，遭受到沉重的打击。然而，他却并未向命运低头，开始以口述(dictation)的方式进行文学创作。而他最重要的两部史诗和一部诗剧(《失乐园》《复乐园》和《力士参孙》: *Paradise Lost*, *Paradise Regained* and *Samson Agonistes*)都是在他失明后创作出来的。

弥尔顿的《失乐园》(*Paradise Lost*, 1667, 1674)是一部著名的以英语写就的史诗，在英国文学史当中占有重要和崇高的地位。《失乐园》记述了撒旦及其党羽在与上帝的征战中被打败，之后被打入地狱，而撒旦为了报复上帝，变成蛇的形象诱惑在伊甸园中生活的亚当和夏娃，使其偷食禁果，最终被逐出乐园，开始在人间的艰辛生活的故事。这也就是《圣经》首卷《创世记》(*Book of Genesis*)当中所记述的人类的堕落的故事(Fall of Man)。有评论家认为，这首史诗反映了弥尔顿对于革命失败的绝望情绪，同时也表达了他对于人类最终获得胜利的坚定信念(Hill,

1977）。

由于篇幅所限，我们在这里仅仅节选了该诗的第一部（*Book 1*）当中的一个片段。该片段讲述了撒旦发誓要报复上帝的故事情节。这一段充分展现出撒旦不畏强权的英雄气概，是历来为文学爱好者们所喜爱的篇章。

请读下面这首诗歌并且回答问题：

Satan's Adjuration
Lines 105 — 124, Book I, Paradise Lost

John Milton

" … What though the field be lost?	105
All is not lost; the unconquerable Will,	
And study of revenge, immortal hate,	
And courage never to submit or yield:	
And what is else not to be overcome?	
That glory never shall his wrath or might	110
Extort from mee. To bow and sue for grace	
With suppliant knee, and deify his power	
Who from the terror of this Arm so late	
Doubted his empire, that were low indeed,	
That were an ignominy and shame beneath	115
This downfall; since by Fate the strength of Gods	
And this empyreal substance cannot fail,	
Since through experience of this great event	
In Arms not worse, in foresight much advanc'd,	
We may with more successful hope resolve	120
To wage by force or guile eternal Warr	

Irreconcilable to our grand Foe,

Who now triumphs, and in th' excess of joy

Sole reigning holds the Tyranny of Heav'n."

思考题：

1. 通过对节选部分的分析，你对撒旦的性格作何评价？
2. 请解释第16行当中的Fate和Gods的含义。
3. 在诗歌中，弥尔顿借撒旦之口称上帝为"the Tyranny of Heav'n"。这表现了诗人怎样的思想状况？

译文鉴赏：

撒旦的誓言

（选自《失乐园》，第1部，第105—124行）

约翰·弥尔顿

"……一场败仗又如何呢？

我们并未失去所有；

我们还有不屈的意志和精心策划的复仇，

我们还有不朽的仇恨和永不言弃的勇气。

还有什么比这些更可贵的吗？   5

他的暴怒和威力休想剥夺我们的荣誉。

这场刚刚结束的恶战已经动摇了他统治的根基；

我们绝不能在他的淫威面前

摇尾乞怜，卑躬屈膝。

那才是真正的羞耻啊；   10

因为，天道轮回，

众神定会重上九霄；

>   历此磨难，我们定会
>   更加的装备精良，更加的深谋远虑。
>   我们要对他发动一场持久的战争，　　　　　　　　　　15
>   满怀胜利的希冀；
>   运用暴力或是计谋，
>   击败这强大的死敌。
>   看呐，
>   他正在天庭欢天喜地，庆祝胜利；　　　　　　　　　　20
>   他正在天庭大权独揽，横行无敌！"

4.2.3 戏剧独白

戏剧独白（dramatic monologue）是叙事诗的一种。这里还需要说明的是，在戏剧当中，剧中角色表达个人思想的独白称为"soliloquy"，也可以翻译成"戏剧独白"，意思是"戏剧当中的独白"（a monologue in the play），例如《王子复仇记》中哈姆雷特（Hamlet）那段非常著名的"To be or not to be..."的独白。通常来讲，作为一种诗歌体裁的戏剧独白是通过诗歌当中的某一个人物所说的话来讲故事；而在此诗歌当中经常还会有另外一个人物，然而他并不讲话。

艾布拉姆斯（M. H. Abrams, 1912 — 2015）在其《文学术语汇编》（*A Glossary of Literary Terms*）当中对戏剧独白的特征做了以下概括：（1）某一个人物，不是诗人本人，在某个特定的情形下或是在某个关键的时间点发表讲话，而讲话的内容则构成诗歌的主体。（2）在戏剧独白当中，读者只能够从讲话人的话语当中推断出听话者的存在以及他们说了什么话或是做了什么事。（3）诗人通过诗歌当中的主要人物讲话的目的，是以某种有趣的方式，向读者展现出说话人的脾气秉性（Abrams, 1999）。

英诗当中较为有名的戏剧独白诗有勃朗宁的《我的前公爵夫人》

（Robert Browning's *My Last Duchess*）、马修阿诺德的《多佛海滩》（Matthew Arnold's *Dover Beach*）、T.S.艾略特的《J·阿尔弗雷德·普鲁弗洛克的情歌》（T. S. Eliot's *The Love Song of J. Alfred Prufrock*）、西尔维娅·普拉斯的《拉撒若夫人》（Sylvia Plath's *Lady Lazarus*），等等。其中最为典型也是最为著名的当数勃朗宁的《我的前公爵夫人》。

罗伯特·勃朗宁（Robert Browning，1812—1889）是英国维多利亚时期最著名的诗人和剧作家之一，是一位戏剧独白和心理刻画大师。他擅长反讽、人物塑造、黑色幽默以及创造性地运用词汇和句法。勃朗宁的代表作包括《戏剧抒情诗》（*Dramatic Lyrics*，1842）、《剧中人物》（*Dramatis Personae*，1864）和《戒指与书》（*The Ring and the Book*，1868—1869），等等。勃朗宁的艺术成就主要体现在他对于"戏剧独白"这种诗歌艺术形式的熟练运用和深刻把握上；此外，他还对许多现代诗人，如弗罗斯特和庞德（Robert Frost and Ezra Pound）等人产生了重要影响。这些诗人都从他的戏剧独白以及创造性地运用语言描写现代生活的多样性等方面汲取了丰富的营养。

这里还值得一提的是罗伯特·勃朗宁和伊丽莎白·巴雷特（Elizabeth Barrett，1806—1861）的爱情故事。巴雷特从小体弱多病，长大后更是深居简出，卧病在床。然而由于她颇具诗才，所以在当时英国的文学圈内有着不小的名气。1845年，与巴雷特神交已久的勃朗宁给她写了一封情书。在信中，勃朗宁直截了当地表达了对于巴雷特的爱慕之情。虽然巴雷特比勃朗宁年长六岁，而且女诗人还长期抱病，但这些都没能阻挡二人爱情的脚步。之后，两位才华横溢的青年便深深地坠入爱河。然而，巴雷特专横而自私的父亲并不赞成这桩婚事，甚至因此剥夺了女儿的继承权。可是二人无惧压力，于1846年9月秘密地结了婚，婚后一周便私奔到了意大利的比萨。自此夫妻二人便开始了长达15年的甜蜜的旅居生活。其间，虽有偶尔的在英国或是法国度假，二人的大部分时光都在意大利的佛罗伦萨度过——直到1861年，女诗人在勃朗宁的怀抱中安详离世。伊丽莎白·巴雷特·勃朗宁留给后世最宝贵的遗产就是她在与勃朗宁恋爱期间创作的、在婚后三年才拿出来给丈夫看并且在1850年最终出版的十四行诗集:《葡萄牙十四行诗集》(*Sonnets from the Portuguese*)。巴雷特去世后不久,勃朗宁便带着他们的儿子回到了英国,继续他的文学创作生涯(Woolford, Karlin, & Phelan, 2010)。

请读下面这首诗歌并且回答问题:

My Last Duchess
Robert Browning

That's my last Duchess painted on the wall,
Looking as if she were alive. I call
That piece a wonder, now: Fra Pandolf's hands
Worked busily a day, and there she stands.
Will't please you sit and look at her? I said   5
"Fra Pandolf" by design, for never read
Strangers like you that pictured countenance,
The depth and passion of its earnest glance,
But to myself they turned (since none puts by
The curtain I have drawn for you, but I)   10
And seemed as they would ask me, if they durst,
How such a glance came there; so, not the first
Are you to turn and ask thus, Sir, 'twas not
Her husband's presence only, called that spot
Of joy into the Duchess' cheek: perhaps   15
Fra Pandolf chanced to say "Her mantle laps
Over my lady's wrist too much," or "Paint

Must never hope to reproduce the faint

Half-flush that dies along her throat": such stuff

Was courtesy, she thought, and cause enough 20

For calling up that spot of joy. She had

A heart — how shall I say? — too soon made glad,

Too easily impressed; she liked whate'er

She looked on, and her looks went everywhere.

Sir, 'twas all one! My favour at her breast, 25

The dropping of the daylight in the West,

The bough of cherries some officious fool

Broke in the orchard for her, the white mule

She rode with round the terrace — all and each

Would draw from her alike the approving speech, 30

Or blush, at least. She thanked men, — good! but thanked

Somehow — I know not how — as if she ranked

My gift of a nine-hundred-years-old name

With anybody's gift. Who'd stoop to blame

This sort of trifling? Even had you skill 35

In speech — (which I have not) — to make your will

Quite clear to such an one, and say, "Just this

Or that in you disgusts me; here you miss,

Or there exceed the mark" — and if she let

Herself be lessoned so, nor plainly set 40

Her wits to yours, forsooth, and made excuse,

— E'en then would be some stooping; and I choose

Never to stoop. Oh sir, she smiled, no doubt,

Whene'er I passed her; but who passed without

Much the same smile? This grew; I gave commands; 45
Then all smiles stopped together. There she stands
As if alive. Will't please you rise? We'll meet
The company below, then. I repeat,
The Count your master's known munificence
Is ample warrant that no just pretence 50
Of mine for dowry will be disallowed;
Though his fair daughter's self, as I avowed
At starting, is my object. Nay, we'll go
Together down, sir. Notice Neptune, though,
Taming a sea-horse, thought a rarity, 55
Which Claus of Innsbruck cast in bronze for me!

思考题:

1. 公爵在对谁讲话？当时是怎样的情形？公爵谈到他的前夫人是跑题了吗？
2. 请根据诗歌的内容分析一下公爵的性格。
3. 公爵为何对他的前公爵夫人不满意？你怎样理解他前夫人的个性？公爵最终对自己的夫人做了什么？
4. 请问这首诗歌体现出意大利文艺复兴时期的哪些特点（例如婚俗、社会阶层、艺术，等等）？公爵对于艺术抱有怎样的态度？此种态度是虚伪的吗？

译文鉴赏：

我的前公爵夫人
罗伯特·勃朗宁

墙上挂的是我的前公爵夫人，
她看上去栩栩如生。
这张画儿是我的最爱：
潘道夫修士忙乎了一整天
于是她就站在那里了。　　　　　　　　　　　　　5
你可以坐下来看看吗？
我刚说过这是"潘道夫修士"的手笔。
像你这样的外来人从来没有见过画上的表情，
她那真诚的眼神深邃而且充满激情，
看过画的人都会转过头来　　　　　　　　　　　10
（只有我才可以拉下遮挡画作的幕布）
似乎要问我，如果他们有胆量问的话，
这样的眼神是怎样画成的？
没错，你不是第一个回过头问这个问题的人。
阁下，即便是她的丈夫不在场，　　　　　　　　15
公爵夫人也一样会喜气洋洋：
潘道夫修士似乎偶然间说过，
"夫人的斗篷把手腕遮住太多了"，或是
"绘画永远都无法表现出您那
逐渐消失在下颌底下的红晕"：　　　　　　　　20
这些话不过是客套一下而已。
然而她却喜形于色。

她的心 —— 我怎么说好呢 —— 太容易高兴了，
太容易被打动了；她看到什么都喜欢，
而且她还什么都喜欢看。 25
阁下，这根本就是一回事！
我对她乳房的夸奖，太阳落下西山，
不知是哪个傻瓜从果园里给她弄来的樱桃树枝，
她在梯田那儿骑的白骡子 —— 所有这一切
都会博得她的欢心，至少是脸上泛起红晕。 30
她感谢那些人 —— 天哪！她居然感谢他们，
尽管我不知道她是怎么说的 —— 似乎
她把我赐给她的九百年的贵族盛名
与其他人的小礼品都一视同仁了。
谁会为这种烂事儿屈尊理论呢？ 35
就算是巧舌如簧 —— 我可没有这两下子 ——
能把自己的想法说得清清楚楚：
"你这么做或是那么做恶心到我了；
你这儿做错了，那儿又越界了"，如此等等。
如果她愿意受教，也不顶撞你或是寻找借口的话， 40
—— 似乎应该屈尊一下；不过
我从来都不会屈尊。对了阁下，她是笑过，
没错，当我经过她的时候；可是
谁走近她的时候她不是一样地笑呢？
这事儿越来越难以容忍；于是我下达了指令； 45
接下来，她所有的笑容就戛然而止了。
你看，她现在站在那儿，栩栩如生。
你可以起身了吗？我们要会见一下下面的客人。
我再说一次，久闻你家伯爵的慷慨大方，

因此，我对于丰盛嫁妆的要求自然是无须讳言了； 50
尽管一开始我就曾声明，
我追求的目标是你家漂亮的小姐本人。
好了，我们一起下去吧。当心，
你身边的那尊尼普顿驯服海马的雕像，
那可是个稀罕玩意儿， 55
是伊斯布鲁克的克劳斯专门为我做的铜雕！

4.3 抒情诗

抒情诗（lyric poetry）是一种通常可以在乐器的伴奏下咏唱的诗歌形式；与叙事诗相较而言，它通常更加侧重表达诗人的某种感受或情绪，并且多数情况下篇幅较短（Britannica, June 27, 2017）。

古希腊的时候，人们是在竖琴（lyre——也称七弦琴、里尔琴）的伴奏下演唱或是朗诵抒情诗的。十四行诗、颂歌以及挽歌（sonnets, odes and elegies）是那一时期抒情诗最为流行的形式。就诗歌的主题而言，"爱"是抒情诗表达最多的情感；同时，其他的情感，例如"悲伤"或是"忧郁"，也经常会以某种抒情诗的形式表现出来。抒情诗的叙事视角一般为第一人称，而内容则多为各种意味深长的思绪而非具体的动作。

因为抒情诗的形式和结构多种多样，所以当我们诵读一首抒情诗的时候，要尽力寻找诗人思想、情感的发展轨迹。这样，我们就会在诗歌的每个诗节或是每个部分当中体会、领悟到诗歌的主旨。此外还需要注意的是，我们对于诗歌的各个部分的划分，通常是建立在对于诗歌的韵律和意象的分析、理解的基础之上的。

下面我们就对十四行诗、颂歌以及挽歌这三种最常见、也是最典型的抒情诗形式分别加以介绍和举例说明。

4.3.1 十四行诗

十四行诗（sonnet）也称为商籁体诗歌，是一种广受读者欢迎的抒情诗类型。十四行诗的英文"sonnet"一词来自意大利语"sonetto"，意为"一支小调"。顾名思义，十四行诗总共包含有十四句诗行；就格律而言，每句诗行大都采用抑扬格五音步的形式，而且通常整首诗歌的格律较为严谨（Jamieson, Aug. 28, 2020）。

作为一种诗体，十四行诗是由13世纪早期的意大利诗人贾科莫·达·伦蒂尼（Giacomo da Lentini, 1210 — 1260）创制并且发展起来的；而后，文艺复兴时期的意大利诗人彼特拉克（Petrarch, 1304 — 1374）使得这一诗歌形式进一步趋于完善并且声名远播。16世纪初，托马斯·怀特爵士（Sir Thomas Wyatt, 1503 — 1542）将十四行诗引入英国；他借用意大利体十四行诗的形式，使用英语进行了诗歌创作。到了16世纪末的伊丽莎白时代，十四行诗开始在英国文坛流行开来；而莎士比亚则对这一诗体的韵律进行了创新，并且推动运用这一诗体进行的诗歌创作达到了顶峰。

传统上来讲，十四行诗的主题（theme）无非是"爱情"（love）；然而随着时代的推移，更多的主题被诗人们用这种形式表现出来，诸如友谊、自然、政治、宗教情感，等等。总之，十四行诗所涉及的主题范围越来越宽泛。

我们再看十四行诗的形式（form）。英语诗歌当中有两种最常见的十四行诗形式，它们分别是意大利体十四行诗，也称为彼特拉克体十四行诗（the Italian, or Petrarchan sonnet）和英国体十四行诗，也称为莎士比亚体十四行诗（the English, or Shakespearean sonnet）。下面我们就具体看一下这两种十四行诗的形式特点。

意大利体十四行诗包括两个部分：第一部分为诗歌的前八行，叫作"octave"，押韵格式为 a b b a, a b b a；第二部分为诗歌的后六行，叫作"sestet"，押韵格式为 c d e, c d e 或是 c d, c d, c d。就诗歌内容而言，通常十四行诗的第一、第二部分之间会发生意思上的转折（叫作"volta"，意大利语"转折"的意思）——这是叙事或是论证方向上的改变，从而对诗歌的第一部分做出回应。这种意思上的转折一般是通过诗歌第二部分第一句诗行开头的单词，例如"But, Yet"或是"And yet"等达成的（Britannica, Nov. 1, 2007b）。

英国体十四行诗的最杰出代表就是莎士比亚所创作的十四行诗。它与意大利体的不同之处就在于，整首诗歌分为三个四行诗（three quatrains）外加一个押韵对偶句（rhymed couplet），共四个部分；其中，前三个部分分别押韵，最后的对偶句将整首诗歌推向高潮（第十二行和第十三行之间也经常发生转折，即所谓的"volta"）。英国体十四行诗的押韵格式为 a b a b, c d c d, e f e f, g g。这里还请各位读者注意的是，英国体十四行诗还有一种变体，即斯宾塞体十四行诗（the Spenserian sonnet）。在斯宾塞体十四行诗当中，诗人会将诗歌的前面三个四行诗节通过连锁押韵（three interlocked quatrains）的方式连接起来，从而使整首诗形成 a b a b, b c b c, c d c d, e e 的押韵格式。当然，除了上述三种十四行诗的形式以外，还存在有很多种十四行诗的变体，只不过是存世数量没有那么多，影响没有那么大罢了。

在熟悉了十四行诗的定义、发展演进的历史、主题和常见形式之后，我们下面就开始举具体的例子帮助大家加深对于十四行诗的理解和认识。

我们先读一首莎士比亚的十四行诗"*Sonnet 18*"。这是收录了莎士比亚154首十四行诗的诗集当中较为著名的一首。它隶属于该诗集的"美少年系列"（Fair Youth sequence——即该诗集的前126首）。该诗是典型的英国体或莎士比亚体十四行诗，历来为广大文学爱好者所喜爱。

请读下面这首诗歌并且回答问题：

Sonnet 18

William Shakespeare

Shall I compare thee to a summer's day?
Thou art more lovely and more temperate:
Rough winds do shake the darling buds of May,
And summer's lease hath all too short a date;
Sometime too hot the eye of heaven shines,   5
And often is his gold complexion dimm'd;
And every fair from fair sometime declines,
By chance or nature's changing course untrimm'd;
But thy eternal summer shall not fade,
Nor lose possession of that fair thou ow'st;   10
Nor shall Death brag thou wander'st in his shade,
When in eternal lines to time thou grow'st:
So long as men can breathe or eyes can see,
So long lives this, and this gives life to thee.

思考题：

1. 请分析这首诗的节奏和韵律。
2. 诗人认为他所赞美的对象与太阳比较起来更加"lovely"和"temperate"。为什么？请结合诗歌内容具体说明。
3. 为什么诗人所赞美对象可以永葆青春，可以永垂不朽？
4. 请分析这首十四行诗的主题思想是如何展开的。

译文鉴赏：

十四行诗·第18首
莎士比亚

我能否将你比作夏天？
你比她更可爱更温婉：
风暴摧折了五月的花瓣，
夏日也总是瞬间流转；
她有时候骄阳似火，   5
有时候又面容黯淡；
岁月无法留住易老红颜，
美人也抵不住风霜修剪：
而你的夏天却永不凋残，
青春的美貌将永驻人间，   10
死神拿你也无可奈何，
因为有我的诗行伴你永远。
直到宇宙洪荒，海枯石烂，
直到还有人诵读这不朽的诗篇。

下面我们再看一首弥尔顿的十四行诗——《致失明》(*On His Blindness*)。

约翰·弥尔顿（John Milton, 1608 — 1674）的这首《致失明》是他最为著名的十四行诗之一。整首诗采用了抑扬格五音步的格律，押韵格式为a b b a, a b b a, c d e, c d e，被称为是弥尔顿体十四行诗（the Miltonic sonnet）。大家一定注意到，所谓"弥尔顿体十四行诗"，其押韵格式和整诗的结构安排（an octave + a sestet）同斯宾塞体十四行诗是一致的。然而相较而言，弥尔顿体十四行诗的题材更为宽泛，经常探讨政治或是道德问题，而且大量地运用"跨行连续"（enjambment）的手法将整首诗歌的结构紧密连接在一起（Robinson, Aug. 14, 2019）。

在下面这首诗歌当中，弥尔顿基于自己的基督教信仰，对如何接纳自己的身体缺陷做出了论证。新教徒认为，人们是响应上帝的感召（calling）才去完成他所承担的世间的工作以取悦上帝从而获得拯救（salvation）的。然而，让弥尔顿感到迷惑不解的是，自己一心要通过诗歌创作来取悦上帝，却被无情地剥夺了视力（诗中第三行：And that one talent which is death to hide）。所以经过剧烈的思想斗争，诗人得出结论：失去光明不是自己完成世间工作的障碍，相反，它是自己工作的一部分；而自己在世间的成就就包括了是否能够耐心地与自己的身体缺陷和平共处——这正如诗歌的最后一行所言："They also serve who only stand and wait"（Baldwin, June 27, 2017）。

这首诗歌其实是诗人对于自身命运思考的结果，体现了诗人对于宇宙人生意义的深入探索。也正是由于弥尔顿在内心深处与自己多舛的命运达成了真正的和解，他才能够真正地获得心灵的安宁，才能够在自己失明之后写出诸如史诗《失乐园》等这样震古烁今的扛鼎之作。

请读下面这首诗歌并且回答问题：

On His Blindness

John Milton

When I consider how my light is spent
Ere half my days, in this dark world and wide,
And that one talent which is death to hide,
Lodged with me useless, though my soul more bent
To serve therewith my Maker, and present   5

My true account, lest He returning chide;

"Doth God exact day-labour, light denied?"

I fondly ask. But Patience, to prevent

That murmur, soon replies: "God doth not need

Either man's work or his own gifts, who best   10

Bear His mild yoke, they serve him best. His state

Is kingly: thousands at His bidding speed,

And post o'er land and ocean without rest;

They also serve who only stand and wait."

思考题：

1. 请注意，诗作的第一行到第七行半为一句话；从第七行半到最后为另一句话。请用自己的话分别复述一下这两句话的意思。
2. 第三行中的"talent"是什么意思？弥尔顿的"talent"又是什么呢？
3. 这首诗歌运用了多种修辞手法，其中就包括"跨行连续（Enjambment）"。请举例分析。
4. 这首诗歌的基调是悲观消极的还是乐观积极的？请论证你的观点。

译文鉴赏：

致失明

约翰·弥尔顿

我未到中年便失去了光明，

跌进这无尽的黑暗；

死神藏匿了我的天赋，

害瞎了我的双眼；

我的灵魂如赤子一般匍匐在造物主前，   5

傻傻问道：

"上帝惩罚我终日劳作，又为何将我打入黑暗？"

忍耐之神立刻打断了我的抱怨：

"上帝不需要人们的劳作，

也不需要他们的贡献；　　　　　　　　　　　　　　　　　　　　10

谁承受得住他温和的羁绊，谁才是他最好的钦犯；

他颁布旨意：于是领命的人们便会成千上万，

他们穿行于陆地和海洋，奔波忙碌；

记住，忍耐与等待同样是向上帝臣服。"

4.3.2 颂歌

颂歌（ode），也称"颂体诗"，是抒情诗中的一种类型。它通常态度庄严，结构精巧，内容多为颂扬或是礼赞某个个人、纪念某个事件或是以较为理性而非感性的方式描绘自然景物。颂歌通常比其他类型的抒情诗的篇幅要更长。诗人往往通过颂歌的形式来表达对于某个主题的严肃而认真的思考。相较其他诗体，颂歌的语言也通常更为文雅一些（Gosse，1911）。

英文"ode"一词来源于希腊语单词"aeidein"，意思是吟唱或歌唱。古希腊的颂歌最初都是有音乐伴奏的诗歌作品，多为民间的集体创作；然而随着时间的推移，颂歌逐渐成了某个诗人个人抒发感情的作品，而表演的形式则多为在乐器的伴奏下的演唱或是朗诵。古希腊颂歌在结构上通常分为三个部分或是诗节，叫作第一诗节、第二诗节和第三诗节（the strophe, the antistrophe, and the epode）。古希腊的颂歌有三种典型的形式：平达体颂歌、贺拉斯体颂歌以及不规则体颂歌（the Pindaric, Horatian, and irregular odes）。由于篇幅所限，有关这三种颂歌形式的特点这里就不再赘述（ibid）。

下面我们就以颂歌体诗歌创作的高手济慈的《夜莺颂》（Ode To a Nightingale）为例，帮助大家理解、认识"颂歌"这一诗体。

约翰·济慈（John Keats，1795—1821）是19世纪初英国杰出的浪漫主义诗人。他1795年出生于伦敦，是家中四个孩子当中的长子。然而他身世凄苦，父母在济慈十五岁前便相继离世了。而济慈本人也只活了25岁便与世长辞。

在如同流星一般划过的短暂一生当中，济慈却给后世留下了诸多名篇佳作，使其如一颗闪耀的恒星一般永远地镶嵌在世界文学史的浩瀚夜空当中。济慈于1821年2月23日在意大利罗马去世。他的遗体葬在该市的新教公墓（Protestant Cemetery, Rome）；英国浪漫主义诗人雪莱后来也安葬于此。济慈对朋友们最后的请求是将自己葬在一块没有名字和日期的墓碑之下，上面只需写这样的文字："Here lies One whose Name was writ in Water."（此地长眠者，声名水中刻。）

济慈是颂歌创作的高手。后世认为，仅凭他1819年先后创作的"五大颂歌"——《夜莺颂》《忧郁颂》《希腊古瓮颂》《普赛克颂》和《秋颂》（Five Great Odes of 1819: Ode to a Nightingale, Ode on Melancholy, Ode on a Grecian Urn Ode to Psyche and To Autumn），就足以奠定其在英国文学乃至世界文学史当中的崇高地位。下面我们选择提供给各位读者研习的颂歌就是他的名作《夜莺颂》。

济慈的挚友查尔斯·布朗（Charles Brown，1787—1842）曾经这样描述济慈创作《夜莺颂》的经过：那是1819年的春天，一只夜莺在我们位于汉普斯特德（Hampstead）的房子附近筑了巢。济慈对于这只夜莺的歌声很着迷——在她的歌声里，济慈似乎能感受到内心的平静和持续的快乐。一天早晨，济慈从餐桌旁搬了把椅子，放到庭院中梅子树下的小草坪那里。然后，他在椅子上连续坐了两三个小时。之后，他回到屋里，手里攥着几张纸片，然后轻轻地把这几张纸片夹在几本书中。我于是过去查看，发现那些纸片，大概四五张的样子，记录了那只夜莺的歌声所唤起的

第四章　英诗的体裁

济慈的诗情（Bate, 1963）。

请读下面这首诗歌并且回答问题：

Ode To a Nightingale
John Keats

My heart aches, and a drowsy numbness pains
　　My sense, as though of hemlock I had drunk,
Or emptied some dull opiate to the drains
　　One minute past, and Lethe-wards had sunk:
'Tis not through envy of thy happy lot,　　　　　　　　　　5
　　But being too happy in thine happiness, —
　　　　That thou, light-winged Dryad of the trees
　　　　　　In some melodious plot
Of beechen green, and shadows numberless,
　　Singest of summer in full-throated ease.　　　　　　　　10

O, for a draught of vintage! that hath been
　　Cool'd a long age in the deep-delved earth,
Tasting of Flora and the country green,
　　Dance, and Provençal song, and sunburnt mirth!
O for a beaker full of the warm South,　　　　　　　　　　15
　　Full of the true, the blushful Hippocrene,
　　　　With beaded bubbles winking at the brim,
　　　　　　And purple-stained mouth;
That I might drink, and leave the world unseen,
　　And with thee fade away into the forest dim:　　　　　　20

Fade far away, dissolve, and quite forget
  What thou among the leaves hast never known,
The weariness, the fever, and the fret
  Here, where men sit and hear each other groan;
Where palsy shakes a few, sad, last gray hairs, 25
  Where youth grows pale, and spectre-thin, and dies;
   Where but to think is to be full of sorrow
    And leaden-eyed despairs,
  Where Beauty cannot keep her lustrous eyes,
   Or new Love pine at them beyond to-morrow. 30

Away! away! for I will fly to thee,
  Not charioted by Bacchus and his pards,
But on the viewless wings of Poesy,
  Though the dull brain perplexes and retards:
Already with thee! tender is the night, 35
  And haply the Queen-Moon is on her throne,
   Cluster'd around by all her starry Fays;
    But here there is no light,
  Save what from heaven is with the breezes blown
   Through verdurous glooms and winding mossy ways. 40

I cannot see what flowers are at my feet,
  Nor what soft incense hangs upon the boughs,
But, in embalmed darkness, guess each sweet
  Wherewith the seasonable month endows
The grass, the thicket, and the fruit-tree wild; 45

    White hawthorn, and the pastoral eglantine;
     Fast fading violets cover'd up in leaves;
      And mid-May's eldest child,
    The coming musk-rose, full of dewy wine,
     The murmurous haunt of flies on summer eves.   50

Darkling I listen; and, for many a time
  I have been half in love with easeful Death,
Call'd him soft names in many a mused rhyme,
  To take into the air my quiet breath;
Now more than ever seems it rich to die,   55
  To cease upon the midnight with no pain,
    While thou art pouring forth thy soul abroad
     In such an ecstasy!
  Still wouldst thou sing, and I have ears in vain —
    To thy high requiem become a sod.   60

Thou wast not born for death, immortal Bird!
  No hungry generations tread thee down;
The voice I hear this passing night was heard
  In ancient days by emperor and clown:
Perhaps the self-same song that found a path   65
  Through the sad heart of Ruth, when, sick for home,
    She stood in tears amid the alien corn;
    The same that oft-times hath
  Charm'd magic casements, opening on the foam
    Of perilous seas, in faery lands forlorn.   70

Forlorn! the very word is like a bell
　　To toll me back from thee to my sole self!
Adieu! the fancy cannot cheat so well
　　As she is fam'd to do, deceiving elf.
Adieu! adieu! thy plaintive anthem fades　　　　　　　　　　75
　　Past the near meadows, over the still stream,
　　　　Up the hill-side; and now 'tis buried deep
　　　　In the next valley-glades:
Was it a vision, or a waking dream?
　　Fled is that music:— Do I wake or sleep?　　　　　　　　80

思考题：

1. 请仔细阅读这首诗，然后用一句话概括出每个诗节的主题思想。
2. 这首颂歌与其他抒情诗在语言和主题思想方面有哪些不同呢？
3. 这首诗的"口吻"（tone）是怎样的？诗人是如何营造出这一"口吻"的呢？

译文鉴赏：

夜莺颂

约翰·济慈

我的心在痛，在昏昏沉沉的麻木中刺痛
　　我的感官，像是喝下了毒酒，
又像是饮尽了鸦片
　　沉入忘川：
不是因为嫉妒你的快乐，　　　　　　　　　　　　　　　　　5
　　而是因为快乐着你的快乐——

你是树木的精灵,轻盈地飞行

　　在夏日里,

在山毛榉树郁郁葱葱的荫影里,

　　引吭高歌。　　　　　　　　　　　　　　　　　　10

哦,一股葡萄酒的香气!似乎

　　经过岁月的洞藏,从深埋的地下飘散了出来,

带着花仙子和绿色乡野的味道,带着

　　舞蹈,普罗旺斯的歌声,以及太阳炙烤下的欢笑!

哦,一只水杯盛满了温暖的南方,　　　　　　　　　15

　　盛满了真正的,让人心动的灵泉之水,

　　　着成串儿的气泡在杯口炸裂,

　　　　将它染成了紫色;

　　我要将它喝下,脱离这真实的世界,

　　　同你一起,渐渐消失在幽暗的丛林深处:　　　20

渐渐远去,消失,直至完全忘却

　　那些你在树叶中从来不知晓的一切,

疲倦,躁动和焦虑

　　这里,人们聚在一起,听着彼此的抱怨;

这里,将死的老人,流露出悲伤和麻痹,　　　　　　25

　　这里,面色苍白的青年,幽灵一般死去;

　　　这里,思考就意味着悲伤

　　　　和满眼的失意,

　　这里,美丽无法保持她温柔而闪亮的双眼,

　　　或是让她新生的爱情活过明天。　　　　　　30

去吧！去吧！我会向你飞去，
　　不是乘着酒神巴克斯豹拉的车子，
而是爬上那隐形的，诗歌的翅膀，
　　穿越愚钝的大脑所设下的层层屏障：
已经和你在一起了！夜色是多么温柔，　　　　　　　　35
　　碰巧，月亮女王登上了她的宝座，
　　　　周围簇拥着星光熠熠的仙子们；
　　　　　　但是这里没有光亮，
　　只有天空中的微风轻轻地吹拂着
　　　　那碧绿幽暗，曲折而长满苔藓的小路。　　　　40

我看不到脚下生长着怎样的花朵，
　　也看不到树枝上挂了怎样柔软的香草，
但在充满香气的黑暗中，猜到，
　　绿草，灌木，以及野生的果木
都在各自的季节中散发着独有的芳香；　　　　　　　45
　　开白花儿的山楂树，牧场上的野蔷薇；
　　　　还有树叶遮盖下快速凋零的紫罗兰；
　　　　　　刚过春天，挂满露水的麝香玫瑰
　　便绽放，如美酒般香甜，
　　　　而成群出没的飞蝇，则在夏日的傍晚呢喃。　　50

我在黑暗中倾听；许多次了
　　几乎爱上了死亡的安逸，
我呼唤着死神的名字，用缪斯的优美旋律
　　希望他将我安静的喘息弥散于空气；
我比任何时候都更接近死亡，　　　　　　　　　　　55

第四章 英诗的体裁

在午夜时分,没有痛苦地停止呼吸,
　　而你正将自己的灵魂之歌宣泄出来
　　　带着狂喜!
你仍将歌唱,而我却已离去——
　　只有你悠扬的安魂曲回荡在我的墓地。　　　　　　60

你永远都不会死去啊,不朽的夜莺!
　　不会有饥馑的世代将你欺凌;
今晚我听闻的歌声
　　古代的皇帝和村夫也曾倾听:
可能,同样悲凉的曲调　　　　　　　　　　　　　　65
　　也曾将露丝打动,当她想家的时候,
　　　站在他乡的田野,泣不成声;
　　　　可能,同样悲凉的曲调
　　也曾回荡在凄凉的幻境,
　　　打开那施了魔咒的窗扉,直面大海的汹涌。　　70

凄凉的幻境!仿佛钟声
　　将我唤醒!
再见吧!幻想的精灵,
　　再美妙的梦境也终会苏醒。
再见吧!再见吧!渐渐消逝的悲伤歌声　　　　　　75
　　飘过附近的草原,掠过寂静的溪流,
　　　攀上高高的山峰;忽而,又沉入到
　　　　下一个林间谷中:
　　告诉我,什么是幻象,什么是真实的梦境?
　　　那歌声消逝了——我是在梦中还是已经清醒?　80

4.3.3 挽歌

现代文学中，挽歌（elegy）是指表达悲伤情绪，特别是表达对于去世的人的哀悼的诗歌（Merriam-Webster, n.d.）。

在希腊和罗马的古典文学当中，挽歌最初是由对联或是对偶句（distichs or couplets）的形式创作而成的。传统意义上的挽歌格律形式特征明显，所涉及的题材也较为广泛。它可以包括爱情、哀悼、政治等诸多方面的内容。古代诗人，诸如古希腊诗人卡利马科斯（Alexandrian Callimachus，310—240, BC）以及古罗马诗人卡图卢斯（Roman Catullus，84—54, BC）都经常运用挽歌这一诗体进行创作（Nagy, 2010）。在现代诗歌当中（16世纪之后），人们主要是以内容而非形式作为区分挽歌的依据——挽歌的内容总是围绕着死亡的主题，呈现出忧郁的色彩。英诗当中最为著名的挽歌当属托马斯·格雷的著名诗作《墓园挽歌》（*Elegy Written in a Country Churchyard*, 1751）。

托马斯·格雷（Thomas Gray，1716—1771）是18世纪中期英国诗坛的领军人物，同时也是英国浪漫主义运动的先驱。格雷出生在一个富裕但并不幸福的家庭。他在家中排行老五，是12个孩子当中唯一一个长大成人的。他的父亲严厉而粗暴，母亲则长期病体缠身，靠经营一家女帽店来供养格雷上学。格雷自小心思细腻、淡泊宁静、学习刻苦。他八岁进入伊顿公学读书，十八岁进入剑桥大学彼得学院，四年后在未获得学位的情况下便离开剑桥开始游历欧洲，并于1742年再次回到剑桥从事教学、科研和文学创作（Britannica, July 26, 2021）。

格雷的诗歌语言成熟、松弛而恰如其分，语调发人深省而感伤，并且经常能够以令人侧目的遣词造句表达出老生常谈的道理。格雷传世的诗作并不多，前期的佳作有《为理查德·韦斯特先生之死而作十四行诗》（*Sonnet on the Death of Mr. Richard West*, 1742）、《春之歌》（*Ode on the Spring*, 1748）、《逆境赞歌》（*Hymn to Adversity*, 1753），等等。然而真正让格雷扬名立万的诗作是于1751年发表的《墓园挽歌》。在这首挽歌当中，格雷所探讨的主题不仅仅是某个个人的死亡；而且，诗歌还对所有的人，包括诗人自己的，不可避免的死亡进行了哀悼——因为无论是王公贵族还是平民百姓最终都会殊途同归。也正因如此，这首诗歌才更加具有普世意义。

《墓园挽歌》中的"墓园"位于英格兰白金汉郡的斯托克波吉斯村（Stoke Poges in Buckinghamshire, England）；而格雷本人也埋葬于此。这首诗的每个诗节都由四句诗行构成，每句诗行大体上都是抑扬格五音步。每个诗节当中，第一行与第三行押韵，第二行与第四行押韵。这种诗歌形式叫作英雄四行体（heroic quatrain），莎士比亚和德莱顿（John Dryden, 1631—1700）都曾经在诗歌创作中使用过此种形式。然而，在格雷的诗名得以确立后，以这种形式创作的诗歌便干脆被叫作"挽歌体"（elegiac stanza）诗歌了。

后世学者对这首《墓园挽歌》的评价甚高，认为它是最为杰出的英语诗歌之一。这首诗将诗歌的结构、韵律、意象以及内容完美地结合在了一起，从而为格雷带来了巨大而长久的声誉。有些学者甚至认为，这首诗所达到的高度已经足以使格雷与莎士比亚和弥尔顿相比肩。

下面我们就看一下这首格雷的《墓园挽歌》。由于原诗作篇幅较长，我们这里仅节选了该诗的前四个诗节（lines 1—16）供各位读者分析、鉴赏。有兴趣的读者也可以通过网络或是其他资源找到整首诗歌的原文并进行深入的研究。

请读下面这首诗歌并且回答问题：

Elegy Written in a Country Churchyard
— an excerpt

Thomas Gray

The curfew tolls the knell of parting day,

The lowing herd winds slow'ly o'er the lea,

The plowman homeward plods his weary way,

And leaves the world to darkness and to me.

Now fades the glimm'ring landscape on the sight.　　　　5

And all the air a solemn stillness holds,

Save where the beetle wheels his droning flight,

And drowsy tinklings lull the distant folds;

Save that from yonder ivy-mantled tow'r

The moping owl does to the moon complain　　　　10

Of such, as wand'ring near her secret bow'r,

Molest her ancient solitary reign.

Beneath those rugged elms, that yew-tree's shade,

Where heaves the turf in many a mould'ring heap,

Each in his narrow cell for ever laid,　　　　15

The rude forefathers of the hamlet sleep.

思考题：

1. 格雷兄弟姐妹众多，却只有他一人长大成人。你认为他兄弟姐妹的早夭对他的诗歌创作是否产生了影响？
2. 请描述一下此处节选的这四个诗节的韵律，并且分析此处的声音和韵律是怎样营造整首诗的氛围的。
3. 诗中都有哪些意象？请分析这些意象与诗歌的音韵所营造的氛围是如何紧密贴合的。

译文鉴赏：

墓园挽歌

（节选）

托马斯·格雷

告别白昼，晚钟悲鸣
畜群低叫，蜿蜒缓行
归家农夫，步履沉重
夜幕降临，孤寂无声

乡村暮色，模糊朦胧　　　　　　　　　　5
庄严寂静，弥漫空中
只有甲虫，嗡嗡飞行
远处羊群，铃碎声声

遥望废塔，藤蔓层层
月光如水，洒进窝中　　　　　　　　　　10
慵懒雕枭，抱怨啼鸣
静谧王国，怎堪扰动

老榆树下，紫杉荫影
草皮隆起，衰败坟茔
狭窄墓穴，棺木之中　　　　　　　　　　15
永远长眠，乡野百姓

接下来我们再看一首罗塞蒂（Christina Georgina Rossetti, 1830 —

1894）的《挽歌》(*A Dirge*, 1896）。

同"elegy"一样，"dirge"也是用来表达悲伤和哀悼情绪的一种诗体。然而，"dirge"通常是在葬礼现场诵读的诗歌；而且，作为抒情诗的一种，与"elegy"相较，"dirge"的篇幅通常更短，更少有对于宇宙人生的苦思冥想。

罗塞蒂的这首挽歌的有趣之处在于，它颠覆了田园牧歌的写作传统——诗人并没有将自然与死亡之间的联系浪漫化或是理想化，而是暗示死亡和出生往往与代表或是象征这些事件的所谓"适当"的季节并不相关。请各位读者仔细体会。

请读下面这首诗歌并且回答问题：

A Dirge

Christina Rossetti

Why were you born when the snow was falling?
You should have come to the cuckoo's calling,
Or when grapes are green in the cluster,
Or, at least, when lithe swallows muster
For their far off flying   5
From summer dying.

Why did you die when the lambs were cropping?
You should have died at the apples' dropping,
When the grasshopper comes to trouble,
And the wheat-fields are sodden stubble,   10
And all winds go sighing
For sweet things dying.

思考题：

1. 请分析这首诗歌的韵律。
2. 诗中的"你"出生在什么季节又是死亡在什么季节呢？
3. 这首诗歌的主旨是什么？诗人的口吻（tone）又是怎样的呢？请结合诗歌的内容加以分析说明。

译文鉴赏：

挽歌
克里斯蒂娜·罗塞蒂

为何你会在雪落的时候出生？
你出生的时候应当有杜鹃的啼鸣，
或是伴着青涩的葡萄挂满藤蔓，
或是，至少有轻盈的燕子在空中飞行
朝着遥远的地方   5
飞离夏末的冷风。

为何你会在剪羊毛的时节死去？
你死去的时候应当正值苹果落地，
当蚱蜢开始蹦来跳去，
当收割后的麦田一片狼藉，   10
当四面八方的风儿吹来声声叹息
当美好的事物即将离去。

4.4 说教诗

说教诗（didactic poetry）通常是指能够为读者提供某种教益的诗歌——这种教益可以是道德方面的，也可以是哲学、艺术，宗教甚至是科学和技术方面的。尽管有些人认为，所有的诗歌从根本上来讲都会为读者提供某种教益；然而，我们这里所说的"说教诗"则特别指那些包含了明确的道德或教育方面信息或目的的诗歌（Poetry-Foundation，2021a）。一般而言，说教诗的主题思想要比叙事诗或是抒情诗的主题思想更容易为读者所发现。而当某首说教诗是以犀利而幽默的口吻对社会或是某个议题进行评论的时候，那么我们就可以称之为"讽刺诗（satire）"。

将抒情诗、叙事诗与说教诗严格区分并非易事。有的时候，一首诗歌可以通过抒发感情的方式进行说教；有的时候，诗人也可以通过讲故事的方式进行说教。所以，某首诗歌到底是说教诗、抒情诗还是叙事诗，在很大程度上要依赖于读者自身的判断。一般而言，如果诗歌的主要目的是解释说明，那么它就是一首说教诗；如果诗歌的主要目的是表达情感，那么它就是一首抒情诗；而当诗歌的主要目的是讲故事的时候，那么它就是一首叙事诗了。

威廉·布雷克创作了很多首说教诗。下面我们就读一首他的代表作之一《杀人树》（*A Poison Tree*）。

《杀人树》最初发表于1794年，后收录于布雷克的诗集《经验之歌》（*Songs of Experience*，1795）。这首诗歌描述了叙述者（narrator，这里是"I"）针对某个人的压抑而愤怒的情绪；而这种愤怒情绪的累积最终导致叙述者设计杀害了那个人。这首诗探讨了愤怒、复仇以及更为宽泛的人类堕落的主题。

请读下面这首诗歌并且回答问题：

A Poison Tree
William Blake

I was angry with my friend:
I told my wrath, my wrath did end.
I was angry with my foe:
I told it not, my wrath did grow.

And I watered it in fears   5
Night and morning with my tears,
And I sunned it with smiles
And with soft deceitful wiles.

And it grew both day and night,
Till it bore an apple bright,   10
And my foe beheld it shine,
And he knew that it was mine —

And into my garden stole
When the night had veiled the pole;
In the morning, glad, I see   15
My foe outstretched beneath the tree.

思考题:

1. 这首诗包含了怎样的寓意?
2. 诗中的"apple"和"garden"有什么引申意义吗?
3. 诗人运用了暗喻的手法使得这首诗歌具有了整体性。请分析诗中这一暗喻的用法。
4. 请找出这首诗第二个诗节当中的意象，并且分析它们传达了怎样的含义。

译文鉴赏：

杀人树

威廉·布雷克

生了朋友的气
说了出来，于是怨恨消弭
生了敌人的气
闭口不提，于是怨恨累积

我日夜对它浇灌　　　　　　　　　　　　　　　　5
用我的恐惧，用我的泪滴
我整日对它照射
用我的谎言，用我的恶意

怨恨一天天长大
直到结出果实，鲜艳无比　　　　　　　　　　　　10
它样子闪闪发光
于是我的敌人，垂涎欲滴

他悄悄溜进我的花园
偷走果实，趁着夜色遮蔽
我早起查看，暗自欢喜　　　　　　　　　　　　　15
他已倒在树下，一命归西

第四章 英诗的体裁

下面我们再读一首弗罗斯特的《未择之路》(*The Road Not Taken*)。

弗罗斯特的《未择之路》于1915年发表于《大西洋月刊》(*The Atlantic Monthly*),后于1916年收录进他的诗集《山间》(*Mountain Interval*)。

弗罗斯特1912—1915年间曾在英国生活。在此期间,他经常同好友兼作家的爱德华·托马斯(Edward Thomas, 1878—1917)一起散步。一天,他们散步的时候遇到了一条岔路口。托马斯犹豫不决,不知道该走哪条路好,而且回来后还常常为他们没有选择另外一条路而感到惋惜。此事触发了诗人的创作灵感,于是弗罗斯特便写下这首《未择之路》,在他返回美国前将这首未发表的诗歌送给了托马斯。然而不幸的是,托马斯认真地读了这首诗,非常喜爱,以至于他下定决心报名参军,于两年后牺牲在第一次世界大战的欧洲战场上(Staff, 2011)。

请读下面这首诗歌并且回答问题:

The Road Not Taken

Robert Frost

Two roads diverged in a yellow wood,
And sorry I could not travel both
And be one traveler, long I stood
And looked down one as far as I could
To where it bent in the undergrowth;　　　　　　5

Then took the other, as just as fair,
And having perhaps the better claim,
Because it was grassy and wanted wear;
Though as for that the passing there
Had worn them really about the same,　　　　　　10

And both that morning equally lay
In leaves no step had trodden black.
Oh, I kept the first for another day!
Yet knowing how way leads on to way,
I doubted if I should ever come back.　　　　　　　　15

I shall be telling this with a sigh
Somewhere ages and ages hence:
Two roads diverged in a wood, and I —
I took the one less traveled by,
And that has made all the difference.　　　　　　　　20

思考题:

1. 本首诗歌当中呈现出了哪些意象？这些意象为诗歌意义的表达发挥了怎样的作用？
2. 诗人在选择了"the one less traveled by"的道路之后是否后悔了？如果没有后悔，那么他为什么要叹息呢？他有什么感到遗憾的地方吗？
3. 为什么在两条看上去很相似的道路间做出选择会在多年以后产生巨大的差异呢？
4. 诗歌的主题思想是什么？诗歌的题目是怎样突出其主题思想的？

译文鉴赏:

未择之路

罗伯特·弗罗斯特

秋林有歧途

行人意踌躇

极目遥望去
路终不知处

选择一路径　　　　　　　　　　5
少有他人行
皆有客往来
两路似相同

落叶盖脚印
晨行第一人　　　　　　　　　　10
长路多岔口
终难再来临

回首长叹息
两路分林中
择其人罕至　　　　　　　　　　15
此生大不同

4.5 传统诗歌和自由体诗歌

　　将英语诗歌划分为传统诗歌和自由体诗歌（closed and open forms of poetry）是从英语诗歌的形式的角度出发的。而诗歌的形式，即诗歌的物理结构，通常是指诗行的长度、诗歌的格律和押韵模式，等等。它既包括诗歌写在纸上的样子，也包括大声朗读诗歌时的声音。有一些诗歌的形式遵循特定的规则，而另外一些则可以更加自由。

诗歌的主要形式包括传统诗歌和自由体诗歌。之所以将"Closed Forms of Poetry"叫作"传统诗歌",是因为在自由体诗歌的形式出现以前,英语诗歌基本上都是传统诗歌;而现代英语诗歌的形式则既可以是"传统诗歌形式"也可以是"自由体诗歌形式"。也有人将"Closed Forms"翻译为"格律诗",这其实不太严谨,因为"格律诗"所对应的英文为"Regulated Verse"——在英文当中是用来特指中文诗歌当中的"近体诗"的,是相对于"古体诗"而言的一种有着严格韵律要求的中文诗歌(B. D. Watson,1971)。

传统诗歌通常拥有较为规整的节奏类型、押韵格式和整体结构。对于此种类型的诗歌一般有着较为严格的形式方面的要求。而与之相反,自由体诗歌在韵律和结构方面的要求则较为宽松。我们甚至可以这样说,如果一首英诗不押韵(rhyme),你可以有90%的把握认为这是一首自由体诗歌;而如果一首诗缺少格律(meter),你可以99%的把握确定它是一首自由体诗歌(A. Lindsay & Bergstrom, June 1, 2019)。

事实上,绝大多数的英语诗歌都可以称为传统诗歌,"传统诗歌"就是"诗歌"的同义词;而所谓"自由体诗歌"是直到19世纪中叶,美国的沃尔特·惠特曼(Walt Whitman,1819—1892)和其他一些法国诗人提出"自由体诗歌(vers libre — free verse)"这个概念,并且在诗歌创作中放弃了韵律之后才开始出现的(ibid.)。

下面我们就分别对传统诗歌和自由体诗歌加以讨论和举例说明。

4.5.1 传统诗歌

与自由体诗歌相较而言,传统英语诗歌更加结构化(structured)——它受制于特定的规则或模式,比如某种特定的格律和押韵格式(meter and rhyme)、诗行的长短(line lengths)以及包含固定行组的诗节(stanzas of set line groupings),等等。

尽管如此，想要严格定义一首诗歌是传统诗歌还是自由体诗歌也并非易事。例如，下面这首威廉·卡洛斯·威廉姆斯（William Carlos Williams，1883—1963）所作的著名的《红色手推车》（*The Red Wheelbarrow*，1923）：

The Red Wheelbarrow
William Carlos Williams

so much depends

upon

a red wheel

barrow

glazed with rain   5

water

beside the white

chickens.

说它是一首传统诗歌，它却没有严谨的韵律：它不押韵，也不具备传统意义上的节奏；说它是一首自由体诗歌，它却有整齐和规律的诗行和诗节形式：共有四个诗节，每个诗节两行诗，每个诗节的第一、第二行的字数都相等——威廉姆斯甚至把单词"wheelbarrow"分解成两个单词来适应他的形式。尽管这首诗的外在形式严谨，然而由于它并未体现出传统英语诗歌的韵律（传统英诗是按照"音节"而非"单词"来衡量诗歌的韵律的），所以我们还是倾向于把类似的诗歌划归为自由体诗歌（ibid.）。

传统英语诗歌的形式多种多样，这其中最为著名的，也是最为典型的恐怕非十四行诗莫属了。下面我们就以济慈的一首十四行诗《当我害怕生命逝去》(*When I Have Fears that I May Cease to Be*) 为例，请各位读者仔细研究一下它的诗歌形式并且回答相应的问题。

约翰·济慈（John Keats，1795—1821）的这首《当我害怕生命逝去》创作于1818年，最早收录于由米尔恩斯（Richard Monckton Milnes，1809—1885）编辑出版的《约翰·济慈的生平、书信和文学遗著》(*Life, Letters, and Literary Remains, of John Keats*, 1848）。

济慈25岁便因罹患肺结核而去世。这首《当我害怕生命逝去》表达了诗人对于死亡的思考。这首十四行诗可以分为两个部分：前面12行提出了问题，最后两行给出了答案。其中，前面12行又可以分为三个四行诗节（three quatrains），探讨了诗人对于死亡的焦虑：生命的终止意味着他将无法继续写作、无法追踪美的真谛、无法享受纯真的爱情；而诗歌最后两行的对句（couplet）则对所有的焦虑和不安给出了答案：一切声名和情爱都会随风而去。

请读下面这首诗歌并且回答问题：

When I Have Fears that I May Cease to Be
John Keats

When I have fears that I may cease to be
Before my pen has glean'd my teeming brain,
Before high piled books, in charactry,
Hold like rich garners the full ripen'd grain;
When I behold, upon the night's starr'd face,   5
Huge cloudy symbols of a high romance,
And think that I may never live to trace

Their shadows, with the magic hand of chance;
And when I feel, fair creature of an hour,
That I shall never look upon thee more,   10
Never have relish in the fairy power
Of unreflecting love; — then on the shore
Of the wide world I stand alone, and think
Till love and fame to nothingness do sink.

思考题:

1. 请描述本首诗歌的节奏和韵律。
2. 请注意，本首十四行诗就是由一句话组成的。请问，这样的安排对于诗歌主题思想的表达有何影响？
3. 诗人为何称他心爱的女孩为"creature of an hour"？与一般人的寿命相较而言，伟大的诗歌可能会更为长久地流传。在这里，你认为诗人在女孩和诗歌中更为看重哪个？诗人对于爱情与名誉中的哪个更为看重？或是你认为这个问题本身并不成立呢？
4. 第12行中，为什么诗人形容爱情是"unreflecting"？
5. 第12、第13行中，诗人说"站在广阔世界的岸边"。请问这里的"shore"有何深意？你是怎样理解的？

译文鉴赏:

当我害怕生命逝去

约翰·济慈

当我害怕生命逝去
手中的笔

还未及收割胸中长满的思绪

还未及写出著作

像成熟的庄稼在谷仓中堆积 5

当我望向满天星斗的夜空

那巨大的浪漫的星云

正在飘去

而我也许再也无法留住她们的身影

用幸运女神吻过的手笔 10

当我感到时日无多

再也无法见到

那美貌易逝的佳人

再也无法享受

那份纯真爱情的魔力 15

于是，我便在这广袤世界的岸边

兀自独立

冥想

直到情爱和声名

随风而去 20

下面我们再读一首同样为传统诗歌的五行打油诗（limerick）。

五行打油诗，顾名思义，是由五个诗行组成的幽默诗歌。英诗当中的五行打油诗的历史可以追溯到14世纪。最初的五行打油诗主要是唱给孩子们听的儿歌、童谣。不过由于这种诗歌篇幅较短，内容通俗易懂，有时还夹杂了草根群众所喜闻乐见的荤段子，所以在15世纪、16世纪以及17

世纪的时候便在英国的市井酒肆当中流行开来，更是通过乞丐们和普通劳动人民的口口相传而延绵不断。

我们再看一下五行打油诗的外在形式。通常情况下，五行打油诗的第一行、第二行和第五行需要有7—10个音节，同时要押尾韵；第三和第四行一般会有5—7个音节，它们也必须彼此押尾韵。所以五行打油诗的押韵格式为ａａｂｂａ；而它的第一、第二、第五行多为抑抑扬格三音步（anapestic trimeter），第三、第四行则多为抑抑扬格二音步（anapestic dimeter）（Britannica, July 5, 2019）。

下面就请读一下这几首五行打油诗。由于五行打油诗的语言相对简单，形式清楚明了，主题也并非宏大深刻，所以我们这里就不再针对每首诗提出思考问题，而只是提供参考译文来帮助大家理解原诗。但是，在读诗的过程当中，还是请各位读者思考一下这样两个问题：五行打油诗的创作意图和叙述口吻通常是什么？它的形式与内容是怎样有机结合的呢？

Limericks

I sat next to the Duchess at tea.

It was just as I feared it would be:

Her rumblings abdominal

Were simply phenomenal

And everyone thought it was me.

* * *

There once was a pious young priest

Who lived almost wholly on yeast.

"for", He said, "It's plain

We must all rise again

That I'd like to get started at least."

* * *

There was a young lady of Niger,

Who smiled as she rode on a tiger.

They returned from the ride

With the lady inside,

And the smile on the face of the tiger.

译文鉴赏：

坐在公爵夫人旁

左顾右盼心发慌

她的肚子咕噜响

引得众人都侧目

以为是我屁上膛

* * *

有个虔诚神父

天天都吃酵母

他说道理简单

既然都会升天

我想升得快点

* * *

非洲少女身姿窈窕

骑着老虎笑弯了腰

溜了一圈连蹦带跳

唯有老虎跑回来了

嘴角流油面露微笑

十四行诗和五行打油诗都只有一个诗节。而有多个诗节的诗歌也可以遵循一定的、规范的韵律安排，例如民歌。所以，传统英语诗歌的形式可以多种多样，远远不止本节中所举例讨论的这两种形式。

4.5.2 自由体诗歌

自由体诗歌创始于19世纪中叶，并且从20世纪开始变得非常流行。尽管一直以来诗人们都在探索以不同的诗歌形式进行创作；然而，只是在近代，诗人们才逐渐感到在旧的诗歌形式基础上进行的演化和再创作的灵感已经接近枯竭，所以，人们必须找到新的诗歌表现形式。有些诗人感到，旧有的诗歌形式无法表达出当今迅速变化的社会和文化现实，新的世界需要新的诗歌表现形式。还有一些诗人认为，诗歌应当是人们思想感情的自然流露，而不应当受到固定诗歌形式的限制（Holcombe，2015）。

因为自由体诗歌不讲求韵律，所以有些人会认为自由体诗歌更容易创作。但事实上，创作自由体诗歌或许更难——这是因为在自由体诗歌的创作中，为了达到预想效果而可供诗人调动的技术手段相比传统诗歌更少。大家知道，在之前的章节中我们介绍了一些有关英语诗歌韵律的知识和技巧。然而在自由体诗歌的创作中，诗人们没有这些技巧可用，他们必须找到其他的方法以达到想要的效果。而且，在传统诗歌的创作中，由于诗歌节奏和押韵的限制，诗人们经常会有新的发现：一些他们不曾想到的语言、表达方式甚至新的思想以及思想间碰撞出的火花。与之相较而言，在自由体诗歌的创作中，诗人们就必须单纯地找到合适的词语，因此在思想的传达上似乎会受到更多的局限。无怪乎奥登（Wystan Hugh Auden，1907—1973）曾经将自由体诗歌的创作者比喻成鲁滨孙（Robinson Crusoe），因为同他一样，这些诗人在创作活动中必须一切都自力更生（Auden，1962）。

下面就请大家读一读这里所选的两首自由体诗歌，并且试着回答以下问题：

1.诗人是通过怎样的方式对重要的思想和词语加以强调的？

2.诗歌的整体形式和结构是通过怎样的方式清晰地呈现给读者的？

3.自由体诗歌的特点以及在思想和情感表达方面的优势和劣势是什么？

第一首是美国著名诗人惠特曼的《啊，我！啊，生活！》(*O Me! O Life!*)。

沃尔特·惠特曼（Walt Whitman，1819—1892）被称为"自由体诗歌之父"，同时他还是一位散文家和新闻记者。惠特曼是一位人文主义者（humanist），是美国文学从超验主义时期（Transcendentalism）过渡到现实主义（Realism）时期的重要作家。

1855年，惠特曼自费出版了他的诗集《草叶集》(*Leaves of Grass*)，并且就此一举成名。这是一部涉及普通美国人社会生活方方面面的史诗级巨著。直到1892年惠特曼去世，他还在不断地扩充和完善这部书。艺术史学家玛丽·贝伦森（Mary Berenson，1864—1945）曾经说过，没有沃尔特·惠特曼，没有《草叶集》，你就无法真正了解美国（Reynolds，1995）。然而作为美国文学史上最具影响力的诗人之一，惠特曼的作品在当时却颇受争议。例如，他的《草叶集》由于过于明显的性描写而被当时许多人认为是淫秽之作，而他的私生活也由于有关他的同性恋传闻而饱受争议。

下面所选的这首《啊，我！啊，生活！》创作于1867年；然而时至今日，它所探讨、表达的主题思想仍然具有重要的现实意义。

请读下面这首诗歌并且回答问题：

O Me! O Life!

Walt Whitman

Oh me! Oh life! of the questions of these recurring,

第四章 英诗的体裁

Of the endless trains of the faithless, of cities fill'd with the foolish,

Of myself forever reproaching myself, (for who more foolish than I, and who more faithless?)

Of eyes that vainly crave the light, of the objects mean, of the struggle ever renew'd,

Of the poor results of all, of the plodding and sordid crowds I see around me,   5

Of the empty and useless years of the rest, with the rest me intertwined,

The question, O me! so sad, recurring — What good amid these, O me, O life?

Answer.

That you are here — that life exists and identity,

That the powerful play goes on, and you may contribute a verse.   10

思考题：

1. 你认为这首诗歌的主题思想和创作意图是什么？诗人达到这一创作目的了吗？请分析。
2. 这首诗歌当中运用了哪些修辞手法？请找到相关诗句并加以分析。
3. 诗歌当中反复使用了"O Me! O Life!"。请分析它的作用和效果。

译文鉴赏：

啊，我！啊，生活！

沃尔特·惠特曼

啊，我！啊，生活！不断地提出这样的问题，

缺少信念的人们坐满一节节车厢，愚蠢的人们挤爆一座座城市，

无休止地斥责自己，（还有谁比我更愚蠢、更缺少信念吗？）

那一双双渴望光明的、徒劳的眼睛，卑微的生活目标，循环往复的挣扎，

所有人的悲凉结局，身边工作辛劳而生活龌龊的人们，   5

还有另一些人虚掷光阴、百无一用，这其中就包括了我，

问题来了，啊，我！如此悲伤，不停追问——活在这其中有何意义，啊，我！啊，生活？

答案。

你就在这里——生活还将继续，

人间大戏还在上演，你也可以高歌一曲。   10

如果说沃尔特·惠特曼是自由体诗歌之父的话，那么艾米莉·狄金森（Emily Dickinson, 1830—1886）则可以称作自由体诗歌之母。

下面我们就看一看这首《草丛中的长虫》(*A Narrow Fellow in the Grass*)。这是一首著名的诗歌，也是仅有的几首在狄金森生前发表的诗歌之一。它最早于1866年发表在《斯普林菲尔德共和党日报》(*Springfield Daily Republican*)上，叙述了诗人遇到一条蛇后所引发的诗思。在这首诗歌当中，狄金森探讨了恐惧和焦虑的本质——特别是对于未知事物以及与之相关的欺骗行为的恐惧。

请读下面这首诗歌并且回答问题：

A Narrow Fellow in the Grass

Emily Dickinson

A narrow Fellow in the grass

Occasionally rides ——

You may have met him? Did you not

His notice sudden is ——

The grass divides as with a Comb ——   5

A spotted Shaft is seen ——

And then it closes at your Feet

And opens further on ——

He likes a Boggy Acre

A Floor too cool for Corn ——   10

Yet when a Boy and Barefoot ——

I more than once at Noon

Have passed I thought a Whip Lash

Unbraiding in the Sun

When stooping to secure it   15

It wrinkled And was gone ——

Several of Nature's People

I know, and they know me ——

I feel for them a transport

Of Cordiality ——   20

But never met this fellow

Attended or alone

Without a tighter Breathing

And Zero at the Bone ——

思考题：

1. 自由体诗歌是不讲求韵律的。但是这不等于说自由体诗歌就一定没有节奏。请结合这首诗歌，分析诗人运用了怎样的方法和表现形式，清晰地表达并且强调了重要的思想？
2. 请找出诗人在这首诗中所运用的修辞手法，并且分析其修辞效果。
3. 请结合诗歌内容分析诗人对待自然的态度是怎样的？

译文鉴赏：

草丛中的长虫

艾米莉·狄金森

草丛中的长虫

偶尔爬行 ——

不知你是否见过

他突然显露行踪 ——

像梳子一样分开草丛 ——

身子如带斑点的细绳 ——

草丛在你脚边瞬间合拢

然后又在远处分开路径 ——

他喜欢潮湿的领地

那里太凉不能生长玉米——　　　　　　　　　　　10
可是我却光着脚丫——
中午时分朝他走去

开始以为是条绳索
在阳光下伸展懒腰
刚要俯身将它捡起　　　　　　　　　　　　　　15
他便缩成一团，逃之夭夭——

我认识一些大自然的子民
他们也与我要好——
我对他们甚是喜欢
他们对我也有同感——　　　　　　　　　　　　20

不过只要见到这个家伙
无论独自一人还是有人陪伴
都会呼吸加速
都会毛骨悚然——

第五章 英诗的题材

5.1 引言

　　诗歌的题材("subjects",也叫作"subject matter")和主题(theme)是极易混淆的两个概念,人们经常将二者混用,比如说"一首诗歌的主题",即是指这首诗歌的题材,又经常用来指它的主题思想。因此,在讨论英诗的题材之前,我们有必要首先对此作出澄清。

　　诗歌的内容可以是我们头脑当中的任何事物。我们经历不同的事件、遇到不同的人群、去到不同的地方、感知不同的情感、产生不同的思想,等等,这些都可以成为诗歌的内容。而诗歌是关于哪方面内容的(What the poem is about?),就构成了它的题材。那么,什么又是诗歌的主题呢?简单说,诗歌对于其内容说了什么(What the poem says about the topic?),就构成了它的主题。诗歌的主题就是诗人要在诗歌当中表达的主题思想(main point),是读者在读完一首诗以后所获得的教益,是一首诗歌的寓意(Jinxia, 2007)。诗歌的题材和主题是密不可分的——当我们确定了一首诗歌的题材后,就会自然而然地思考它的主题思想;而要明确诗歌的主题思想则需要我们调动自己有关诗歌的所有知识来对这首诗歌进行具体的分析、解读。

　　于是我们就可以用下面这两句话来概括一下上述这两个概念:诗歌所描写、叙述、讨论的对象就是诗歌的题材;诗歌对于上述对象所表达出的观点、主旨或是寓意就是诗歌的主题,完整的表述应当是"主题思想"。本书当中,为了方便起见,我们仍然沿用了"主题"的说法来代指"题材"。

在本章接下来的内容里面,我们将英语诗歌的题材划分为四个主要类别加以讨论:有关自然主题的诗歌;有关爱情主题的诗歌;有关死亡主题的诗歌;有关哲思主题的诗歌。

5.2 有关自然主题的诗歌

"自然"是英语诗歌最古老的主题之一。自古以来,自然之美都是伟大艺术家寻求创作灵感、汲取精神营养的不竭源泉。例如,当一颗敏感的心灵在看到自然的景物时可能会提出下面这些疑问:海浪撞击或轻抚海岸的不同方式说明了什么?当滚滚江水在脚下不停奔流的时候我们的感觉是什么?娇艳的花朵从乱石堆中冒了出来意味着什么?等等。总之,自然界的景物常常会使我们联想到人性之美或是人性的不完美。因此,诗人们常常会在诗歌当中以某些自然现象象征人类的特性,抑或是将某种人类的特性赋予自然景物。

下面就请各位读者阅读一些有关自然主题的英语诗歌并且思考以下这些问题:

1. 在诗歌当中,诗人描绘了什么自然景物?他们描绘这些自然景物的目的是什么?
2. 诗人在描绘自然的时候是否运用了象征的手法?
3. 在诗歌当中,诗人是否借助了自然景物来映射或是解释人生呢?

第一首是济慈的《秋颂》(*To Autumn*)。

《秋颂》创作于1819年,是济慈同年创作的系列颂歌(Five Great

Odes of 1819）当中的最后一首。这首诗歌既是济慈诗歌创作的巅峰之作，同时也标志着诗人创作生涯的结束，因为他在1821年初便与世长辞了。

在1819年9月21日写给朋友约翰·汉密尔顿·雷诺兹（John Hamilton Reynolds，1794—1852）的信中，济慈描述了那天他沿着温彻斯特附近的伊琴河（River Itchen of Winchester）散步时看到的景象：现在的季节多么美丽，空气多么清新。给人一种温和、爽利的感觉⋯⋯我从来没有像现在这样喜欢这收割过后的田野⋯⋯不知怎的，这收割后的田野给人一种很温暖的感觉，就像某些油画所带来感觉一样（Milnes，1848）。

请读下面这首诗歌并且回答问题：

To Autumn
John Keats

1

Season of mists and mellow fruitfulness,
    Close bosom-friend of the maturing sun;
Conspiring with him how to load and bless
    With fruit the vines that round the thatch-eves run;
To bend with apples the moss'd cottage-trees,   5
    And fill all fruit with ripeness to the core;
        To swell the gourd, and plump the hazel shells
With a sweet kernel; to set budding more,
And still more, later flowers for the bees,
Until they think warm days will never cease,   10
    For summer has o'er-brimm'd their clammy cells.

2

Who hath not seen thee oft amid thy store?
    Sometimes whoever seeks abroad may find
Thee sitting careless on a granary floor,
    Thy hair sort-lifted by the winnowing wind;   15
Or on a half-reap'd furrow sound asleep,
    Drows'd with the fume of poppies, while thy hook
        Spares the next swath and all its twined flowers:
And sometimes like a gleaner thou dost keep
    Steady thy laden head across a brook;   20
    Or by a cyder-press, with patient look,
        Thou watchest the last oozings hours by hours.

3

Where are the songs of spring? Ay, where are they?
    Think not of them, thou hast thy music too —
While barred clouds bloom the soft-dying day,   25
    And touch the stubble-plains with rosy hue;
Then in a wailful choir the small gnats mourn
    Among the river sallows, borne aloft
        Or sinking as the light wind lives or dies;
And full-grown lambs loud bleat from hilly bourn;   30
    Hedge-crickets sing; and now with treble soft
    The red-breast whistles form a garden-croft;
        And gathering swallows twitter in the skies.

思考题：

1. 你能在这首诗当中找到多少种意象呢？请一一举例说明。
2. 这首诗当中的意象是精心安排的还是随意为之的呢？请说明原因。回答这个问题时请从以下三个方面考虑：第一，每个诗节对应了秋天的哪个方面；第二，每个诗节当中的最主要的意象类别是什么；第三，每个诗节都代表了秋天的什么时间。
3. 第二个诗节当中，诗人将秋天比拟成了什么？其他两个诗节是否也运用了拟人的手法呢？
4. 除了描写秋天的景色，诗人还表达了怎样的诗歌主题？

译文鉴赏：

秋颂
济慈

你是薄雾的季节，果香四溢
太阳的光线依旧温暖
而你与他密谋，用葡萄
挂满茅草屋檐上攀爬的藤蔓
用苹果，将村舍周边的树枝压弯　　　　　　　　　　　5
所有的果实都熟透了心儿
葫芦们吃得腰饱肚圆
甜香的果仁也将榛子壳胀满
更多，更多的新芽
更多，更多的花瓣　　　　　　　　　　　　　　　　10
直到蜜蜂们以为暖和的日子会永远没完

因为夏日已用蜜汁

将它们黏湿的巢穴溢满

你经常徘徊在自家的谷仓周边

闲逛的人们看到 15

你惬意地坐在粮仓的地板

箕扬的微风吹动你的发梢,有时

你就睡在犁了一半的沟田

罂粟花的刺鼻气味将你灌醉

长柄的镰刀丢到一边 20

同庄稼一起生长的花儿也因此幸免

有时你变身拾穗的人儿

低着头,越过小溪的身子让麦穗压弯

有时,你又站在榨汁机旁耐心观看

任由苹果的汁水 25

一滴一滴地流干

你不停地问询哪里有春天的歌声

可你忘了,自己的乐曲同样动听——

寂静的傍晚暗潮涌动

收割后的田野被彩霞染红 30

小虫随着微风的起伏

从柳叶儿中发出集体的悲鸣

那声音时而在低处盘旋,时而又抛向空中

远处的山坡上传来

肥硕羔羊的咩咩叫声 35

树篱下的蟋蟀也寂寞难耐

那百转千回的

是农场花园里知更鸟的低唱

燕子在天上成群地飞过

叽叽喳喳，叫个不停。   40

　　第二首是华兹华斯的《我独自游走如浮云》(*I Wandered Lonely as a Cloud*)。

　　这首诗既是华兹华斯诗歌的代表作之一，也是英国浪漫主义诗歌当中的经典作品。这首诗创作于1804年，最早发表于1805年出版的《诗集·两卷本》(*Poems, in Two Volumes*)。

　　这首《我独自游走如浮云》的创作灵感来自1802年4月15日诗人和妹妹多萝西（Dorothy Mae Ann Wordsworth, 1771—1855）在英格兰西北部"湖区"的第二大湖厄尔斯沃特湖的格林可因湾（Glencoyne Bay, Ullswater, in the Lake District）漫步时所看到的景象。据说，两年后，华兹华斯偶然间看到妹妹多萝西散步那天所写的日记，因此受到启发，才写下了这首诗。多萝西在1802年4月15日当天的日记中这样写道：我从来没有见过这么漂亮的水仙花。它们生长在长满苔藓的石头之间，将它们团团围住。有些水仙花靠在石头上，就像人累了之后靠在枕头上休息；其余的水仙花则随着湖面吹过的风儿频频点头或是左右摇摆，像是与风儿配合着发出一阵阵的欢笑声（Knight, 1897）。

　　请读下面这首诗歌并且回答问题：

I Wandered Lonely as a Cloud
William Wordsworth

I wandered lonely as a cloud
That floats on high o'er vales and hills,

When all at once I saw a crowd,
A host, of golden daffodils;
Beside the lake, beneath the trees,   5
Fluttering and dancing in the breeze.

Continuous as the stars that shine
And twinkle on the milky way,
They stretched in never-ending line
Along the margin of a bay: 10
Ten thousand saw I at a glance,
Tossing their heads in sprightly dance.

The waves beside them danced; but they
Out-did the sparkling waves in glee:
A poet could not but be gay,   15
In such a jocund company:
I gazed — and gazed — but little thought
What wealth the show to me had brought:

For oft, when on my couch I lie
In vacant or in pensive mood,   20
They flash upon that inward eye
Which is the bliss of solitude;
And then my heart with pleasure fills,
And dances with the daffodils.

思考题：

1. 英诗当中经常会有一个最主要的意象。这首诗当中的最主要的意象是什么？在这首诗歌当中，华兹华斯所创造的意象与我们的哪些感官相联系？
2. 哪些词语表明了诗人看到景物后的感受？
3. 最后一个诗节与其他诗节是怎样联系的？何为"a vacant or pensive mood"？何为"the inward eye"？为什么它是"the bliss of solitude"？
4. 这首诗的主题思想是什么？是在诗中哪里提出的？

译文鉴赏：

我独自游走如浮云

华兹华斯

我独自游走如浮云
漂荡在溪谷和群山，
突然，我看到
一丛金黄色的水仙；
在树下，在湖畔，　　　　　　　　　　　　　　5
随着微风摇摆，震颤。

它们如星星般眨眼
如银河般绵延，
它们一望无际
生长在溪谷岸边：　　　　　　　　　　　　　　10
它们密密匝匝，
欢快地起舞，翩跹。

一旁的湖水也在舞蹈；然而
花儿的舞姿胜过那波光点点：
此时的我难掩欣喜， 15
因为有这样的快乐相伴：
我看啊，看啊，心中了无挂牵
只因此时美景胜过那金山银山：

我时常躺在长椅上
茫然若失，抑或是愁绪万千， 20
此时，那些花儿会突然闪现
在我孤寂的心中掀起波澜；
于是，我的心中便充满了喜悦，
舞动，如那水仙。

5.3 有关爱情主题的诗歌

爱情是亘古不变的诗歌创作题材之一，是激发诗人创作灵感的最重要的源泉。下面我们选择两首经典的、有关爱情主题的英语诗歌。请各位读者仔细阅读并思考下面这些问题：什么是爱情？是什么引发了爱情？恋爱中的人会有哪些表现？诗人是如何歌咏爱情的？

第一首是勃朗宁夫人的《我是怎样的爱你》(Sonnet 43: How Do I Love Thee?)。

这首《我是怎样的爱你》选自勃朗宁夫人的《葡萄牙十四行诗集》(Sonnets from the Portuguese, 1850)，是其中的第43首。该诗集收录了勃朗宁夫人在与丈夫罗伯特·勃朗宁 (Robert Browning, 1812—1889) 恋爱期间所作的44首以爱情为主题的十四行诗。由于勃朗宁夫人认为这些十四行诗的内容涉及隐私，所以迟迟不愿将其发表。后来在勃朗宁的劝说下，她才同意假说这些十四行诗是翻译的葡萄牙语十四行诗旧作，将其发表出来（Browning, 1850）。这些诗歌一经发表便广受好评，时至今日已经成了爱情主题诗歌当中的经典之作。我们下面所选的这首《我是怎样的爱你》则是经典中的经典。

请读下面这首诗歌并且回答问题：

Sonnet 43: How Do I Love Thee?

Elizabeth Barrett Browning

How do I love thee? Let me count the ways.
I love thee to the depth and breadth and height
My soul can reach, when feeling out of sight
For the ends of Being and ideal Grace.
I love thee to the level of everyday's   5
Most quiet need, by sun and candlelight.
I love thee freely, as men strive for Right;
I love thee purely, as they turn from Praise.
I love thee with the passion put to use
In my old griefs, and with my childhood's faith.   10
I love thee with a love I seemed to lose
With my lost saints — I love thee with the breath,
Smiles, tears, of all my life! — and, if God choose,
I shall but love thee better after death.

思考题：

1. 请仔细阅读本首诗的第二到第四行的三个句子。每个句子分别表达了怎样的思想？
2. 请看第十三行。单词"smiles"和"tears"有哪些引申意义？
3. 请看第七到第十行。分析一下诗人是如何通过比较和引入宗教思想的方法突出诗歌主题的？

译文鉴赏：

我是怎样的爱你

伊丽莎白·巴瑞特·勃朗宁

我是怎样的爱你？
让我细说端详。
我爱你至深，至广
我爱你直到灵魂
触到天堂，将　　　　　　　　　　　　　　　5
宇宙人生的真谛，冥想。
我爱你平静而琐碎的生活，
我爱你在白天，也在晚上。
我自由地爱着你，
如勇士般坚强；　　　　　　　　　　　　　10
我纯洁地爱着你，
无论得到赞誉还是诽谤。
我的爱热情激荡，
如孩子一般痴情，如陈年的感伤。
我的爱无处不在，　　　　　　　　　　　　15

时而绽出笑脸，时而热泪盈眶。
啊！上帝呀，
如果我死了，我的爱
将会十倍的癫狂！

下面再看一首彭斯的《一支红红的玫瑰》(A Red, Red Rose)。

《一支红红的玫瑰》是苏格兰民族诗人罗伯特·彭斯（Robert Burns, 1759—1796）所作。众所周知，彭斯毕生致力于保护、发掘、整理苏格兰民歌，而这首《一支红红的玫瑰》便是其中著名的一首。

这首诗歌最初收录于苏格兰歌手皮耶罗·乌尔巴尼（Pietro Urbani, 1749—1816）于1794年出版的《苏格兰民歌选》(A Selection of Scots Songs)当中。在这本歌集当中，乌尔巴尼这样解释这首诗：……这首《一支红红的玫瑰》的歌词是一位著名的苏格兰诗人交给我的。他说听到一位乡下的小姑娘唱起这首歌，自己被震撼到了，于是赶紧记下了歌词。由于对原来的曲调不太满意，所以他便恳求我根据苏格兰的曲风重新谱曲。而我便这样做了（M. Lindsay，1996）。

请读下面这首诗歌并且回答问题：

A Red, Red Rose

Robert Burns

O My Luve's like a red, red rose,
    That's newly sprung in June;
O My Luve's like the melodie
    That's sweetly played in tune.

As fair art thou, my bonnie lass,

  So deep in luve am I;
And I will luve thee still, my dear,
  Till a'the seas gang dry.

Till a' the seas gang dry, my dear,
  And the rocks melt wi' the sun: 10
O I will luve thee still, my dear,
  While the sands o' life shall run.

And fare thee weel, my only luve,
  And fare thee weel awhile!
And I will come again, my luve,   15
  Though it were ten thousand mile.

思考题：

1. 这首诗歌当中运用了哪些修辞格？
2. 为什么诗人会使用"红玫瑰"这个意象来表达自己的主题思想？
3. "Till a' the seas gang dry"的重复使用有何作用？
4. 这首诗歌在表达爱情主题方面是否成功？为什么？

译文鉴赏：

一枝红红的玫瑰

罗伯特·彭斯

哦，我的爱像一枝红红的玫瑰，
  在六月里初绽花蕾；
哦，我的爱像一曲和谐的旋律，

奏响如天籁般甜美。

你是如此的美丽啊，可爱的姑娘，　　　　　　　　　　5
　　让我望眼欲穿；
我会永远爱着你啊，亲爱的，
　　直到大海枯干。

直到大海枯干啊，亲爱的，
　　直到岩石腐烂：　　　　　　　　　　　　　　　10
我会永远爱着你啊，亲爱的，
　　任凭时光流转。

再见吧，我唯一的爱人，
　　不过是片刻的别离！
我会再次来到你的身边，亲爱的，　　　　　　　　15
　　即使相隔万里。

5.4 有关死亡主题的诗歌

　　死亡是一颗敏感心灵所无法回避的思考题。尽管人们都知道死亡是自然的规律，是人生不可避免的最终结局；然而在人们的心目中，死亡仍然充满了恐怖的、神秘的和令人敬畏的色彩。在开始阅读有关死亡主题的诗歌之前，我们不妨先思考一下下面这些问题：什么是死亡？你害怕死亡吗？为什么？你相信存在死后的世界吗？

　　事实上，千百年来人们一直不断地追问着这些问题。而对于这些问题的回答则可见于歌曲、舞蹈、故事传说、绘画、雕塑等诸多的艺术形式当中，这其中自然也包括诗歌。下面我们就看一下英语诗歌都是如何对此进行讨论的。

我们先看一首莎士比亚的《歌：不再惧怕太阳的酷热》(Song: *"Fear No More the Heat o' the Sun"*)。

莎士比亚在他的戏剧作品中掺杂了一百多首歌曲（Songs）——可以伴着音乐唱的诗歌。各位读者请注意，音乐是伊丽莎白时代的人们的生活中不可或缺的一部分。那时的书商们经常会出版民谣、情歌和合唱作品；而大多数受过教育的人都懂音乐，并且在竖笛、鲁特琴或是古大提琴（recorder, lute, or viola da gamba）上一试身手。莎士比亚笔下的人物正是反映了在他们所处的那个时代，人们会在人生悲欢离合的时刻借助音乐表达情感（Lindley, 2006）。

下面这首《歌：不再惧怕太阳的酷热》选自莎士比亚的戏剧《辛白林》（Cymbeline）的第四幕、第二场，是他众多戏剧诗歌当中非常有名的一首。尽管人们对于这出戏剧当中朗诵这首诗歌时的背景大都没有什么深刻的印象，然而，这首优美的诗歌以及它所传达的主题思想——死亡的好处就在于你永远不用再为生活的艰辛而感到恐惧了——却历来为广大文学爱好者们所传颂（Tearle, 2019）。

请读下面这首诗歌并且回答问题：

Song: "Fear No More the Heat o' the Sun"

William Shakespeare

(*From* Cymbeline, Act IV, Scene 2)

Fear no more the heat o' the sun,

Nor the furious winter's rages;

Thou thy worldly task hast done,

Home art gone, and ta'en thy wages:
Golden lads and girls all must,　　　　　　　　　　　　　　5
As chimney-sweepers, come to dust.

Fear no more the frown o' the great;
Thou art past the tyrant's stroke;
Care no more to clothe and eat;
To thee the reed is as the oak:　　　　　　　　　　　　　10
The scepter, learning, physic, must
All follow this, and come to dust.

Fear no more the lightning flash,
Nor the all-dreaded thunder stone;
Fear not slander, censure rash;　　　　　　　　　　　　　15
Thou hast finished joy and moan:
All lovers young, all lovers must
Consign to thee, and come to dust.

No exorciser harm thee!
Nor no witchcraft charm thee!　　　　　　　　　　　　　20
Ghost unlaid forbear thee!
Nothing ill come near thee!
Quiet consummation have;
And renownèd be thy grave!

思考题:

1. 请分析这首诗歌的主题思想。

第五章　英诗的题材

2. 这首诗歌当中运用了大量的修辞手法，例如"呼语""典故"和"重复"。请具体说明诗人在哪里运用了这些修辞手法，并且分析它们所达到的修辞效果。
3. 诗歌的最后一个诗节运用了与前面三个诗节不同的押韵格式和标点符号。这样做的目的和效果怎样？

译文鉴赏：

歌：不再惧怕太阳的酷热

威廉·莎士比亚

选自《辛白林》，第四幕，第二场

不再惧怕太阳的酷热，
不再惧怕凛冽的寒冬；
你已完成今生的职责，
满载着收获回到家中：
无论锦衣玉食的男女，　　　　　　　　　　　5
抑或是扫烟囱的孩童，
都将化为尘土，消失无踪。

不再惧怕权贵的淫威；
不再惧怕暴君的鞭刑；
不再担心吃饭和穿衣；　　　　　　　　　　　10
不再留意高傲或谦恭：
无论是帝王还是学者，
抑或是救人命的医生，
都将化为尘土，消失无踪。

不再惧怕天空的闪电，　　　　　　　　　　　　　　15
不再惧怕吓人的雷鸣；
不再惧怕无端的诽谤，
不再惧怕草率的批评；
你已经阅尽世间苦乐：
所有花季的痴情男女，　　　　　　　　　　　　　　20
都将化为尘土，消失无踪。

不再惧怕邪祟的伤害！
不再惧怕妖魔的扰动！
游魂也无法向你靠近！
野鬼也远离你的坟茔！　　　　　　　　　　　　　　25
愿你在寂静中获得圆满；
愿你在坟墓中收获尊崇！

  第二首是狄金森的《因为我不能停下来等待死神》(*Because I could not stop for Death*)。

  这首诗是在诗人去世后的1890年收录在诗集《诗歌：第一集》(*Poems：Series 1*)当中公开发表的。在此版本中，该诗歌被加上了标题：《马车》(*The Chariot*)，而且每个诗行的末尾都加上了标点（参见：Poem IV.XXVII（page 138）in：Higginson, T. W. & Todd, Mabel Loomis, ed. *Poems by Emily Dickinson*. Boston：Roberts Brothers, 1890）。我们这里选用的是1999年"雷丁版"的文本（参见：Poem 479 in：Franklin, R. W., ed. *The Poems of Emily Dickinson：Reading Edition*. Cambridge, MA：The Belknap Press, 1999）。下面就请各位读者同狄金森一起登上"死亡的马车"，开启一段神游之旅。

  请读下面这首诗歌并且回答问题：

Because I could not stop for Death–(479)

Emily Dickinson

Because I could not stop for Death —
He kindly stopped for me —
The Carriage held but just Ourselves —
And Immortality.

We slowly drove — He knew no haste   5
And I had put away
My labor and my leisure too,
For His Civility —

We passed the School, where children strove
At Recess — in the Ring —   10
We passed the Fields of Gazing Grain —
We passed the Setting Sun —

Or rather — He passed Us —
The Dews drew quivering and Chill —
For only Gossamer, my Gown —   15
My Tippet — only Tulle —

We passed before a House that seemed
A Swelling of the Ground —
The Roof was scarcely visible —
The Cornice, in the Ground —   20

Since then — 'tis centuries — and yet

Feels shorter than the Day

I first surmised the Horses' Heads

Were toward Eternity —

思考题：

1. 诗歌当中的车马之行有何寓意？
2. 诗歌的第七行运用了怎样的语音技巧？概括了诗人怎样的生活？
3. 诗歌在第二行和第八行分别使用了"kindly"和"civility"。这是怎样的修辞手法？
4. 在这首诗歌当中，狄金森将死亡拟人化为一位绅士，他悠闲地坐着马车召唤诗人一起走向坟墓。这首诗当中还有其他地方运用了拟人的修辞手法吗？请分析。

译文鉴赏：

因为我不能停下来等待死神

艾米莉·狄金森

因为我不能停下来等待死神 ——
他体贴地停下来等我 ——
于是我们一起坐上了马车 ——
车上还有永生同坐。

我们慢慢地前行 —— 他并不着急
而我也已抛却了
所有的烦劳和安逸，
因为他的彬彬有礼 ——

我们路过了学校，那里的孩子们
在课间 — 做游戏 —   10
我们路过了谷物丰收的田野 —
又路过了夕阳下山 —

或许 — 是夕阳路过了我们 —
露水带来一丝寒战 —
因为我的长袍薄如蝉翼 —   15
而我的披肩 — 不过是一块绢网 —

我们来到一座房前
似乎是地面的隆起 —
屋顶若隐若现 —
房檐 — 垂到地面 —   20

从那时起 — 倏忽百年 — 然而
竟觉得比一天还短
我想那马头所指
定是永远 —

5.5 有关哲思主题的诗歌

除了"自然""爱""死亡"等主题外，诗人们还要回答其他一些宇宙人生的大问题，诸如"我是谁?""何为命运?""是否存在永恒?"，等等。对于这些问题的探讨和回答就是哲理诗（philosophical poems）的主要内容。哲理诗是通过诗歌的语言和形式表达诗人对于宇宙人生的思考，是优美的艺术形式与深刻的思想完美结合的产物。

我们先看一首雪莱的《奥兹曼迪亚斯》(Ozymandias)。

先说说诗人雪莱。珀西·比希·雪莱（Percy Bysshe Shelley，1792—1822）是英国19世纪初著名的浪漫主义诗人。谈情说爱和文学创作贯穿了雪莱的一生——他经历两次私奔，与多名女性有染；他英年早逝，却留给后世许多脍炙人口的诗篇。

雪莱幼时家境优渥，作为家中长子备受宠溺。1802年雪莱进入赛昂宫学院（Syon House Academy），两年后进入伊顿公学（Eton College）开始了长达六年的学习生活。上学期间雪莱经常受到同学们的欺负，据说主要是由于他孤芳自赏同时又桀骜不驯的性格所致；以至同学们给他取了个外号，叫作"疯子雪莱"（Mad Shelley）(Bieri, 2004)。

1810年10月，雪莱进入牛津大学学习。在牛津大学期间他很少上课，而是花了大把的时间读书或是关在自己的房间里做实验。此外，他还结识了友人托马斯·杰斐逊·霍格（Thomas Jefferson Hogg, 1792—1862），并且在其影响下形成了激进的政治和宗教观点。1811年3月，由于雪莱拒绝对校方承认之前匿名发表的包含激进言论的诗歌和短文是自己所写，而被牛津大学开除。

1822年8月，雪莱乘坐自己的新船"唐璜号"（Don Juan）去会见拜伦，然而在返航途中遭遇风暴而船毁人亡。雪莱的骨灰葬在意大利罗马的新教公墓（Protestant Cemetery, Rome），墓碑中央镌刻着这样的文字：众心之心（Cor Cordium — Heart of Hearts）。

《奥兹曼迪亚斯》是一首十四行诗，最初发表于1818年。奥兹曼迪亚斯是古代埃及的一位暴君。雪莱在这首诗中探讨了这样一个主题：即便是最伟大的人和他们所缔造的帝国也不可能永垂不朽，他们所遗留的一切注定会消散于历史的长河之中。

请读下面这首诗歌并且回答问题：

Ozymandias

Percy Bysshe Shelley

I met a traveller from an antique land,

Who said — "Two vast and trunkless legs of stone

Stand in the desert … Near them, on the sand,

Half sunk a shattered visage lies, whose frown,

And wrinkled lip, and sneer of cold command,　　　　　5

Tell that its sculptor well those passions read

Which yet survive, stamped on these lifeless things,

The hand that mocked them, and the heart that fed;

And on the pedestal, these words appear:

My name is Ozymandias, King of Kings,　　　　　10

Look on my Works, ye Mighty, and despair!

Nothing beside remains. Round the decay

Of that colossal Wreck, boundless and bare

The lone and level sands stretch far away."

思考题：

1. 诗歌的第七行和第八行是理解的难点，请说一说你的理解。"survive"是一个及物动词，后面的"hand"和"heart"是它的直接宾语。请问是谁的"手"，又是谁的"心"呢？此处的"hand"和"heart"运用了怎样的修辞手法呢？
2. 请描绘一下奥兹曼迪亚斯的性格特征。
3. 奥兹曼迪亚斯象征了什么？在雪莱的时代，这首诗可能有什么所指呢？
4. 这是一首十四行诗。它的结构是前八行为一个部分，后六行为一个部分。

请问，前八行和后六行分别呈现出怎样的画面，传达了怎样的思想呢？
5. 这首诗运用反讽的手法表达了思想。它告诉读者，外表的东西与内在的现实是不同的。请分析这首诗歌的主旨是什么，诗歌是怎样表达其主旨的？

译文鉴赏：

曾经枭雄
珀西·比希·雪莱

偶遇异乡客
见闻大不同
巨人横荒漠
身躯无所终

石匠巧手雕　　　　　　　　　　5
面容露狰狞
觑得人无物
生杀一念中

匠人已作古
王者自凋零　　　　　　　　　　10
唯留此头颅
震撼我心灵

细看雕像座
文字刻分明
吾乃王中王　　　　　　　　　　15
上帝亦尊崇

> 风沙漫漫起
> 世间有枭雄
> 孤寂残骸处
> 淹没长河中　　　　　　　　　　　　20

我们再来看一首戴维斯的《闲暇》(Leisure)。

威廉·亨利·戴维斯（William Henry Davies, 1871 — 1940）出生于威尔士，父亲早亡，母亲改嫁，他由祖父母抚养成人。戴维斯生性热爱冒险，曾多次乘船前往北美，在一次加拿大旅行中因为跳火车而导致一条腿膝盖以下截肢。回到英国后，他靠打零工维持生计，同时开始积极从事写作，并最终成了一名受人爱戴的诗人。

戴维斯的诗歌多以自然或旅途生活为主题，呈现出自然的、质朴的写作风格。除了诗歌，他还写了两部小说和其他一些自传体文学作品。其中，他的《一个超级流浪汉的自传》(The Autobiography of a Super-Tramp, 1908) 最为著名。这本书是在萧伯纳（George Bernard Shaw, 1856 — 1950）的帮助下出版的，记录了戴维斯在美国的旅行生活。

下面这首《闲暇》最初发表于1911年出版的诗集《快乐的歌声及其他》(Songs of Joy and Others) 当中，是戴维斯最为有名的代表作之一。在诗歌当中，戴维斯警告世人，现代生活忙忙碌碌的节奏会给人类的精神世界带来损害，因为这种生活方式会使得现代人无暇亲近自然。

请读下面这首诗歌并且回答问题：

Leisure

William Henry Davies

What is this life if, full of care,
We have no time to stand and stare?

No time to stand beneath the boughs,
And stare as long as sheep and cows:

No time to see the woods we pass,　　　　　　　　　　　5
Where squirrels hide their nuts in grass:

No time to see, in broad daylight,
Streams full of stars, like skies at night:

No time to turn at Beauty's glance,
And watch her feet, how they can dance.　　　　　　　10

No time to wait till her mouth can
Enrich that smile her eyes began?

A poor life this if, full of care,
We have no time to stand and stare.

思考题：

1. 请分析这首诗的韵律。
2. 诗中反复重复了哪些短语？这一重复的目的是什么？
3. 诗人在这首诗歌的最后两行回答了最初两行所提出的问题。请问，诗人提出的问题是什么？答案又是什么？
4. 请分析这首诗歌的主题思想。

译文鉴赏：

闲暇
W.H. 戴维斯

生活中少了凝视和驻足
就只剩下庸庸碌碌

我们无暇徜徉树下
像牛羊一样
无牵无挂　　　　　　　　　　　　　　　　　　　　　5

我们无暇欣赏走过的森林
那儿的松鼠
正用草叶把坚果遮住

我们无暇凝视那流淌的溪水
白日里它波光晃动　　　　　　　　　　　　　　　　10
恰如夜空中闪烁的繁星

我们无暇回首佳人的一颦一笑
忽略了她曼妙的身姿和那欢颜
才下眉梢却又盈上嘴角

生活是如此庸庸碌碌　　　　　　　　　　　　　　　15
只因为我们无暇凝视和驻足

第六章　经典英语诗歌选注

前面五章我们以不同历史时期、不同题材、不同体裁的英语诗歌作为例子佐证、说明了如何理解、分析、鉴赏英语诗歌。然而，相对于汗牛充栋的英语诗歌宝库来讲，这里所选的诗歌只能算是九牛一毛。因此，在最后一章中，笔者尝试着再多收录十余首经典英语诗歌，并且对这些诗歌进行较为详细的注解，从而希望能够起到弥补缺憾、抛砖引玉、启发读者进一步阅读英语诗歌的作用。

第一首

Song: "Sigh no more, ladies, sigh no more"[1]

William Shakespeare

(from *Much Ado About Nothing*)

Sigh no more, ladies, sigh no more.
　　Men were deceivers ever,
One foot in sea, and one on shore,
　　To one thing constant never.
Then sigh not so, but let them go,
　　And be you blithe[2] and bonny[3],
Converting all your sounds of woe
　　Into hey nonny, nonny[4].

> Sing no more ditties[5], sing no more
>   Of dumps[6] so dull and heavy.
> The fraud of men was ever so
>   Since summer first was leafy.
> Then sigh not so, but let them go,
>   And be you blithe and bonny,
> Converting all your sounds of woe
>   Into hey, nonny, nonny.

Notes:
1. 这首戏剧诗选自莎士比亚的喜剧《无事生非》(*Much Ado About Nothing*, 1598—1599)，最早发表于1623年，收录在《第一对开本》(*First Folio*)当中。这是一首欢快的小调——一方面谴责了男人们轻率和欺骗的行为，另一方面鼓励女孩们不要沮丧，而是以积极和快乐的心态继续她们的生活。
2. blithe: happy, not anxious.
3. bonny: very pretty, attractive.
4. nonny: meaningless word, used to imitate a cheerful song (hey nonny, nonny没有实在意义，经常以副歌的形式出现在伊丽莎白时代的民歌歌谣诗节末尾，代指欢乐的歌声).
5. ditty: a short simple song.
6. dumps: sad songs.

第二首

To His Coy Mistress[1]

Andrew Marvell

Had we but world enough and time,
This coyness, lady, were no crime.
We would sit down, and think which way
To walk, and pass our long love's day.
Thou by the Indian Ganges'[2] side
Shouldst rubies[3] find; I by the tide
Of Humber[4] would complain. I would
Love you ten years before the flood,
And you should, if you please, refuse
Till the conversion of the Jews[5].
My vegetable love[6] should grow
Vaster than empires and more slow;
An hundred years should go to praise
Thine eyes, and on thy forehead gaze;
Two hundred to adore[7] each breast,
But thirty thousand to the rest;
An age at least to every part,
And the last age should show your heart.
For, lady, you deserve this state[8],
Nor would I love at lower rate.

    But at my back I always hear
Time's wingèd chariot[9] hurrying near;
And yonder[10] all before us lie

Deserts of vast eternity.

Thy beauty shall no more be found;

Nor, in thy marble vault[11], shall sound

My echoing song; then worms[12] shall try

That long-preserved virginity,

And your quaint[13] honour turn to dust,

And into ashes all my lust;

The grave's a fine and private place,

But none, I think, do there embrace.

  Now therefore, while the youthful hue

Sits on thy skin like morning dew,

And while thy willing soul transpires[14]

At every pore[15] with instant fires,

Now let us sport[16] us while we may,

And now, like amorous birds of prey[17],

Rather at once our time devour

Than languish[18] in his slow-chapped power[19].

Let us roll all our strength and all

Our sweetness up into one ball,

And tear our pleasures with rough strife[20]

Thorough[21] the iron gates of life:

Thus, though we cannot make our sun

Stand still, yet we will make him run.

Notes:

1. 这首发表于1681年的《致羞怯的情人》是马维尔最为著名的诗作，也是英国玄学派诗歌的代表作之一。这首诗歌以抑扬格四音步的对偶句写成（iambic tetrameter in couplets），其主题思想是"及时行乐"（carpe diem（Latin），"seize the day"）。整首诗的结构采用逻辑上的"三段论"（syllogism）方式组织——假如……然而事实上……所以……（Had we but … But … Now therefore … ）。

2. Ganges: River in Asia originating in the Himalayas and flowing southeast, through India, to the Bay of Bengal. The young man here suggests that the young lady could postpone her commitment to him if her youth lasted a long, long time. She could take real or imagined journeys abroad, even to India（印度的恒河。这里男青年假设这位小姐的青春可以不朽，那么她就可以拒绝自己的求爱，并且有充足的时间游历世界各地）.

3. rubies: gems that may be rose red or purplish red. In folklore, it is said that rubies protect and maintain virginity.

4. Humber: River in northeastern England. It flows through Hull, Andrew Marvell's hometown.

5. flood...Jews: Resorting to hyperbole, the young man says that his love for the young lady is unbounded by time. He would love her ten years before great flood that Noah outlasted in his ark (Gen. 5: 28-10: 32) and would still love her until all Jews became Christians at the end of the world（运用夸张的手法表明男青年对于这位小姐的爱可以不受时间的束缚）.

6. vegetable love: love cultivated and nurtured like a vegetable so that it flourishes prolifically（我的爱像植物一般缓慢生长）.

7. adore: to love sb/sth very much.

8. this state: This lofty position; this dignity（这种礼遇）.

9. Time's winged chariot: In Greek mythology, the sun was personified as the god Apollo, who rode his golden chariot from east to west each day. Thus, Marvell here associates the sun god with the passage of time（太阳神阿波罗驾驶着金色战车飞驰的形象，预示着时不我待）.

10. yonder: overthere.
11. marble vault: The young lady's tomb（大理石雕的墓室。这里指美女的葬身之地）.
12. worms: a morbid phallic reference（蛆虫。这里很可能暗指男性生殖器）.
13. quaint: attractive in an unusual or old-fashioned way（稀奇古怪的。这里是调侃的口吻）.
14. transpires: erupts, breaks out, emits, gives off（透露出欲望的蠢动）.
15. pore: 毛孔。
16. sport: to play in a happy and lively way（及时行乐）.
17. amorous birds of prey: birds showing sexual desire and love towards others（发情的猛禽）.
18. Languish: to be forced to stay somewhere or suffer sth unpleasant for a long time（忍受煎熬）.
19. slow-chapt power: the power of chewing or eating slowly（时光缓慢的吞噬）.
20. strife: angry or violent disagreement between two people or groups of people.
21. Thorough: Through.

第三首

The Chimney Sweeper[1]

William Blake

A little black thing among the snow,
Crying weep, weep, in notes of woe[2]!
Where are thy father & mother? say?
They are both gone up to the church to pray.

Because I was happy upon the heath,

And smil'd[3] among the winters snow,

They clothed me in the clothes of death,

And taught me to sing the notes of woe.

And because I am happy, & dance & sing,

They think they have done me no injury,

And are gone to praise God & his Priest & King,

Who make up a heaven of our misery[4].

Notes:

1. 布雷克的《扫烟囱的孩子》共有两首。第一首收录于1789年出版的《天真之歌》(*Songs of Innocence*)；第二首收录于1794年出版的《经验之歌》(*Songs of Experience*)。我们这里所选的是第二首。这两首诗的创作背景是18世纪末、19世纪初的英格兰，那时普遍存在雇佣童工的现象。而四五岁的男孩由于个头矮小，经常被雇佣去扫烟囱。这些孩子在扫烟囱的过程中经常被烫伤或是由于吸入过量的煤灰而患上肺病，有时甚至失足跌落而被摔死。在这首诗中我们看到一个浑身漆黑的扫烟囱的孩子站在洁白的雪地上，而他的父母则去教堂歌颂上帝。整首诗歌讽刺意味浓厚，意象鲜明而生动。

2. notes of woe: sweep 与 weep 谐音，所以说孩子们的叫卖声是 "notes of woe"（悲伤的音符）。

3. smil'd: smiled.

4. a heaven of our misery: God & his Priest & King live in the heaven built upon our misery（他们的天堂建立在我们的痛苦之上）。

第四首

Auld Lang Syne[1]

Robert Burns

Should auld acquaintance be forgot,
And never brought to mind?
Should auld acquaintance be forgot,
And auld lang syne?

(Chorus)

For auld lang syne, my dear,
For auld lang syne.
We'll tak a cup o' kindness yet[2],
For auld lang syne.

And surely ye'll be your pint-stowp[3]!
And surely I'll be mine!
And we'll tak a cup o'kindness yet,
For auld lang syne.

We twa hae run about the braes[4],
And pou'd the gowans fine[5];
But we've wander'd mony a weary fitt[6],
Sin' auld lang syne.

We twa hae paidl'd in the burn[7],

Frae[8] morning sun till dine[9];

But seas between us braid[10] hae roar'd

Sin' auld lang syne.

And there's a hand, my trusty fiere[11]!

And gie's a hand o' thine[12]!

And we'll tak a right gude-willie waught[13],

For auld lang syne.

Notes：

1. 这首《友谊地久天长》（又译《过去的时光》）是经彭斯搜集整理而来的一首以苏格兰方言写成的民歌，后经人谱曲传唱至今。传统上，英语国家的人们经常在除夕夜钟声敲响的时刻唱起这首歌曲。"Auld Lang Syne"翻译成标准英语就是"Old Long Since"，意为"since long ago or for old times' sake"。这首民歌讲述了老友相聚，推杯换盏，共同回忆往日时光的情形。

2. We'll tak a cup o' kindness yet：we'll drink another cup of wine of friendship（再干一杯友情之酒）。

3. pint-stowp：能盛一品脱酒的酒壶（stoup）。你喝你的，我喝我的，我们一醉方休。

4. We twa hae run about the braes：we two have once run about the slopes（我们曾经一起游遍山坡）。

5. pou'd the gowans fine：pulled the fine wild daisies（我们曾经一起采摘雏菊的花朵）。

6. we've wander'd mony a weary fitt：we have wandered many a weary foot（我们曾经一起长途跋涉）。

7. We twa hae paidl'd in the burn：we two have paddled in the stream（我们

曾经一起蹚过小河）.

8. Frae: from
9. dine: dinner
10. braid: broad
11. my trusty fiere: my trusty friend. Fiere: comrade.
12. gie's a hand o' thine: give us your hand.
13. gude-willie waught: a draught of good will: a drink of friendship（为我们的友谊干杯）.

第五首

We Are Seven[1]

William Wordsworth

A simple Child[2],

That lightly draws its breath,

And feels its life in every limb,

What should it know of death?[3]

I met a little cottage Girl:

She was eight years old, she said;

Her hair was thick with many a curl

That clustered round her head.

She had a rustic, woodland air[4],

And she was wildly clad[5]:

Her eyes were fair, and very fair;

— Her beauty made me glad.

"Sisters and brothers, little Maid,
How many may you be?"
"How many? Seven in all," she said,
And wondering looked at me.

"And where are they? I pray[6] you tell."
She answered, "Seven are we;
And two of us at Conway dwell,
And two are gone to sea.

"Two of us in the church-yard lie,
My sister and my brother;
And, in the church-yard cottage, I
Dwell near them with my mother."

"You say that two at Conway dwell,
And two are gone to sea,
Yet ye are seven! I pray you tell,
Sweet Maid, how this may be."

Then did the little Maid reply,
"Seven boys and girls are we;
Two of us in the church-yard lie,
Beneath the church-yard tree."

"You run about, my little Maid,

Your limbs they are alive;

If two are in the church-yard laid,

Then ye are only five."

"Their graves are green, they may be seen,"

The little Maid replied,

"Twelve steps or more from my mother's door,

And they are side by side.

"My stockings there I often knit,

My kerchief there I hem[7];

And there upon the ground I sit,

And sing a song to them.

"And often after sun-set, Sir,

When it is light and fair[8],

I take my little porringer[9],

And eat my supper there.

"The first that died was sister Jane;

In bed she moaning lay[10],

Till God released her of her pain;

And then she went away.

"So in the church-yard she was laid;

And, when the grass was dry,

Together round her grave we played,

My brother John and I.

"And when the ground was white with snow,
And I could run and slide,
My brother John was forced to go[11],
And he lies by her side."

"How many are you, then," said I,
"If they two are in heaven?"
Quick was the little Maid's reply,
"O Master! we are seven."

"But they are dead; those two are dead!
Their spirits are in heaven!"
'Twas throwing words away[12]; for still
The little Maid would have her will,
And said, "Nay, we are seven!"

Notes:

1. 《我们七个》收录于华兹华斯的《抒情歌谣集》(*Lyrical Ballads*, 1798)。这首诗讲述了诗人同一个农村小女孩偶遇并且讨论她到底有几个兄弟姐妹，要不要把她死去的兄弟姐妹算在内的故事。1793年的一个萧瑟的秋天，华兹华斯与友人分别后独自一人在英格兰的乡间漫步。此时的他心中愁绪万千、情绪低落，不能自拔。恰巧这时，华兹华斯在古德里奇城堡（Goodrich Castle）遇到一个小女孩儿，并且同她攀谈起来。这个小女孩儿便是这首诗歌中乡村女孩儿（a little cottage Girl）的原型。

2. 第一句诗行的音步并不完整。在有的版本当中第一句诗行是这样的："A little child, dear brother Jim,"——这其实是柯勒律治建议华兹华斯修改成的诗句，而非他的原作（Wordsworth, 1907）。

3. 诗人以提问开头：一个幼小的、充满活力的生命怎么会理解死亡呢？

4. air：the particular feeling or impression that is given by sb（小女孩儿神态淳朴）.

5. clad：clothed；wildly clad：穿着散乱，充满野性。

6. pray：to hope very much.

7. hem：锁边。

8. light and fair：晴朗的夜晚。

9. porringer：a small dish, often with a handle, for soup, porridge, etc.

10. she moaning lay：she lay moaning.

11. to go：to die（euphemism）.

12. 'Twas throwing words away：白费唇舌。

第六首

Sonnets from the Portuguese 14: If thou must love me, let it be for nought[1]

Elizabeth Barrett Browning

If thou must love me, let it be for nought[2]

Except for love's sake only. Do not say

"I love her for her smile — her look — her way

Of speaking gently, — for a trick of thought[3]

That falls in well with mine[4], and certes[5] brought

A sense of pleasant ease on such a day"[6] —

For these things in themselves, Belovèd, may

Be changed, or change for thee[7], — and love, so wrought,

May be unwrought so[8]. Neither love me for

Thine own dear pity's wiping my cheeks dry[9], —

A creature might forget to weep, who bore

Thy comfort long, and lose thy love thereby[10]!

But love me for love's sake, that evermore[11]

Thou may'st[12] love on, through love's eternity.

Notes:

1. 这是一首勃朗宁夫人恋爱期间写给丈夫的十四行诗，收录于《葡萄牙十四行诗集》(*Sonnets from the Portuguese*, 1850)，是其中的第14首。在诗中，女诗人表达了对于爱情的理解：相爱的原因可能多种多样，然而这些原因终究会变化、消失，所以请"以爱的名义爱我"（love me for love's sake）。这是一首意大利体的十四行诗（Petrarchan or Italian sonnet）：由一个八行诗节（octave）加上一个六行诗节（sestet）组成，押韵格式为：abba, abba, cdcdcd。

2. nought: zero or nothing.

3. a trick of thought: the way of thinking.

4. falls in well with mine: to add to my thought or to make it more perfect.

5. certes: certainty, truly.

6. 第2、第3、第4、第5、第6行为跨行连续（enjambment）：Do not say "I love her for her smile — her look — her way of speaking gently, — for a trick of thought that falls in well with mine, and certes brought a sense of pleasant ease on such a day" ——列举了爱一个人的种种具体原因。

7. change for thee: you may change your enjoyment of these things.

8. and love, so wrought, May be unwrought so: 建立在此基础上的爱情也会因此而消失。

9. Thine own dear pity's wiping my cheeks dry: 见我流泪而心生怜悯。

10. lose thy love thereby: as the result, you may lose your love.
11. evermore: for all the time in the future.
12. may'st: 也作mayst；古英语，may的第二人称单数现在式，仅与thou连用。

第七首
Dover Beach[1]
Matthew Arnold

The sea is calm tonight.
The tide is full, the moon lies fair
Upon the straits; on the French coast the light
Gleams and is gone; the cliffs of England stand,
Glimmering and vast, out in the tranquil bay.
Come to the window, sweet is the night-air![2]
Only, from the long line of spray[3]

Where the sea meets the moon-blanched land[4],
Listen! you hear the grating roar
Of pebbles[5] which the waves draw back, and fling,
At their return, up the high strand,
Begin, and cease, and then again begin,
With tremulous cadence slow, and bring
The eternal note of sadness[6] in.

Sophocles[7] long ago
Heard it on the Ægean[8], and it brought

Into his mind the turbid ebb and flow

Of human misery[9]; we

Find also in the sound a thought[10],

Hearing it by this distant northern sea.

The Sea of Faith

Was once, too, at the full, and round earth's shore

Lay like the folds of a bright girdle furled.

But now I only hear

Its melancholy, long, withdrawing roar,

Retreating, to the breath

Of the night-wind, down the vast edges drear

And naked shingles of the world[11].

Ah, love[12], let us be true

To one another! for the world, which seems

To lie before us like a land of dreams,

So various, so beautiful, so new,

Hath really neither joy, nor love, nor light,

Nor certitude, nor peace, nor help for pain[13];

And we are here as on a darkling plain[14]

Swept with confused alarms of struggle and flight,

Where ignorant armies clash by night[15].

第六章　经典英语诗歌选注

Notes：

1. 《多佛海滩》最早发表于1867年出版的诗集《新诗歌》(*New Poems*)。多佛海滩位于英国肯特郡的多佛港附近，与法国的加来隔海相望。此处海域被称为多佛海峡，是英吉利海峡的最窄处。这首诗是马修·阿诺德（Matthew Arnold, 1822—1888）的代表诗作。在这首诗中，阿诺德一方面表达了对宗教信仰式微的忧虑；另一方面也表达了对人类自相屠戮的悲惨命运的感叹。

2. 诗人此时突然同另外一个人说话，并且邀请他来到窗前同自己一起感受夜晚甜美的气息。

3. spray：浪花，泡沫。

4. moon-blanched land：moonlit land.

5. the grating roar Of pebbles：海浪反复推送、拽回海滩上的卵石所发出的刺耳的摩擦声。

6. The eternal note of sadness：诗人认为这种反复的摩擦声是亘古不变的悲伤之音。

7. Sophocles：古希腊悲剧诗人索福克勒斯。诗人想象古希腊剧作家索福克勒斯在大海中听到了和自己现在听到的同样的悲伤之音。

8. Ægean：爱琴海。

9. the turbid ebb and flow Of human misery：人类的悲苦如同潮起潮落，反复出现——折戟沉沙铁未销，自将磨洗认前朝（杜牧：《赤壁》）。

10. a thought：诗人发现了另外一种情思。

11. 这一诗节的意思是：宗教信仰（Sea of Faith）曾经如涨潮的海水一样将世界紧紧围绕；然而现在它却偃旗息鼓，黯然消退了。

12. love：诗人对另外一名同伴的称呼（见Note 2）。

13. "for the world, which seems … nor help for pain"：这是一个充满梦想的、矛盾的、纷繁复杂的新世界。

14. a darkling plain：世界就像是眼前这片黑暗的平原。

15. ignorant armies clash by night：在黑暗的掩盖下，各种无知的势力在进行着殊死争斗。

第八首

Remember[1]

Christina Rossetti

Remember me when I am gone away[2],
　　Gone far away into the silent land[3];
　　When you can no more hold me by the hand,
Nor I half turn to go yet turning stay[4].
Remember me when no more day by day[5]
　　You tell me of our future that you plann'd:
　　Only remember me; you understand
It will be late to counsel then or pray[6].
Yet if you should forget me for a while
　　And afterwards remember, do not grieve[7]:
For if the darkness and corruption[8] leave
　　A vestige[9] of the thoughts that once I had,
Better by far[10] you should forget and smile
　　Than that you should remember and be sad.

Notes：

1. 这首《记住我》是克里斯蒂娜·罗塞蒂（Christina Rossetti, 1830—1894）于1849年创作的一首十四行诗。这首诗中，女诗人先是要求自己的爱人在自己离开后记住她；然而在诗歌的后半部分又告诉自己的爱人，如果记住她会带给他悲伤的话，那么就请将自己忘记，笑对人生。这首诗的结构分为两个部分：第一部分为前八行（Octave），是典型的意大利体十四行诗（押韵格式为：abba, abba）；第二部分为后六行，意思发生转折（Volta），韵脚也发生转变（罗塞蒂自己的独创押韵格式：cdd, ece）。

2. gone away：euphemism, referring to death.
3. silent land：heaven or hell.
4. Nor I half turn to go yet turning stay：I could not stop and turn back halfway.
5. Remember me when no more day by day：remember the days when we were together.
6. It will be late to counsel then or pray：it will be useless for you to counsel or pray after my death.
7. do not grieve：暂时停止悲伤。
8. darkness and corruption：death and decaying body.
9. vestige：a small part of sth that still exists after the rest of it has stopped existing（残存之物——一些对我的残存的记忆）。
10. Better by far：I think it will be better.

第九首

Mending Wall[1]

Robert Frost

Something there is that doesn't love a wall,
That sends the frozen-ground-swell under it,
And spills the upper boulders[2] in the sun;
And makes gaps even two can pass abreast[3].
The work of hunters is another thing:

I have come after them and made repair
Where they have left not one stone on a stone,
But they would have the rabbit out of hiding,
To please the yelping[4] dogs. The gaps I mean,
No one has seen them made or heard them made,
But at spring mending-time we find them there.
I let my neighbor know beyond the hill[5];
And on a day we meet to walk the line
And set the wall between us once again.
We keep the wall between us as we go.
To each the boulders that have fallen to each[6].
And some are loaves and some so nearly balls[7]
We have to use a spell[8] to make them balance:
'Stay where you are until our backs are turned!'
We wear our fingers rough with handling them.
Oh, just another kind of out-door game,
One on a side. It comes to little more[9]:
There where it is we do not need the wall[10]:
He is all pine and I am apple orchard[11].
My apple trees will never get across
And eat the cones[12] under his pines, I tell him.
He only says, 'Good fences make good neighbors.'
Spring is the mischief in me, and I wonder
If I could put a notion in his head:
'Why do they[13] make good neighbors? Isn't it
Where there are cows? But here there are no cows.
Before I built a wall I'd ask to know

What I was walling in or walling out[14],

And to whom I was like to give offense.

Something there is that doesn't love a wall,

That wants it down.' I could say 'Elves'[15] to him,

But it's not elves exactly, and I'd rather

He said it for himself. I see him there

Bringing a stone grasped firmly by the top

In each hand, like an old-stone savage armed[16].

He moves in darkness as it seems to me,

Not of woods only and the shade of trees.

He will not go behind his father's saying[17],

And he likes having thought of it so well

He says again, 'Good fences make good neighbors.'

Notes:

1. 《修墙》收录在弗罗斯特（Robert Frost, 1874 — 1963）的第二部诗集《波士顿以北》（*North of Boston*）当中，于1914年发表，是该诗集中的第一首诗。写这首诗时弗罗斯特就生活在美国东北的新英格兰乡村地区，所以这首诗的创作背景和灵感就来自那里的地理环境、风土人情和生活方式。这首诗描述了讲话人同他的邻居每年春天一起修葺两家之间的围墙的情形。这看似简单的活动却引起了诗人对于人际关系以及人类社会当中存在的各种边界的深入思考。这又是一首典型的弗罗斯特式的，看似简单实则复杂并且极其耐人寻味的诗作。

2. upper boulders: 墙头上的大石头。

3. breast: side by side.

4. yelping: 嚎叫。

5. beyond the hill: 邻居住在山的那一边。

6. 这两句的意思是：我们各自沿着自家的一侧走，从自己一侧修葺毁坏的石墙。
7. 有些石头是长的，有些是圆的。
8. spell：咒语，魔法（指的是下一句："Stay where you are until our backs are turned!"）。
9. It comes to little more：nothing more（仅此而已）。
10. There where it is we do not need the wall：There's no need for a wall to be there.
11. apple orchard：苹果园。
12. cones：锥形的松果。
13. they：指代 fences。
14. walling in or walling out：to keep in or out of the wall.
15. Elves：精灵。
16. like an old-stone savage armed：like an ancient warrior carrying stones.
17. go behind his father's saying：超越先人的智慧。

第十首

Do not stand at my grave and weep[1]

Mary Elizabeth Frye

Do not stand at my grave and weep：
I am not there; I do not sleep.
I am a thousand winds that blow,
I am the diamond glints[2] on snow,
I am the sun on ripened grain,
I am the gentle autumn rain.
When you awaken in the morning's hush[3]

I am the swift uplifting rush

Of quiet birds in circling flight.

I am the soft starshine[4] at night.

Do not stand at my grave and cry:

I am not there; I did not die.

Notes：

1. 这首《不要站在我的墓前哭泣》是美国女诗人玛丽·弗莱（Mary Elizabeth Frye，1905 — 2004）的代表作。因为这首诗从未公开发表过，而且坊间也有多个版本流行，所以关于这首诗的作者历来有争议。20世纪90年代玛丽·弗莱宣称这是一首她于1932年创作的诗歌；后经多方考证，确认了她的说法。弗莱这首诗的创作灵感来自她的一位祖籍是德国的犹太裔友人母亲的去世——这位朋友因为未能见上母亲最后一面，也未能亲临墓地去凭吊而异常悲痛，于是弗莱便写了这首诗安慰她受伤的心灵。这是一首以抑扬格四音步押韵对偶句（rhyming couplets of iambic tetrameter）写成的诗歌。全诗共十二行，两两成对。整首诗歌表达了诗人对于死亡的看法：死亡不是墓穴中的尸体，而是生者化作了狂风、宝石、阳光、雨露、飞鸟和星光，所以请你不要为我哭泣，因为我不曾离去。这首仅仅十二行的短诗，以其真诚、直白而且治愈的语言深深地打动了、抚慰了无数人的心灵。
2. glints：to produce small bright flashes of light.
3. hush：a period of silence.
4. starshine：star+shine.

参考文献

1. Abrams, M. H. (1999). *A Glossary of Literary Terms* (7th ed.). Boston: Thomson Learning.
2. Abrams, M. H. (2000). The Romantic Period *The Norton Anthology of English Literature* (7th ed., Vol. 2A). New York: W. W. Norton & Company.
3. Attridge, D. (1982). *The Rhythms of English Poetry*. London: Longman.
4. Aubrey, J. (1898). *'Brief Lives'*: *Chiefly of Contemporaries* (Vol. 1). Oxford: Clarendon Press.
5. Auden, W. H. (1962). *The Dyer's Hand and other essays*. New York: Random House.
6. Baldwin, E. (April 3, 2019). Silver by Walter de la Mare. *Poem Analysis*, from https://poemanalysis.com/walter-de-la-mare/silver/.
7. Baldwin, E. (June 27, 2017). Sonnet 19 – (On His Blindness) When I Consider How My Light Is Spent by John Milton. *Poem Analysis*, from https://poemanalysis.com/john-milton/when-i-consider-how-my-light-is-spent/.
8. Balfour, G. (1906). *The Life of Robert Louis Stevenson*. London: Methuen.
9. Barry, P. (2013). *English in Practice*: *In Pursuit of English Studies*. London: Bloomsbury Publishing.

10. Bate, W. J. (1963). *John Keats*. Cambridge, Massachusetts: Belknap Press of Harvard University Press.
11. Bell, J., & Millar, V. (2011). Farjeon, Eleanor (1881–1965), children's writer: Oxford University Press.
12. Bevington, D. (2002). *Shakespeare*. Oxford: Blackwell.
13. Bieri, J. (2004). *Percy Bysshe Shelley: A Biography: Youth's Unextinguished Fire, 1792–1816*. Newark: University of Delaware Press.
14. Britannica, T. E. o. E. (April 25, 2018). Metre. *Encyclopedia Britannica* Retrieved 28, Dec. 2022, from https://www.britannica.com/art/metre-prosody.
15. Britannica, T. E. o. E. (Aug. 4, 2017). Topographical poetry. *Encyclopedia Britannica* Retrieved 28, Dec.2022, from https://www.britannica.com/art/topographical-poetry.
16. Britannica, T. E. o. E. (Feb. 4, 2020). Rhyme. *Encyclopedia Britannica* Retrieved 28, Dec.2022, from https://www.britannica.com/art/rhyme.
17. Britannica, T. E. o. E. (Jan. 15, 2020). Allusion. *Encyclopedia Britannica* Retrieved 28, Dec.2022, from https://www.britannica.com/art/allusion.
18. Britannica, T. E. o. E. (July 5, 2019). limerick. *Encyclopedia Britannica* Retrieved 28, Dec.2022, from https://www.britannica.com/art/limerick-poetic-form.
19. Britannica, T. E. o. E. (July 26, 2021). Thomas Gray. *Encyclopedia Britannica* Retrieved 28, Dec.2022, from https://www.britannica.com/biography/Thomas-Gray-English-poet.
20. Britannica, T. E. o. E. (June 27, 2017). lyric. *Encyclopedia Britannica* Retrieved 28, Dec.2022, from https://www.britannica.com/art/lyric.
21. Britannica, T. E. o. E. (May 22, 2013). Symbolism. *Encyclopedia*

Britannica Retrieved 28, Dec.2022, from https://www.britannica.com/art/Symbolism-literary-and-artistic-movement.

22. Britannica, T. E. o. E. (Nov. 1, 2007a). Poetic diction. *Encyclopedia Britannica* Retrieved 28, Dec.2022, from https://www.britannica.com/art/poetic-diction.

23. Britannica, T. E. o. E. (Nov. 1, 2007b). volta. *Encyclopedia Britannica* Retrieved 28, Dec.2022, from https://www.britannica.com/art/volta-poetry.

24. Browning, E. B. (1850). *Sonnets from the Portuguese and other love poems* (reissue, 1990 ed.). New York: Doubleday.

25. Burns, A. D. (2002). *Thematic Guide to American Poetry*. Westport, Connecticut: Greenwood Press.

26. Calhoun, C. (2004). *Longfellow: A Rediscovered Life*. Boston: Beacon Press.

27. Child, F. J. (1965). *The English and Scottish Popular Ballads*. New York: Dover Publications.

28. *Collins English Dictionary*, T. E. o. (2021). ballad. Collins English Dictionary, from https://www.collinsdictionary.com/zh/dictionary/english/ballad.

29. Crossley-Holland, P. (Nov. 12, 2020). rhythm. *Encyclopedia Britannica*, from https://www.britannica.com/art/rhythm-music.

30. Culler, J. (1996). *Literary Theory: A Very Short Introduction*. New York: Oxford University Press.

31. Cummings, M. J. (2006). Meter in Poetry and Verse: A Study Guide Retrieved 23/09, 2021, from https://www.cummingsstudyguides.net/xmeter.html.

32. Cummings, M. J. (2008). She Walks in Beauty. *Cummings Study Guides*

Retrieved 24/09, 2021, from https: //www.cummingsstudyguides.net/ Guides5/SheWalks.html.

33. Feng, C. (1995) . *English Rhetorical Options: A Handbook of English Rhetorical Devices*. Beijing: Foreign Language Teaching and Research Press.

34. Ford, T. W. (1966) . *Heaven Beguiles the Tired: Death in the Poetry of Emily Dickinson*. Tuscaloosa: University of Alabama Press.

35. Friedman, A. B. (Dec. 1, 2016) . ballad. *Encyclopedia Britannica*, from https: //www.britannica.com/art/ballad.

36. Fussell, P. (1979) . *Poetic Meter and Poetic Form*. New York: Random House, Inc.

37. Glatch, S. (Sep. 21, 2021) . Repetition Definition: Types of Repetition in Poetry and Prose Retrieved March 5, 2022, from https: //writers.com/ repetition-definition.

38. Gosse, E. (1911) . Ode. In H. Chisholm (Ed.) , *Encyclopædia Britannica 20* (11th ed.) . London: Cambridge University Press.

39. Greene, R., & Cushman, S. (2016) . *The Princeton Handbook of Poetic Terms: Third Edition. Princeton*, NJ: Princeton University Press.

40. Hainton, R. (1996) . Derwent Coleridge — The Romantic Child. *The Coleridge Bulletin, New Series* (8) , pp. 24–46.

41. Harmon, W., & Holman, C. H. (1999) . *A Handbook to Literature* (8th ed.) . Hoboken: Prentice Hall.

42. Hart, J. (Ed.) . (1976) . *Ayres & Observations: selected poems of Thomas Campion*. Cheadle: Carcanet Press.

43. Hassett, J. M. (2010,) . *W.B. Yeats and the Muses*. New York: Oxford University Press.

44. Hecht, A. (1996) . The Riddles of Emily Dickinson. In J. Farr (Ed.) ,

Emily Dickinson: A Collection of Critical Essays (pp. 149–162). Hoboken: Prentice Hall.

45. Hill, C. (1977). *Milton and the English Revolution*. London: Faber.
46. Holcombe, C. J. (2015). Open Forms in Poetry, from https://www.textetc.com/modernist/open-forms.html.
47. Hutchinson, G. (Sep. 14, 2021). Harlem Renaissance. Encyclopedia Britannica. Retrieved 24/09, 2021, from https://www.britannica.com/event/Harlem-Renaissance-American-literature-and-art.
48. James, W. (2001). *A Fierce Hatred of Injustice: Claude McKay's Jamaica and His Poetry of Rebellion*. London: Verso.
49. Jamieson, L. (Aug. 28, 2020). What Is a Sonnet?, from https://www.thoughtco.com/what-is-a-sonnet-2985266.
50. Jinxia, Z. L., Kang; Han, Liu (2007). *An Introduction to English Poetry*. Baoding: Hebei University Press.
51. Kelly, J. (1996). SOME GRAVESTONE EPITAPHS OFFER COMICAL INSIGHTS. *The Morning Call* Retrieved 20/09, 2021, from https://www.mcall.com/news/mc-xpm-1996-11-04-3120391-story.html.
52. Kennedy, J. G. (1993). Poe, 'Ligeia,' and the problem of Dying Women. In K. Silverman (Ed.), *New Essays on Poe's Major Tales*. New York: Cambridge University Press.
53. Knight, W. (Ed.). (1897). *Journals of Dorothy Wordsworth* (Vol. 1). London: Macmillian and Co., Ltd.
54. Kumar, D. (March 11, 2017). A Birthday by Christina Rossetti, from https://poemanalysis.com/christina-rossetti/a-birthday/.
55. Lindley, D. (2006). *Shakespeare And Music*. London: Bloomsbury Academic.
56. Lindsay, A., & Bergstrom, C. (June 1, 2019). Poetic Form: Open

and Closed. *An Introduction to Poetry*, from https: //introtopoetry2019. pressbooks.com/chapter/chapter-8-poetic-form-open-and-closed/.

57. Lindsay, M. (1996). Urbani, Pietro (1749-1816). *The Burns Encyclopedia* Subsequent edition. Retrieved 24, Feb., 2022, from http: // www.robertburns.org/encyclopedia/UrbaniPietro17491511816.871.shtml.

58. Literary Devices, T. E. o. (2021). *Epic. Literary Devices: Definition and Examples of Literary Terms*, from https: //literarydevices.net/epic/.

59. Maycock, A. L. (1938). *Nicholas Ferrar of Little Gidding*. London: Society for Promoting Christian Knowledge.

60. McNally, F. (Dec. 5, 2014). Frank McNally on Yeats in love: An Irishman's Diary on a new book about an old affair, *The Irish Times*. Retrieved from https: //www.irishtimes.com/news/frank-mcnally-on-yeats-in-love-1.2025984.

61. Merriam-Webster. (n.d.). Elegy. *Merriam-Webster.com dictionary*, from https: //www.merriam-webster.com/dictionary/elegy.

62. Meyer, M. (2015). *The Bedford Introduction to Literature: Reading, Thinking, and Writing* (11th ed.). Boston: Bedford/St. Martin's.

63. Meyers, J. (1992). *Edgar Allan Poe: His Life and Legacy*. New York: Cooper Square Press.

64. Milnes, R. M. (Ed.). (1848). *Life, Letters, and Literary Remains of John Keats*. New York: G. P. Putnam.

65. Myers, J. (1996). *Robert Frost: A Biography*. Boston: Houghton Mifflin Company.

66. Nagy, G. (2010). Ancient Greek elegy. In K. Weisman (Ed.), *The Oxford Handbook of the Elegy* (pp. 13-45). Oxford: Oxford University Press.

67. Nemerov, H. (2021). poetry. Encyclopedia Britannica Retrieved 17/09,

2021, from https: //www.britannica.com/art/poetry.

68. Nespor, M., Shukla, M., & Mehler, J. (Ed.). (2011). *Stress-timed vs syllable-timed languages*. Malden, MA: Blackwell.

69. Pavel, T. (2003). Literary Genres as Norms and Good Habits (JSTOR). Retrieved 27 Dec. 2022, from The Johns Hopkins University Press http: //www.jstor.org/stable/20057776.

70. Poetry-Foundation. (2021a). Didactic poetry. *Glossary of Poetic Terms* Retrieved 2, Feb. 2021, from https: //www.poetryfoundation.org/learn/glossary-terms/didactic-poetry.

71. Poetry-Foundation. (2021b). Edgar Allan Poe: 1809–1849. Poets Retrieved 15, Jan. 2021, from https: //www.poetryfoundation.org/poets/edgar-allan-poe.

72. Poetry-Foundation. (2021c). Edmund Spenser: 1552–1599. Poets Retrieved 10, Jan. 2021, from https: //www.poetryfoundation.org/poets/edmund-spenser.

73. Poetry-Foundation. (2021d). Robert Burns: 1759–1796. Poets Retrieved 21, Jan. 2021, from https: //www.poetryfoundation.org/poets/robert-burns.

74. Poets, A. o. A. (2021). W. H. Auden. Poets Retrieved 21 July, 2021, from https: //poets.org/poet/w-h-auden.

75. Reynolds, D. S. (1995). *Walt Whitman's America: A Cultural Biography*. New York: Vintage Books.

76. Riffaterre, M. (1973). The Self-Sufficient Text. *Diacritics*, 3 (3), pp. 39–45.

77. Robinson, A. (Aug. 14, 2019). The 8 Types of Sonnets and How to Tell Them Apart Retrieved 21, Feb., 2023, from https: //blog.prepscholar.com/types-of-sonnets.

78. Romano, T. (2014). The Lives of a Poem. *The English Journal*, 103(5), 24–29.

79. Schoenbaum, S. (1991). *Shakespeare's lives*. Oxford: Clarendon Press.

80. Sewall, R. B. (1974). *The Life of Emily Dickinson*. New York: Farrar, Straus, and Giroux.

81. Shakespeare, W. (1609). Sonnet 55: Not Marble nor the Gilded Monuments. Literary Devices Retrieved 20/09, 2021, from http://www.shakespeare-online.com/sonnets/55detail.html.

82. Sharp, W. (1895). Some Reminiscences of Christina Rossetti. *Atlantic Monthly*, 75(6), p. 749.

83. Shaw, R. B. (2007). *Blank Verse: A Guide to its History and Use*. Athens: Ohio University Press.

84. Sigler, D. (Feb. 16, 2017). Claude McKay and "The White House" Retrieved 18/10, 2021, from https://sites.utexas.edu/ransomcentermagazine/2017/02/16/claude-mckay-and-the-white-house/.

85. Staff, H. (2011). Behind the Poem: "The Road Not Taken", from https://www.poetryfoundation.org/harriet-books/2011/08/behind-the-poem-the-road-not-taken.

86. Stine, J. C., Broderick, B., & Marowski, D. G. (Eds.). (1983). *Contemporary Literary Criticism* (Vol. 26). Detroit: Gale Research.

87. Team, U. (2021). Imagery in Literature: Tools for Imagination. *Soft Skills*, from https://blog.udemy.com/imagery-in-literature/.

88. Tearle, O. (2019). A Short Analysis of the Shakespeare Song 'Fear No More the Heat o' the Sun'. *Interesting Literature*, from https://interestingliterature.com/2019/08/a-short-analysis-of-the-shakespeare-song-fear-no-more-the-heat-o-the-sun/.

89. Thomas, D. N. (2008). *Fatal Neglect: Who Killed Dylan Thomas.*

Bridgend: Seren.

90. Tsykynovska, L. (May 5, 2017). Apostrophe. *LitCharts LLC*, from https://www.litcharts.com/literary-devices-and-terms/apostrophe.

91. Twitchell, J. (2004). An English Teacher Looks at Branding. *The Journal of Consumer Research*, 31(2), 484–489.

92. Valéry, P., & Guenther, C. (1954). Poetry and Abstract Thought. *The Kenyon Review*, 16(2), 208–233.

93. Vaughan, H. (1652). *The Mount of Olives: or, Solitary devotions*. London: William Lcake.

94. Vivian, P. (1909). Introduction. In P. Vivian (Ed.), *Campion's Works*. Oxford: Oxford University Press.

95. Wallenstein, B. (1993). JazzPoetry/jazz-joetry/'jazzjoetry' ??? *African American Review*, 27(4), pp. 665–671.

96. Watson, B. D. (1971). *CHINESE LYRICISM: Shih Poetry from the Second to the Twelfth Century*. New York: Columbia University Press.

97. Watson, T. (2009). Buoy & Marker Messages Retrieved 20/09, 2021, from https://paddling.com/learn/buoy-marker-messages.

98. White, P. A. (1993). *Psychological Metaphysics*. London: Routledge.

99. Woolford, J., Karlin, D., & Phelan, J. (Eds.). (2010). *Robert Browning: Selected Poems*. London: Routledge.

100. Wordsworth, W. (1802). Preface to Lyrical Ballads Retrieved 17/09, 2021, from https://web.english.upenn.edu/~jenglish/Courses/Spring2001/040/preface1802.html.

101. Wordsworth, W. (1907). *Poems by William Wordsworth*. New York: McClure Phillips.

后　记

　　历时三年，积累半生，才写完这本小书。笔者个人天资一般，不算勤快，工作也没什么效率，所以能完成这本书实属侥幸。

　　记得几年前有出版社联系笔者翻译一本有关藏族历史、文化的长篇小说。笔者很喜欢那本小说，但对小说里面的藏族的风俗习惯和历史文化却知之甚少，就更别提再翻译成英文了。所以笔者足足准备了三个月，甚至为了保证译文的质量千方百计地寻到了一本《汉英—英汉藏学翻译词典》和其他一些珍贵资料。然而就在要签翻译合同时，对方才告知要在一年以内完成。笔者大吃一惊，告诉对方，要笔者来翻至少要两年。当然对方也不会"惯着你"，于是就另找其他人去做了。其间还有朋友好心提醒笔者：找几个研究生弄一下，你再把把关，一年都用不了啊。可笔者觉得，既然译者是自己的名字，便宁可不做，也不能放宽标准。这大概是有些强迫症在作祟吧。有时自己也在想，或许错的是自己，跟不上时代的脚步了。

　　给这本书起名字其实也颇费了一些脑筋。曾经想叫《英诗鉴赏》，后来又想叫作《英诗赏析入门》，而最终叫作《理解英语诗歌》。这个名字其实是有些浮夸了——英语诗歌博大精深，想凭借这样一本小书就能帮助读者"理解"它，显然是有些不自量力。但是，联想自己写这本书的初衷——帮助英语文学爱好者和高校英语专业的学生学习有关英语诗歌的基础知识，获得英语诗歌赏析的基本方法，提高对于英语诗歌及其汉译的审美能力，等等，笔者便斗胆确定了现在的书名，希望能激发读者更进一步探究英语诗歌奥秘的决心。

　　本书内容的重点是英语诗歌基本知识和进行赏析的不同角度，例如

"英语诗歌的韵律""英语诗歌的语言",等等。本书内容的难点有两个:第一是英语诗歌相关重要概念的辨析,特别是那些在翻译成中文后容易引起歧义或是理解错误的重要概念(例如什么是"rhythm",它和"meter"有何不同?再如什么是"theme",它和"subject matter"有何不同?等等);第二则是英语诗歌的翻译。

本书中作为例证进行翻译、赏析的英语诗歌多达好几十首;而笔者则包办了所有这些英语诗歌的翻译。其中,有些诗歌的译文甚至采用的是笔者还是大学生时的旧作(例如,彭斯的那首《一支红红的玫瑰》,就是笔者三十年前大学二年级时翻译的。在整理旧书时,笔者发现夹在书里面那张发黄的,写有诗歌译文的旧信纸,于是便稍加润色,用于书稿当中);有些诗歌的译文是笔者在给学生上"英诗赏析"课的时候翻译的,断断续续也有十多年的历史了;而有些诗歌的译文则是笔者在写这本书时才翻译的,例如济慈的《秋颂》和《夜莺颂》,等等。所有这些参考译文,笔者都少则三五遍,多则十多遍地,在不同时间段里,进行了修改和润色。虽然笔者能力有限,才思不足,但是一颗热爱英语诗歌的赤子之心则是袒露无遗。

在作为例证的英语诗歌的选择方面,笔者遵循了两个基本原则:第一,诗歌与对应章节所讨论的基础知识和基本方法要尽可能地匹配;第二,所选诗歌英美兼顾,古今兼顾,以经典作品为主,同时适当照顾一些稍显冷门的诗作。当然,所选诗歌也有笔者本人的喜好,比如诗人叶芝、济慈、狄金森等的作品就占比略高。

为了帮助读者更好地理解每首诗歌,笔者特意在每篇诗作前加入了诗人和诗歌的创作背景的介绍;这里面涉及诗人的成长经历、历史地位、婚恋趣事,等等,同时也包括诗歌作品的创作背景。这些奇闻逸事有的是诗人的自述,有的是朋友视角的描写;但无论是哪种情况,都绝非是笔者的杜撰。感兴趣的读者可以根据相关参考文献一探究竟。

本书的读者对象为英语专业的大学生或是广大英语文学特别是英语诗

后 记

歌的爱好者。鉴于此，笔者对本书所列举的所有章节题目、历史人物、历史事件、外国地名、文学专有词汇都附加了英文对照，为的是防止隔靴搔痒，防止不同翻译措辞带来误解或是曲解，从而方便读者进行更深入的研究。

　　本书也存在一些缺点和不足。例如，笔者所参考的网络文献当中，有些没有作者，有些没有具体的创作时间，有些原本是纸质图书，可是在网页上却没有显示具体页码，等等。这些缺憾都使得本书的科学性、严谨性有一定的不足。所以希望广大读者能在看到书后不吝赐教，多提宝贵意见，以便本书再版的时候加以改正、提高。

笔者
2023/2/26